Careers for Women

ALSO BY JOANNA SCOTT

Careers
for
Women

A Novel

Joanna Scott

Little, Brown and Company

New York Boston London

The characters and events in this book are fictitious. Any similarity to real persons, living or dead, is coincidental and not intended by the author.

Copyright © 2017 by Joanna Scott

Hachette Book Group supports the right to free expression and the value of copyright. The purpose of copyright is to encourage writers and artists to produce the creative works that enrich our culture.

The scanning, uploading, and distribution of this book without permission is a theft of the author's intellectual property. If you would like permission to use material from the book (other than for review purposes), please contact permissions@hbgusa.com. Thank you for your support of the author's rights.

Little, Brown and Company
Hachette Book Group
1290 Avenue of the Americas, New York, NY 10104
littlebrown.com

First Edition: July 2017

Little, Brown and Company is a division of Hachette Book Group, Inc. The Little, Brown name and logo are trademarks of Hachette Book Group, Inc.

The publisher is not responsible for websites (or their content) that are not owned by the publisher.

The Hachette Speakers Bureau provides a wide range of authors for speaking events. To find out more, go to hachettespeakersbureau.com or call (866) 376-6591.

ISBN 978-0-316-36383-9

LCCN 2016957618

10 9 8 7 6 5 4 3 2 1

LSC-C

Printed in the United States of America

For Jim
Reccan moste
þicce ond þynne…

Careers for Women

I

THE GOLDEN DOOR

"My dears, it goes without saying that there are advantages to being a woman." Mrs. J spoke in a voice strong and clear enough to be heard over the noise of other diners. I was sitting to her left and fixed my gaze on the powdery segment that clung to the end of her cigarette like a young bear hanging on a branch too narrow to support its weight. She tapped the cigarette on the rim of the ashtray. The branch wobbled; the cub slipped and fell.

"Still," she continued, "one's sex is sometimes a handicap, especially in our own institution, where those few of us who have not served as commanders of a large navy vessel are expected to prove our worth in riskier ways. It's a fine line one has to walk to survive the executive gauntlet. A woman must give the impression that she is confident and never let down her guard. She must be poised and unflappable. Her clothes and accessories should come from the finest stores. Regarding the field of public relations, a woman can earn what she is worth, provided she possesses tact, resourcefulness, personality, and imagination. But if you have an aversion to nerve strain and don't want to work late into the night, there are more suitable professions for you to consider, such as horticulture or ornithology. Why not become a chemist or a garden photographer? There are all sorts of careers open to women these days. I met a woman just last month who is a director at a home for girls who are misfits. I asked her if she ever felt demoralized by the behavior of the residents in her care. She assured me that the work of straightening out something twisted is entirely satisfying."

There were eleven of us at the table, plus Mrs. J. We were the clerical girls in the Office of Public Relations at the Port Authority; Mrs. Lee K. Jaffe was our director, and she was launching an annual tradition that would continue until her retirement. While treating us to a lavish lunch at the Golden Door, the high-end restaurant at the New York International Airport, Mrs. J took advantage of the opportunity to offer the kind of advice that would be useful to anyone who wanted to follow in her footsteps.

In reality, most of us had no interest in a career in public relations. It was 1958, and we had come to New York in search of husbands. Mrs. J seemed to understand as much, but she wanted to make sure we knew what we'd be in for in case we changed our minds.

Some of the girls sipped martinis. Others bit into generous dollops of red caviar spread on triangles of toast. I gazed toward the window and watched a plane roll slowly along a runway in the distance.

Jessie Putnam raised her hand, as if in a classroom.

"Yes, Jessie?"

We were already a little drunk by then. Among us, Jessie

Putnam was the most ready to be reckless. "I have a question," she announced.

"Go ahead." There was no shred of impatience in Mrs. J's tone, yet I sensed a private calculation going on as she considered Jessie Putnam's future role in her department.

"What's the most difficult part of your job?" Jessie asked.

"If I told you that the most difficult part is also the easiest part, can any of you guess what it is?"

"Dictating letters," proposed Brenda Dowdle.

"Good answer," said Mrs. J, "but no."

"Going back to work after drinking three martinis," Jessie Putnam said with a giggle.

"I never have more than one martini at lunch. You, Miss Putnam, should show similar restraint." We all froze for an awkward moment, embarrassed for Jessie, until Mrs. J added, "Today, of course, is an exception—cheers," and she lifted her glass in a toast.

"Is it meeting with . . ." This from shy Eugenia Gilmore, who never raised her voice above a whisper. "With . . ." She said something I couldn't make out.

Trudy Frizzell, sitting beside Eugenia, repeated the word that had been inaudible to the rest of us: "Newspapermen?"

"Oh, that is just difficult, I'm afraid."

Other wrong guesses offered by the girls included managing the department's budget, going to Washington to testify before Congress, and telling a roomful of copywriters—all male— what to do.

I was the only one who kept my mouth shut, and Mrs. J noticed. "Miss Gleason," she said, turning to me, "don't you want to wager a guess?"

"I think," I said, looking down at my hands, curling my fingers to hide my gnawed nails, "it must be difficult to have to perform in front of a crowd. Giving a speech and all...in public...that's hard, I imagine." I struggled against my instinct to shut up. "And maybe it's easy, too, if you're used to pretending to be someone you're not."

I was instantly horrified, aware, too late, that I had effectively accused one of the city's most powerful businesswomen of hypocrisy...to her face. Good Lord, had I left my cozy home in Cleveland just to be thrown out on the street in New York? I had no family in the city and not a penny of savings. Yet I had boldly revealed my capacity for rudeness to the woman who was in charge of my livelihood. Pack your bags now, Maggie Gleason.

I should have known that Mrs. J would never fire anyone for failing one of her pop quizzes. Anyway, it appeared I hadn't failed.

"Touché," she said, grinding out her cigarette. "Now, girls, let's talk about what it means to pretend in this business."

SCALE BAR

When I started working for the Port Authority in the spring of 1958, the headquarters was on Eighth Avenue, Austin Tobin was executive director, and Lee K. Jaffe was the chief of the Public Relations Department. I had been hired as a secretary and so was not surprised that one of my first assignments was to fetch coffee for Mrs. J. I *was* surprised when she ordered me to make a mock-up of a detailed map, with individual shops listed, of the downtown blocks between West and Greenwich Streets. I knew nothing about how to make a map, and Mrs. J didn't take the time to give me instructions; she just warned me to be discreet when I visited the neighborhood to gather information.

The best method, I decided, was to trace the designated area of an existing map of Manhattan on a separate piece of paper. I used the largest map I could find, so the neighborhood I was supposed to include filled nearly the whole sheet. I wrote in the street names by hand, then spent a morning downtown exploring the blocks from Fulton to Liberty and from West Street to Greenwich, charting the major businesses, among them Syms Men's Apparel, Cantor the Cabinet King, Arrow Electronics, McInnes Restaurant and Bar. I went inside them all in an effort to gauge their dimensions. I walked out to the end of West Street to count the piers, then had a hamburger at McInnes. My last stop was Oscar's Radio Shop.

I discovered in Oscar's something between a hardware store and a curiosity shop. I felt an urge to comb through the boxes filled with rotary switches, clamps, hooks, and dials. Huge spools of copper wire were propped against the walls. Heating pipes pinged gently. Abandoned televisions and radios beckoned to be adopted. Scattered without any evidence of order along the shelves were terminal strips and boards, metal plates, vacuum tubes, and other oddly shaped objects with inscrutable functions.

Though I wasn't a radio enthusiast myself, I found Oscar's to be an unexpectedly restful place amid the hubbub of downtown. I liked the atmosphere of the shop so much that I lingered for a long while. I pretended to be interested in the antique radios on display, but in truth I just enjoyed being among people who were so quietly purposeful. Customers arrived with their broken machines. Clerks climbed ladders and dug into the depths of cabinets in search of parts needed to make repairs. A boy in oversize overalls and a dingy felt cap pulled low on his forehead sat on a stool in a back corner, entranced by a manual he was reading, a kitten asleep on his lap.

Back at the P.A., I colored squares on my map to indicate the different businesses and drew dotted lines to connect them to the names I wrote in pen. I hesitated before delivering the map to the printer, wondering if I should give it to Mrs. J to look it over. I decided that she wouldn't want to be bothered.

When I saw the finished map, I thought it looked clean and professional. Mrs. J did not agree. She took one short glance at the copy I handed her and tossed it back to me. I failed to catch it and was forced to stoop to lift it from the floor. By the time I was upright again, Mrs. J had already swiveled in her chair and was reaching for the handle of a file cabinet. With her back to me, she told me to redo the map and make sure to put in the missing scale bar.

I admit my humiliation was out of proportion to the situation. Mrs. J hadn't even raised her voice. She'd been entirely reasonable—a map without a scale bar isn't very useful. Still, I felt as if my application for admission to some prestigious college had been turned down. And I wasn't even planning to go to college. Yet Lee Jaffe had such power over me that a word of praise from her kept me glowing all day, and her disappointment broke my heart.

From the start, I tried desperately to please her. I can't really explain why she assumed such importance in my mind. I'd always been obedient to my superiors without giving them much thought. My parents were sensible Presbyterians who aimed to raise their daughter to be a good citizen. I didn't feel the need for another authority figure in my life. But Mrs. J loomed large in my imagination, for reasons I will never fully understand. And when I had the opportunity to choose between a better-paying job in a different department or the same salary as an assistant to Mrs. J, I chose to stick with Mrs. J. That's why I'm the one telling this story.

Careers for Women

Picture this: Six men, four of them in short-sleeved tailored white shirts, two of them in suits, only one wearing a tie, all of them holding signs protesting the latest landgrab by the Port Authority. PORT AUTHORITY HAS NO AUTHORITY TO CONFISCATE PRIVATE PROPERTY ITS UNCONSTITUTIONAL reads one sign. And another: PORT AUTHORITY HAS NO PERMISSION FROM CONGRESS TO BUILD WORLD TRADE CENTER.

The men are standing outside Oscar's Radio Shop. Through a corner of the window, you can see a jumble of radios and televisions. The grinning face of a white-haired man is visible between the shoulders of two of the protesters. The rest of the crowd in the rear is blocked by the men and their signs.

On the sidewalk in the foreground of the photograph is a coffin, the hinged lid open to show the face of the occupant. Though the sign on the coffin says HERE LIES MR. SMALL BUSI-NESSMAN. DON'T LET THE P.A. BURY HIM, in fact the role of Mr. Small Businessman is played by a female mannequin borrowed from a department store. With her hair cut short and dressed in a suit, she resembles a beautiful boy more than an owner of one of the local businesses.

If you look carefully at the photograph, you will see shadows of onlookers on the left side of the sidewalk opposite the coffin. There are two shadows in particular to note, one much smaller than the other. These are the shadows of a woman named Pauline Moreau and her daughter, Sonia, who was not quite four at the time, young enough to think that the occupant of the coffin had once been alive.

WHAT IF

I met Pauline Moreau in 1964, after Lee Jaffe hired her to organize files. I'm told she had been a familiar figure around the piers near the neighborhood the P.A. had designated as the future site of the World Trade headquarters. In her pencil skirt, chiffon blouse, and silly tin tiara, she aimed to solicit the workmen at lunchtime, though she liked to hang around the area all day to keep her claim on it, for it was popular with other hustlers.

I was accompanying Mrs. Jaffe and a large entourage of foreign journalists from a variety of European countries when Pauline appeared among a group of prostitutes who had been rounded up and handcuffed by the police; they were being dragged by a chain to the rear cage of a van. One of the women was screaming obscenities. Another one kicked out at a cop, who responded by knocking her on the buttocks with his club, causing her to collapse and nearly pull the other prostitutes to the ground with her. There was a loud, gabbling outcry as the women tried to steady themselves. Bystanders, too, began yelling, and the scene threatened to explode into chaos until one of the cops appeared with a bucket and tossed water on the women, shocking them into a silence that lasted long enough for the one who had been hit with the club to clamber back to her feet.

You can imagine how excited the foreign visitors were to come upon such spicy street drama in a city they would go on to characterize as filthy, crime-ridden, and corrupt. As it happened, there were no photographers present, but the reporters were busy writing notes on their pads. I stood mutely, stupidly, embarrassed by everything—the prostitutes with their deep, sweaty cleavage and cheap clothing, the brutality of the police, the smell of the garbage in the street, the journalists who were happy to be entertained without paying the price of a ticket. I didn't even notice that Mrs. J had left us until I saw her deep in conversation with a police sergeant, leaning so close to him that she seemed to be kissing him on the ear. Whatever she was saying, it obviously made an impression. The sergeant signaled to a fellow officer, who proceeded to unlock the handcuffs, setting the women free.

In minutes, the crowd had dispersed, the reporters had put away their notepads, and we were following Mrs. J back on our tour. Only when we were returning to the bus supplied by the P.A. did I see Pauline Moreau sitting on a doorstep, hugging her scabby shins, her blouse drenched, her hair flying free from that crown of a tiara. She was rocking back and forth with a crazed, lost expression. As we passed her, Mrs. J slowed and slipped to the rear of our party. The journalists didn't seem to notice, and I know they didn't see Mrs. J hand Pauline a business card, for none of them asked about it once we were settled on the bus.

Sometimes I try to imagine how my life would have been different if Pauline had never been hired by Lee Jaffe. I come up with all sorts of scenarios, though none of them seems convincing.

A THEORY OF ILLUSIONS

Unlike Pauline, I had my parents' blessing when I left for New York. My mother regretted that she hadn't seen more of the world when she was younger; she understood why I wanted to leave Cleveland and quietly encouraged me to go. My father, who liked to say that an eligible girl needs a wide field to find a husband, predicted that I would be engaged before Christmas.

I was twenty-one years old in 1958—four years older than Pauline and, unlike her, looking forward to marriage. I figured I would find a temporary job, something that would give me a chance to meet single young men. I hadn't thought to question the ethos I'd inherited from generations of housewives. My mother, my grandmother, my aunts all made it clear that they pitied workingwomen. Successful ladies did not have to work for a living.

Secretly, I admit, I used to page through magazines and hungrily read profiles of women who had established themselves in one profession or another. I remember one article in particular that captured my interest. It was by a woman who identified herself as an "Artist of Tropical Research." She loved her job, and she recommended it for anyone who had keen powers of observation, a steady hand, and an ability to recognize essentials that deserved emphasis. She explained that a scientific artist must be ready to draw anything from an amoeba to a whale. She promised that the work would be rewarding for those who were suited to it, though she warned that the financial return was variable, ranging, she said, from a moderate salary to nothing at all. Of course, I would need to earn more than *nothing*. But I had always loved to draw and was good at it. I told myself that if I was doing something I loved, I wouldn't mind scrimping to make ends meet.

I pored over the classifieds but didn't see any opportunities for a scientific artist. Instead, I found plenty of listings for clerical girls. I applied to several. Within two weeks of my arrival in New York, I was employed by the Port Authority.

I didn't immediately warm to the job. It was drudgery typing other people's letters regarding business that didn't interest me. I didn't like having to correct my mistakes on both the original sheet and the carbon copy. I felt awkward answering phones. More than anything else, I hated taking dictation. I had never properly learned shorthand, and it was all I could do to keep up with Mrs. J when she rattled off multiple memos.

Soon, though, I found myself getting used to the routine. In her imperious commitment to the task at hand, Mrs. J made it seem that the goals of her department were of weighty importance. Under her supervision, I felt more valued than I ever had in my life. I enjoyed gossiping with the other girls over our coffee breaks. I liked getting a regular paycheck. I dreaded the end of the workday, when I had to go back to the rooming house on Second Avenue. On the weekends, I couldn't wait for Monday morning. Office work became such a comfortable habit that I would stick to it for more than thirty years.

In contrast to me, Pauline spent some time trying out other ways of making money—always with the expectation that with minimal effort, she'd get filthy rich and never have to work again—before coming to the Port Authority.

I arrived in New York many months before Pauline did, and it would be years before we met. I picture our two paths as converging lines. At our origins, the space between us is vast. As we get closer, the angle shrinks. We head toward each other, slowly approaching our inevitable intersection, but with certain physical realities keeping us separate.

Represented on graph paper, converging lines create a trick of perspective. Draw two bars of equal length between them, and the bar closer to the point of convergence will look longer, proving that illusion can have its own kind of truth.

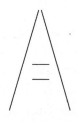

Joanna Scott

PAULINE ARRIVES IN THE BIG CITY

A girl with an umbrella, so excited about the world that she can hardly breathe. A girl walking in the rain through Times Square, dazzled by the lights, stopping at an open door and peering down the dark corridor of an establishment advertising itself with a poster of a stripper pinching her own cherry-red nipples. A girl whose private reflections on the meaning of XXX as she walks on are interrupted when she sees a dollar bill in the gutter. She peels the bill off the pavement and pockets it, intending to keep it as a memento, her lucky dollar. Now, her first day here, she has eight hundred and fifty-one dollars.

Correction: She spent five dollars on a train ticket. Fifty cents on a sandwich at the station in Albany. A dollar plus change for the umbrella. The deposit of thirty dollars for her room on West Eighty-Second Street. How much does that leave her? She has lost track. It is all a blur—her fortune, her life, the lights of Broadway. Blurred by the sweet spring rain. Drops lit by neon, as though from within. Neon veiled by the drops. Sucking sounds of tires. A girl just walking along. A girl beginning to thicken around the waist. A girl who is happy to be free. Walking downtown under her umbrella, then uptown as the sky clears and a velvety breeze blows away the dampness.

What a beautiful night. She pretends that her closed umbrella is a fancy walking stick. She keeps her chin up. She tries to look like a blue blood.

At Columbus Circle she stops to watch a juggler throwing plastic batons into the air. The crowd *oohs* when he catches a baton under his lifted knee, *aahs* when he spins and catches a baton behind his back. How is a human being capable of such dexterous actions? The show embodies the magic of New York. The girl can't believe what she sees. The buildings are taller

14

than she would have thought possible. The people are more beautiful than anywhere else on earth. Even the dogs are stylish in their doggy raincoats, their puffed tails raised like the sickle feathers of proud roosters.

She is just a girl from Albany who finally is discovering the taste of freedom. A girl who walks uptown along Broadway and turns west on Seventy-Seventh, intending to zigzag to Eighty-Second and West End Avenue. A girl who is seen as easy bait. A girl who doesn't think about the dangers of a deserted block and who, before she knows what is happening, is grabbed from behind.

She is not just afraid; she is appalled! Don't men get enough without having to steal what's not theirs? She is a mother-to-be, for God's sake. Fortunately, she has a handy weapon in the shape of an umbrella.

Swipe sting pound kick rage of the eons power bestowed as if from above you prick get off my back you stinking garbage pit you maggot you better lay off mister the girl will put a hole in your foot she will poke out your eye if you don't stop with your groping she will gallop at you with the spear of her umbrella pointed straight at your pathetic heart you pervert take that and that and that from a girl who will show no mercy so you better run while there's still time you better get away from the girl before she turns you into mincemeat.

Idiot, whoever he was. He should have known better.

A girl smoothing her ruffled skirt, tugging it back over her knees. A girl who isn't just anyone. A girl who is proud. A tough girl. A girl who refuses to think of herself as vulnerable. A girl unwilling to learn what it really means to be alone in this world.

A PROBLEM NAMED SONIA

October 1959:, Pauline Moreau has come out of her paraldehyde-induced stupor in the maternity ward at New York Hospital and is waiting to meet her child. She doesn't know how long she's been sedated, or where the baby is, or even whether it is a girl or a boy. What is taking the nurses so long to introduce her to her little one?

Money is taking them so long. Money—or the lack thereof—makes nurses inattentive and doctors downright brutal, or so they were in Pauline's case if her fuzzy memory is at all accurate.

Jesus, shut her up, I can't think.

They shouldn't have talked like that in front of her, not before she fell asleep!

Hear you got a breech there, Doc.

A breech? She vaguely wondered then, and wonders again now, if she would have to pay extra. She had come straight to the hospital after her water broke without calling ahead to her doctor. The truth is, she doesn't have a doctor. Doctors are something she hasn't bothered with, being relatively new to the city. She has been here only five months, and already her money is getting low. But she doesn't want to fret about finding a job. Right now, she wants to meet her baby. Where is he? Or she? She can't name it if she hasn't met it.

"Yoo-hoo?" she calls in the direction of the open door.

From the opposite side of the room, behind the curtain hiding the second bed, a voice replies, "Keep your trap shut!"

Other women might be offended, but not Pauline, who has seen enough of the world to know not to expect kindness from strangers. All her life, people have been telling her to keep her trap shut. Even the man she nicknamed Bobo, the one who fathered the child she has yet to meet, told her to keep her trap shut. But Pauline Moreau is no pushover. Bobo understood that she could make trouble for him, given that he already had a legal wife and worked for a boss "who doesn't smile at perfidy." That's a quote from Bobo himself. Pauline had to guess at the meaning of *perfidy,* but at least a baby on the way gave a girl leverage, and it earned Pauline enough to set herself up in a boardinghouse in New York City and lie around watching her belly swell.

"I want to see my baby," Pauline says to the curtain.

"Plenty of time for that," says the curtain to Pauline. "Get some shut-eye while you can because you won't be getting much coming up."

With the speaker hidden, the statement has the force of prophecy. Pauline reflects for a moment, then asks, "Is this your first?"

"Fifth. Now stop pestering me."

Pauline has more she wants to ask the curtain, but she is distracted by the entrance of a nurse, who proceeds to check Pauline's vitals without a word, squeezing her arm with the blood-pressure cuff, taking her pulse.

"Where is my baby?" Pauline asks.

The nurse, who has her forefinger on Pauline's wrist, glances up from her watch with an inscrutable expression.

"What?" Pauline asks.

"I didn't say anything," the nurse replies. After a minute, she picks up the clipboard and jots down numbers.

"Why can't I see my baby?" Pauline persists.

The nurse's smooth face doesn't match her white hair. "Honey, there's a problem," she says quietly.

Problem. That's a word Pauline has never liked. She associates it with math classes she couldn't keep up with and fights between her uncle and his succession of wives that culminated in dishes crashing onto the floor.

"What's wrong?"

"Don't worry, the doctors have it under control. Everything will be fine."

"No, it won't," Pauline announces. How can she be so sure? It must be her first blast of a mother's intuition. She, who is hardly more than a child herself—somehow she knows that everything will not be fine, not ever again.

Fortunately, Pauline Moreau gave up the feeling of sadness years ago. The worst she feels is annoyed, which is definitely unpleasant, worth avoiding whenever possible, but more tolerable than sadness. And sometimes it can't be helped.

How annoyed she is when she says, "I want to see my baby."

"You will soon."

"Now."

The nurse contemplates her patient for a moment. "Can you walk?"

"I think so."

"Then come on."

Pauline doesn't bother to secure the rear ties of her hospital gown as she follows the nurse down the hall. She is too irritated to care whether some old lech on call gets an eyeful, plus she has to concentrate on staying upright because she still feels wobbly from the medication. There is a dreamlike sensation to the whole march past the nurses' station, through the swinging double doors, around the corners of the labyrinthine corridor, through another set of double doors, and into a ward that has the look of a laboratory, with small plastic boxes containing babies.

She can see at a glance that there's a problem with each of them. A *problem*—there's that stupid word again. Poor things.

Some of them aren't much bigger than her hand. Others are the color of ripe bananas. Yet, look here, there's no problem she can see with the one she recognizes as her own even before the nurse identifies it. How she knows who is hers without reading the charts is hard to figure. Chalk it up to more mother's intuition, or maybe just the luck of a good guess, but she gets it right, she knows her baby when she sees it and is immediately filled with pride for the plump, bald creature, her little snoozing angel with wrinkly legs sprouting from the diaper, knees spread in the shape of a butterfly, a tube to its nose held in place with a brown Band-Aid. Who dares to say that Pauline's little butterfly has a problem?

The nurse does. "She had some trouble breathing at the start, unfortunately."

"She?" A baby girl. A daughter.

"There will be motor issues, I'm afraid."

Pauline is willfully slow to process the information.

"She'll need extra care."

All Pauline wants is to take her home and care for her forever. No matter that Pauline doesn't have a proper home. Now she has something better.

"She's pretty," Pauline says.

"She's darling," says the nurse.

"Her name is Sonia," Pauline declares, as if she's been planning to have a daughter named Sonia all along—she who never plans anything. "Can I hold her?" She doesn't wait for a response but lifts her baby from the box, nearly dislodging the tube from her nose.

"Careful!" the nurse says sharply, though she doesn't try to stop Pauline from cradling her newborn baby in her arms.

Long ago, Pauline taught herself to produce tears by swallowing as she gave an imperceptible yawn and then briefly squeezing her eyes shut. It's a handy trick when she wants sympathy. That the tears come without effort this time surprises her. She hasn't cried for real for as long as she can remember. And now she's crying out of happiness because she has a problem named Sonia all to herself.

PRETTY BOY

What I remember best about the day that Pauline Moreau started working as a filer in the Department of Public Relations at the Port Authority is that Mrs. J arrived at work in a limousine, and she brought a large cage with her.

Inside the cage was Pretty Boy, a mynah bird that fluffed his feathers and made a sound like a dog's growl when Jessie Putnam wiggled a finger at him. I was a little afraid of the bird after that. With Mrs. J, however, Pretty Boy was quite the gentleman. She opened his cage door and let the bird fly around her office. He spent much of the day perched on the desk, taking every opportunity to demonstrate his linguistic skills. At the sound of a ringing phone, he would say, "Hello, Pretty Boy here." When Mrs. J tapped the miniature silver hammer on the silver anvil she had received for being named the premier public relations executive in the country, he would give a long whistle and then call out, "Order in the courtroom!"

Mrs. J had brought Pretty Boy to work to show off to her friend Guy Tozzoli, who directed another department at the P.A. and was well liked by all. When Mrs. J told Mr. T about the conversations she carried on with the bird, he'd said he would have to see it to believe it. After inviting him to meet Pretty Boy that day, Mrs. J called the staff into her office to witness the event.

Mr. T stood with his arms folded over his chest, obviously skeptical. Mrs. J beckoned him to come closer and say hello to Pretty Boy.

"Hello, Pretty Boy," said Mr. T without moving.

Pretty Boy gave a grunting sound. A few of the girls giggled. Mr. T said, "Well, I'm not sure I would call that a conversation."

"He takes his time to warm up to strangers. Isn't that right, Pretty Boy?"

Pretty Boy fluffed his feathers. We thought he would growl. Instead, he let out a series of odd clicks and bit hungrily at his talon.

"Is it a beautiful day, Pretty Boy?" Mrs. J coaxed.

Pretty Boy cocked his head and looked in the direction of the window, then went back to biting his talon. We stared at him, waiting for him to perform. Pretty Boy lowered his leg and looked around at his audience. With a little farting noise, he deposited creamy droppings on Mrs. J's desk.

"He's a real smart bird," said Mr. T.

I'd seen Guy Tozzoli around our department often enough to know that he and Mrs. J had the somewhat prickly relationship of two star players on a team. They respected each other, but there was an air of rivalry in their exchanges.

"Mrs. J, I found the report!" It was Pauline, the only employee in the department who hadn't heard the invitation to come into Mrs. J's office. She had been in the storage room for the past hour, searching through old file cabinets. In her eagerness to announce that she'd located a report thought to be lost, she had flung open the door and burst into our midst. Now, instead of staring at Pretty Boy, we stared at Pauline Moreau. I felt the mortification I would have expected her to feel. To my surprise, she seemed amused by us, happy to be the center of attention.

"Whatcha all doing in here?" she asked.

She was a coarse woman, and even after she started to work for Mrs. J, she wore those revealing blouses. Though she had bought a longer skirt for herself and given up the tiara, you could tell at a glance that she lacked class. I don't think I was alone that day in resenting Mrs. J for bringing her into our ranks.

Mrs. J was unfazed by the interruption and answered Pauline in a motherly tone. "We're trying to get Pretty Boy to speak. But he seems rather reticent today."

"Really? You, Pretty Boy," Pauline said sternly. She seemed so stupidly unaware of the impression she was making that I rolled my eyes in disbelief. "Say something," she commanded the bird.

Pretty Boy cocked his head and looked with interest at this new visitor. "Something," the bird said in echo.

"You smart aleck. Say something else."

"Something else."

We all were laughing by then, even Mrs. J, who was usually too dignified to laugh aloud in public.

"You can do better than that, Pretty Boy," said Pauline, as if she and the bird had a long history together. "Tell us something we don't know."

"You're a cutie," declared the bird, kicking out a leg in Pauline's direction.

"Oh, you men are all alike," Pauline said. She blew Pretty Boy a kiss, then turned on her high heel and did her suggestive runway walk in the direction of the door before remembering why she'd come to the office. She whirled around, clattered over to Mrs. J's desk, and handed her the file. Then she headed back across the room with a wiggling stride that captivated us all. Pretty Boy let out a wolf whistle, and Pauline was gone.

Based on Pauline's display that day, I predicted she would rise faster than the rest of us. What she lacked in sophistication, she made up for in swagger, which appealed to Mrs. J. Besides, Mrs. J had a soft spot for anyone approved of by Pretty Boy.

Just as I forecast, Pauline got special treatment in the department and was moved from filing to reception. She seemed to enjoy the work of answering phones, though often the person on the other end had to wait for her to exhale a lungful of cigarette smoke before she spoke. And she frequently called in sick or left early. But Mrs. J didn't seem to mind. For a while, Pauline was golden. She would have stayed golden if she hadn't gone looking for trouble.

II

WHEREABOUTS

In 1988, twenty-four years after Pauline came to work at the P.A., a fire broke out in the foundry of an aluminum plant in Visby, St. Lawrence County. According to the investigators' preliminary report, one of the pots in the production line pulled loose from its scaffold, spilling its molten contents. The flames quickly spread across the floor and up the wall. The night crew managed to escape moments before the fire set off a series of powerful explosions deep inside the foundry. By the time the local volunteer fire department arrived with its two trucks, the roof had collapsed. The firefighters concentrated on containing the blaze, soaking the surrounding ground and chasing sparks that flew off, saving the two adjacent warehouses. Though on that windless night the toxic smoke rose in a thick column and dispersed harmlessly across the heights of the troposphere, the sheriff took the precaution of ordering an evacuation of nearby apartments.

By dawn, the foundry had burned to the ground. The first responders finally went home to grab an hour of sleep before heading off to their day jobs. The evacuated residents, sheltering overnight in a Super 8 in nearby Massena, drank themselves into a stupor. After giving their testimony to police, the members of the plant's night crew fled town, fearing that they would be held responsible for the devastation. It didn't help that the fire had broken out late on the night before Easter, when the plant's supervisor was away for the weekend. Those inhabitants of Visby who hadn't left were occupied with church and holiday feasts. No one came to survey the ruins. The industrial yard remained deserted through the rest of the weekend. Though the smoke had dissipated safely over the St. Lawrence, no living thing appeared within a radius of a mile. No telephones rang. No radio announcers could be heard through open car windows. The only sound, I imagine, was the occasional clatter when a gentle breeze unsettled a small piece of debris.

By Monday morning, the crows were back, soaring far overhead, while down below, cars sped along Route 82. A commissioner from the EPA took readings with a particle counter to verify that the air was safe to breathe. Around Visby, people gathered to talk about the fire and make bets about the future of Alumacore. But it wasn't until investigators began sifting through the soggy ash later in the day that anyone thought to ask about the whereabouts of Robert Whittaker Jr., director of the plant, and his wife, Kay.

MEET THE WHITTAKERS

Allow me to introduce you to the Whittakers. Bob Whittaker had been employed by Alumacore since January of 1957 and early on worked in their Albany headquarters as a low-level accountant. Five years later he was appointed a managing director, a promotion that came with perks, including a substantial raise, but involved moving north to the St. Lawrence River Valley to oversee the construction and operation of the corporation's newest aluminum-production facility. By 1988, he was stout, double-chinned, mostly bald, with his remaining hair shaved short, looking like a circlet of brushed gray velvet attached by Velcro above his ears.

His wife, Kay, was a woman who carried herself with the poise that came from having once been considered beautiful. She had a springy step and perfect teeth she liked to frame with lipstick a bright shade of red. When she was younger, she had twice been stopped as she walked along the street in Albany and asked if she was Doris Day. She tried to perfect a friendly manner but sometimes inadvertently gave the impression of being standoffish.

Kay had been married once before, briefly, to a high-school sweetheart who died abruptly at the age of twenty-five from a congenital heart condition that had gone undiagnosed. Shortly after his death, their first child was born. The boy, coincidentally named Robert, was later adopted by Kay's second husband and became third in the line of Robert Whittakers.

Kay was a resilient woman, and while waiting to remarry she whiled away her time by writing, with some success. She published an original Harlequin paperback that brought in a little money she didn't need, since her wealthy parents made sure she was comfortable. She came up with a whole series of promising plots and planned to go on to produce dozens of romance novels under her pseudonym, Patricia Linwood. After her second marriage, however, her hobby lost its allure. Miss Linwood was obliged to give up her place to Mrs. Robert Whittaker Jr.

Kay had been happy living in Albany. In her opinion, Visby, up near the Canadian border, was a hardship post. She would rather have lived more frugally and stayed in Albany. When her husband came home with news of the promotion, she pleaded with him to turn it down and offered to ask her parents to make up for the loss of the raise he'd been promised.

Nope. The move was a done deal, Bob said. The alternative would have involved starting his career from scratch, and he wasn't interested in scratch.

The first year in Visby, Kay was unabashedly miserable. She sat in the living room of their shabby rental house sipping her vodka tonics and looking out the window at the construction pit in the distance. She watched brown clouds of dust rise like steam from a hot spring. She watched the rain turn to snow and the snowdrifts pile up to the windowsills. She watched talk shows and soap operas on television and waited for her son to come home from kindergarten.

Her mood improved when Bob announced that he had bought ten acres adjacent to the golf course of the Visby Country Club. Kay had little interest in golf, but she was enthralled by the new property. The land was spread over a hilltop with views to the south of an open meadow full of hollyhock and cornflowers sloping down to a winding stream and to the north, beyond the rolling greens of the golf course, the silver slab of the St. Lawrence River. The long driveway from the road cut through a grove of old-growth hardwoods that had been spared by the local lumber company.

Kay set out to ensure that they would have the perfect house to complement the land and stand as a testament to the industry that had doubled the Whittakers' wealth. In consultation with a team of architects based in Montreal, she settled on a post-and-beam structure with signature aluminum details, including an aluminum-paneled roof, aluminum siding, aluminum shelving and counters. Interior walls were surfaced with anodized aluminum in different-textured patterns. Recessed ceiling lights created a soft glow, muting the shine. Between the garage and the house was an enclosed courtyard lined with tree ferns in aluminum pots.

The project completely absorbed Kay, with increasingly minute details demanding her attention long after the house was built and the Whittakers had moved in. She had the kitchen floor resurfaced twice. She kept changing the faucets in the bathroom and the hinges on their bedroom door. She returned three sets of drapes before settling on burgundy hand-woven silk to complement the silver color of the walls. The ferns in the courtyard died the first winter, so Kay replaced them with a single Japanese maple encircled by hardy philodendrons.

After several years of concentrated work, she looked around at her beautiful aluminum home and declared it finished. She considered how it reflected the larger picture of her life. Who wouldn't be envious? She had an adorable son and a successful husband and lived in splendor. She was in charge of her time and could occupy herself in Visby just as she pleased. And though Visby might not have been Albany, Albany didn't have the views of the sun setting over clumps of little islands in the distance, giving the metallic expanse of the St. Lawrence a lavender cast.

That summer, she decided to throw a party and invite her friends from Albany to come stay for a weekend. She set a date and mailed the invitations. The responses came quickly. Friends were grateful for the invitation and so sorry to have to decline, but they didn't have the time to travel all the way to Visby.

With her son at boarding school by then and her husband at work from dawn to dusk, Kay Whittaker went back to her vodka tonics. She watched the meadow turn brown and the snow start to fall. She studied her reflection in the mirror of her powder compact. She smoked two packs of menthol Virginia Slims every day. Her friendly GP wrote her a prescription for Valium. She looked forward to nothing more than the end of the day so she could lose herself in her dreams. By nightfall, sufficiently medicated, she would finally reach a state of tranquillity; when she fell asleep, nothing could wake her.

Her misery proved contagious—either that or her husband used it as an excuse to let his affections wander. In August of 1974, he came home after a night of carousing, looking ragged and hung over. Kay didn't hold back—she made it plain that she knew what he was up to. At first he tried to deny his guilt, but, under the pressure of Kay's suspicion, he couldn't hide the truth, finally admitting he'd been—his word—*perfidious*. She surprised herself with how little she wanted to hear all the wretched details of his betrayal. In the end, there was nothing to do but forgive him.

In atonement, he spirited his wife away to Italy for a second honeymoon, promising to spare no expense. They stayed in a luxury hotel above the Spanish Steps in Rome. When the shutters were open in their lavish suite in Florence, they could see the bulb of the great cathedral in the distance without even getting out of bed. In Venice, they sipped champagne on their balcony overlooking a small canal, the quiet broken only by the occasional call of a gondolier as he steered his boat around a corner.

The trip seemed to have the intended effect. Back in Visby, Bob returned to his job with a fresh sense of purpose, and Kay found new ways to keep busy. She continued to write long letters to her friends in Albany—a habit she'd begun while traveling. She planted a vegetable garden and tended it herself. She drove up to Montreal several times a year to shop for clothes. She subscribed to the Book of the Month Club and read every book she received in the mail. She remembered the satisfaction writing had given her and started thinking about reviving Patricia Linwood and putting her back to work.

I should mention that in the late seventies, Kay followed a story in the local newspaper about human remains that had been discovered in the woods to the west of Raquette Point, not far from an old lumber road. It was the first murder reported in Visby in over a decade—if it was a murder at all. The skeleton was in such a state of decomposition that the coroner could not ascertain a cause or time of death; he could say only that the bones belonged to a woman somewhere between twenty and thirty years of age. Two Mohawk boys had found the body, and when no one came forward to claim it, the tribe assumed the responsibility of burial, sparing the deceased a pauper's grave.

With so little information available, the story soon disappeared from the newspaper, and from Kay's consciousness. She remembered it only several years later, when she was trying to come up with an idea for her second novel. She had time on her hands, and here was something to keep her busy—a murder mystery just waiting to be written.

Unplayable Lie

Several hours before the Alumacore plant in Visby went up in flames, Kay closed herself in the study and made a few revisions to the pages she'd penned the day before. She was delighted at how naturally the process came to her again, how instinctually she figured out a rhythm that had her writing new material one day, making changes the next day, and then moving forward. True, she had no experience as a writer of mysteries, but she liked to point out to others with a laugh that her maiden name was Doyle. Was it such a stretch to imagine that the creator of Sherlock Holmes was an ancestor?

She usually knew just what she wanted to reveal next in the story. Unfortunately, that day she realized she'd made a mistake in the plot, and an event that was supposed to happen in an ongoing scene couldn't happen because the characters hadn't yet met. She was stumped. The fleeting burst of red as a cardinal flew past the window distracted her. She reread the opening pages, trying to regain direction.

She had not bothered to show the portion she had written to anyone. She had given it a title, however: *Unplayable Lie*— a term used in golf to describe a ball that lands too inconveniently to be hit.

In the pages Kay left behind, a local industrialist plays in a golf tournament in a fictional town in Upstate New York. He is battling it out with the mayor when his ball lands wide of the eighth green in a swampy gully. After using his club to break a path through the reeds, the industrialist sees the waxy, dimpled white patch of his golf ball. As he reaches for it, he also sees the lump of a human leg in the mud. He follows the leg with his eyes and sees that it is attached to the corpse of a dark-haired woman wearing a belted, lemon-colored dress. Her face is turned to the ground.

It was apparent right from the first chapter that the author had an impressive ability to turn the plot in unexpected directions. I was intrigued to read that the local industrialist pockets the ball but then, instead of shouting to alert others to the presence of the body, he eases his way out of the reeds and quietly returns to the mayor. He announces that his ball was an unplayable lie, and he would take the penalty and redo the shot. The two players resume their game. For reasons that I'm sure would have become clear if Kay Whittaker had ever finished the book, the industrialist never says anything about his discovery. The body is left to rot for years, and the remains are finally found again by a group of Mohawk boys hunting for lost golf balls, setting in motion an investigation conducted by a bumbling local detective named Theo, who, by the end of the third chapter, hasn't even begun to figure out the identity of the dead woman and, in the incomplete manuscript, never will.

ENGAGED

The phone rang shortly before eleven o'clock a.m. on the day of the Visby fire. Although it was Saturday, Bob had gone off to his office to finish up a report, and Kay was taking advantage of the time to work on her book. She was irritated by the interruption of the call but glad to hear her son on the other end. Her dear, gifted Robbie, who had recently been appointed an assistant professor of history at Rutgers University—a plum job for a young man fresh out of graduate school. Who cared what else Kay did with her life as long as she had Robbie to show off! Handsome Robbie, the spitting image of Phil Pressman, her first husband, may he rest in peace. She didn't need a photograph to remember Phil. She had Robbie to remind her. Sometimes the reminder had a sting to it; more often, the resemblance seemed only right and good, like a tribute.

Sweet Robbie. He would have been entirely perfect if his friends hadn't put all those socialist ideas in his head. In Robbie's view, capitalism was the villain destroying civilization, stealing from the poor, corrupting the rich, and filling the earth with toxic chemicals. On visits home, he couldn't stop talking about Alumacore and the sins of industrial pollution. All injustice in the world would end, in Robbie's mind, if the whole Alumacore corporation would just shut down.

Sooner or later he would come to his senses and appreciate the salary his adoptive father received from Alumacore. Until then, it was all Kay could do to keep the ongoing argument between her son and her husband from escalating into violence.

"Robbie, it's so good to hear from you! How are you?"

He said he was just fine and had some happy news to report. He and Brigid were engaged! They were planning a December wedding, nothing extravagant, just a small gathering of close friends and family.

There was something wrong with the phone connection, and his words were repeated in a tinny echo. "Honey, what did you say?" In fact, she had understood him fully. She just needed a moment to reflect on the news. Robbie was marrying Brigid Finney, his childhood sweetheart and the eldest daughter of the plant's maintenance supervisor, Tom Finney, who had succumbed several years earlier to a brain tumor. The poor Finneys had run through their savings to pay Tom's health-care costs and were left destitute. The Whittakers had contributed generously to the college fund set up for the Finneys' children.

"I said, Mom, that Brigid and I are engaged."

"Brigid Finney?"

"What other Brigid do I know? Aren't you going to congratulate me? Aren't you going to say you're thrilled?"

Thrilled? Why, of course she was. Brigid was a nice girl, thoughtful and considerate, though perhaps a little too stern for Kay's taste, the kind of girl who had a look in her eyes like a judge just waiting to hear the evidence against you.

"I thought Brigid had gone off to Paris for the year." She heard the sharpness in her voice dinging across the line. The secret truth was, she had been hoping that her son's devotion to his girlfriend would cool while Brigid was abroad.

"She is. We got engaged there."

"You were in Paris?"

"Last week."

"Why didn't you tell us?"

"Mom, you sound so suspicious. Aren't you happy for me?"

"Oh, Robbie, of course I am. I'm overjoyed, but you went to—"

"You'll tell Dad for me?"

She was looking for hurdles to put in his way. "You should tell him yourself," she said.

"I'd rather not."

"He would want to hear the news from you, Robbie."

"He won't want to hear the news at all. He wants nothing to do with the Finneys. You remember what he said about Brigid last summer? He called her a charity case! Whittakers aren't supposed to marry charity cases, are they, Mom? Well, I say it's time for Dad to admit his responsibility for Tom Finney's death. Dad knew what he was doing when he supposedly forgot to install proper filters at the plant. What a convenient lapse in memory. Gee, you can save a lot of money by forgetting. Thanks to Dad, Alumacore poisoned the land and the water for miles around. Alumacore poisoned Tom Finney. Dad might as well have killed Tom Finney with his own hands!"

"Don't say that," Kay hissed. "Never, ever say that again."

"I'm going to marry Brigid, and Dad better not try to stop me." His heaving breath made him sound like a little boy on the verge of breaking into sobs. "I love her!"

Of course he should marry the girl he loved. He would not let his future be dictated by his parents; they belonged to his childhood, like the arrowheads he used to scavenge from the woods and still kept on his shelf at home. Kay could do nothing but promise to support him, to cherish Brigid, and, yes, to relay the news to her husband. But first she needed to calm herself...and calm her son. She took a sip of water, then said cheerily that she wanted to hear all about the trip to Paris. Where did he stay? What did he see? Did he try escargot and coq au vin? Was the table wine as good as its reputation?

She would have to wait to hear about Paris. Robbie was too upset to continue. His mother could tell he was fabricating the excuse that he had work to do, but she didn't want to challenge him. He promised to call her back later.

After Robbie had hung up, Kay listened to the buzzing disconnection, and then the recorded voice advising her that somewhere, a phone was off the hook.

Setting down the receiver, she considered the news. Robert Whittaker III was to be married to Brigid Finney. She surveyed her emotions and decided she wasn't disappointed. Indeed, she was truly happy for her son, who, after all, was a full-fledged adult. And though it would take time, her husband would get used to the fact that Brigid was his daughter-in-law.

Kay remained free of disappointment through her lunch, which she ate at the kitchen table looking out at the garden dotted with crocuses and snowdrops. She wondered how many grandchildren she would have. She pictured Brigid and Robbie walking along a cobbled street in Paris, arm in arm. She decided to suggest to her husband that on their next trip, they should go to Paris. She felt more satisfied with each successive bite of her sandwich. She would not allow herself to wish that her son had fallen in love with another girl. Brigid would make a good wife. And Robbie had a promising career ahead of him. He was a strong and passionate young man in search of good causes.

Kay was glad she had work of her own to do. She turned her mind to her book and the chapter she'd left unfinished. She thought she might write something about Detective Theo's breakfast. How about bacon and two eggs over easy at the local diner? She had to give the waitress a name and took a moment to reflect. Was the waitress old or young? Maybe she could be a member of the local Indian tribe. Yes, Kay liked that idea and would have written more about the waitress if the phone hadn't started ringing once more. She assumed it was Robbie. She hoped he was calling to apologize for what he'd said about his father and Tom Finney.

"Robbie, dear, hello again."

Robbie did not respond. The only answer Kay received was a taut silence.

"Hello? Hello, who's there?"

Someone was on the line, Kay could tell. She clearly heard traffic in the background, which meant that there wasn't a problem with the connection. She could have heard the caller just fine if the caller had chosen to speak.

I don't have time for games, she felt like saying but refrained, because she did not want to give the impression that she was easily ruffled. She just offered a curt good-bye to whoever was on the line and hung up the phone.

There had been too many interruptions for her to recover her concentration. She decided she was done writing for the day. She thought she might go for a walk across the golf course. First, though, she would see if the mail had arrived.

THE SIEGE OF ALESIA

"We should have known how it would turn out," said one Cyrus Blandford, retired high-school social studies teacher, two weeks after the Alumacore plant in Visby burst into flames. Cy was sitting on a bench in front of the boarded-up Tastee-Freez when the journalist from Watertown happened upon him. Distinguished by his habit of running a faded blue washcloth over his bald head as if to wipe away the freckles, he was proud to serve as the town spokesman in the wake of the fire.

The journalist had been sent to Visby to investigate the environmental impact of the fire, which turned out to be so minimal that the paper didn't even bother to run the story. But Cy took advantage of the opportunity to offer the journalist a little history lesson. "Consider, if you will, the Siege of Alesia," he began, unfurling his washcloth. "Surely you've heard of it. No? Then here's your chance to learn something." He cleared his throat. "Roman troops led by Julius Caesar constructed a series of fortifications and moats to trap the soldiers and civilians inside the hilltop town of Alesia. It was only a short time before the inhabitants began to run out of food. To save what was left of their supplies as well as to encourage the Romans to let down their guard, the soldiers of Alesia expelled their women and children from the town. But the merciless Romans refused to let the poor exiles pass, and the Alesian soldiers would not risk reopening the gates. They left their helpless families to perish in the no-man's-land below the walls...imagine. Well, the siege went on. The relief force that arrived to save the day for the Alesians was summarily defeated by the Romans. Finally, on the verge of death, the starving Gauls inside Alesia gave up and surrendered. They stepped over the bones of their wives and children, waving white flags." Cy paused to give the scribbling journalist a chance to catch up. "What can we learn from the Siege of Alesia? you might ask," he said when he resumed. "I'll tell you. A doomed company must be ready to surrender. It must not sacrifice its loved ones to fleeting profit and empty pride. From the day Alumacore first dumped its poisonous waste into Turtle Creek, it was doomed." Massaging the crown of his head with the washcloth, he said, "They should have known better." After a moment he added, "But we never have figured out how to learn from our mistakes, now, have we?"

HOWDY

As it happened, a postcard came with the Whittakers' mail that fateful day of the Alumacore fire. The picture on the front of the postcard was an aerial view of lower Manhattan, with a greeting—*Howdy from New York City*—printed in bold yellow letters across the sky. On the back, besides the address of Mr. Robert Whittaker, there were just four words written in black ink with the distinctive width of a felt-tip marker. Kay Whittaker pulled out the swing arm of the wall lamp in the hall and held the card under the light to examine the writing more closely. The flat cursive suggested that the sender had written slowly, with special effort to form each letter perfectly.

I will be there.

Kay remembered a popular song that had been on the radio a few years back. She used to like to sing along to it when she was driving.

Don't matter if the sky is clear
Or the thunder's crackin'

When you want me near
I will be there.

Who was the singer? It bothered her that she couldn't re-member. She felt stupid and careless. Why didn't she pay closer attention to things that were important?

She studied the writing again. It wasn't unusual to receive a postcard without a return address. She wondered, though, why the sender hadn't signed the card. The effect of the unidentified *I* was not so much to prompt Kay to guess at the missing name but, rather, to consider the implied familiarity. Whoever *I* was must have felt sufficiently known, making the personal name redundant. *I*, in the common form of the nominative case, was functioning more like *we*, and *we*, Kay thought, was a pronoun that rarely needs to be explicated. The *I*, then, was read by Kay as a gesture toward the *we*, who, as was claimed on the card, *will*, meaning "at some unspecified time in the future." *Will* was both promise and prediction, not as formal as *shall*, but with its own stiff insistence. *Will be*. Not modal in the sense of *will meet* or *will see*, but emphatically *be*, insisting on the fact of being and, again by implication, taking for granted that the *you* was necessarily looking forward to being with the *I*, a presumption that led directly to the locative culmination: *there*. Where?

I will be there.

She searched the front of the postcard. She recognized the Woolworth Building and the Twin Towers. There were cranes atop a skyscraper under construction. The harbor was oddly empty of barges.

The more she stared at the image, the more an explanation crystallized in her mind until it acquired the status of certainty. How obvious it was! Any wife would recognize the implication of the message, especially Kay, who had already been through this once before. Her husband was at it again, repeating his old cheating ways—Kay had no doubt. *There* was a place of assignation. Bob often went on business trips to New York. New York! Her imagination took flight as she tried to determine which building in the skyline was a hotel and which window hid the bed where a naked woman lounged, smoking a cigarette and waiting for her lover to arrive.

She might as well as have caught her husband in the hotel elevator on the way up to the room—that's how sure Kay was that she knew his secret. She felt a cold, rational acuity about it all. The clarity was appealing. After she had caught him straying the first time, she had almost given up on him. He had sworn he would be faithful forevermore. She had wanted to believe him, yet through the subsequent years, she could not stop looking for evidence to feed her gnawing suspicion. At last, in the postcard that had appeared in the mail that day, she had something close to proof to put in front of her husband and demand from him...

What? In 1988, she was fifty-nine years old. Bob was fifty-seven. What did she hope to gain by accusing him of adultery? Did she want to live the remainder of her life alone? What would a generous alimony earn for her that she didn't have already?

All possible answers to these questions only strengthened the appeal of inaction. She sat there in reflection while the numbers kept changing on the desktop clock. She paid no attention to the time. She needed to think. Her thoughts moved rhythmically, with effort, as if she were paddling along a river. Sometimes she moved with the current, sometimes against it.

She spent a long while anticipating a showdown with her husband and just as long coming to the decision to do nothing. She liked her routines too much to disrupt them. She was comfortable in her marriage. Why blame Bob for what was probably just a passing moment of weakness? She had her own faults, after all. Contrary to what the neighbors might think, Visby's Doris Day was no model of virtue. Bob himself could have reminded her of picking her up off the bathroom floor after she had occupied a lonely day with a bottle of Absolut. Kay and Bob had looked after each other, in their fashion. Now wasn't the time to turn on him.

Marriage was a fragile thing, beautiful when it was intact but easily damaged. Like a rare vase, it could be bumped accidentally off its pedestal and shatter into pieces. It could be thrown against the wall. It could be forgotten in a corner, left to gather dust.

Better, Kay decided, to give her marriage the attention it deserved—to polish it lovingly and set it in a central place where it could be admired by everyone.

LAVENDER SERENADE

Let's say it's late on a winter's day, a Friday around six, and dark as midnight on the streets of Albany, a gentle snow falling, the flakes big and feathery, hiding the grimy drifts beneath a new white coat. The windows of the company headquarters are lit, suggesting busy activity within, though in fact most of the employees have put on their coats and are already heading out to their cars. Only a handful remain finishing up work—a pair of commercial controllers on the fifth floor who are struggling with the wording on their department's self-assessment, a team of advisers on the eighth floor who are tinkering with a list of cost-control recommendations, and an accountant on the seventh floor who, with the help of his secretary, is inputting numbers in an inventory report.

The secretary is new on the job. Although she has worked only three days of the five-day week, she is looking forward to the weekend as much as if she'd started on Monday. This isn't the kind of gig where she can type two reports in an hour and be done for the day. She's never done, not with a boss who produces a new report before she has typed up the last. She is thinking she'll be glad to be out of his sight for the weekend. Plus there's a good happy-hour deal at Paradiso's, and she plans on joining her girlfriends there as soon as her boss decides enough is enough and gets off her case.

For now he's got her pinned in that position not uncommon for a young female secretary when a nearsighted boss leans over from behind her chair so he can better examine a document in her typewriter, creating with his torso a wall that reeks of aftershave while his arms are like two sides of a split-rail fence set there to keep in the livestock. With his hands gripping the ends of the typewriter roller, his fingers are taut, the skin blotched; a gold band beneath a bony knuckle shines in the light now that the boss has tilted the desk lamp to illuminate the numbers she has typed so far.

She can smell his cigar breath when he murmurs, "Good, good." She can hear a rumbling in his belly, which makes her wonder if he's hungry. She can feel the stubble on his chin when he kisses the back of her neck. She can feel the vise of his hands pressing now on her shoulders instead of the carriage of her typewriter, holding her in the chair while he goes on nuzzling her.

She who was the ward of her alcoholic uncle until his death the previous year and since then has been dependent on her uncle's third wife for room and board...she who is no more than a nuisance among young cousins still in diapers and whose worst fear is that when she turns eighteen, in six months, she will have nowhere to go...this girl who has been unwanted for as long as she can remember can't be blamed if her first thought when her boss makes advances is *What can I get out of this?*

This is not a scene in the unfinished novel Kay Whittaker began writing in Visby, nor is it exactly like the scene in Kay's first novel, *Lavender Serenade,* in which a handsome viscount grabs a reluctant and inexperienced milkmaid, pulls her bloomers down to her ankles, climbs on top of the girl, and plunges into her.

In the reality that is proceeding on the seventh floor of the Alumacore headquarters on a late-winter afternoon in January of 1959, Pauline Moreau would not consider having sex on the desk. There is a nice, soft couch in her boss's office, and that's where she leads him, taking him by the hand with a firm grip so he will know that she is the one in charge.

III

BUSINESS CARDS

Before I even knew Pauline's name, when she was just one of the prostitutes rounded up by the police, I remember that she stood out because of that silly tiara she was wearing, made of tin and rhinestones. It was something a child would wear when she was pretending to be in a beauty pageant. Like I said, Pauline always welcomed attention. I suppose that during her stint downtown, attention helped to pay her rent.

My memory often returns to the image of Pauline being led by a chain to the paddy wagon. I felt humiliated for her, and for the other women, especially when the officer came with that bucketful of water and doused them like they were a campfire.

The women sputtered, faded, turned gray as ash. The worst part was when those members of Mrs. J's entourage of foreign journalists started to laugh.

I've already told you how Mrs. J came to the rescue, whispering secretly, almost coyly, into the sergeant's ear, threatening him in some clever way, I bet. A miniature key appeared, and an officer went down the row of prostitutes unlocking their handcuffs.

After she was released, Pauline made her way along Church Street and onto the side street connecting Liberty and Cedar. She found a stoop of a bricked-up doorway to collapse on, and she crouched there, hugging her knees, rocking back and forth to the silent chant in her head, *I can't take it anymore I can't take it anymore,* until, out of the comforting repetition of her acknowledged defeat, she envisioned a way out. All she had to do was walk over to the Brooklyn Bridge and throw herself off. She would have done it too, she later admitted to me, if it hadn't been for the problem of Sonia. Whether she could fix the problem by reframing the prospect of abandoning her daughter as something positive for the girl, she wasn't entirely sure. She tried telling herself that Sonia would be all right, maybe even better than all right, or maybe not, Pauline couldn't decide; would it be better or worse for the girl to be deprived of her shameful mother?

Pauline never liked to contemplate the future. She felt so muddled as she rocked on the stoop, convinced that the best alternative was to end her life, unsure about her right to do so, rocking back and imagining herself falling a great distance, rocking forward and thinking of Sonia, when up the little street came our group, Mrs. J leading the way, business cards in a leather holder tucked in the breast pocket of her jacket, ready to hand out.

Mrs. J's business card was printed on premium eggshell matte stock, bordered in silver, with a photograph of New York Harbor on one side and information on the other side identifying Lee K. Jaffe as DIRECTOR OF PUBLIC RELATIONS AT THE PORT OF NEW YORK AUTHORITY. She distributed her cards liberally at meetings and conventions. Many people didn't realize, however, that Mrs. J actually had two sets of cards in her holder, one that listed the department's general phone number, and the other with the number for her direct line. This latter card, which she gave out only on rare occasions, was the one she handed to Pauline.

I've often pictured the scene from both perspectives. To Pauline, Mrs. J loomed large, arriving in her field of vision backlit by the sun, so her features would have been hard to make out. Having narrowly escaped an extended visit to a house of detention, Pauline could only feel threatened by the approach of a stranger. The fact that the stranger was female lessened Pauline's fear without diminishing her distrust. Only minutes earlier, when she was one of the pack being paraded along the street, the loudest jeers had come from female bystanders. Now, the silhouette that stood in front of her had the imposing presence of someone who was taking time out of her day to pass harsh judgment. But this impression was offset by a slight hesitation on the stranger's part before she took an additional step forward, suggesting that she wanted to make sure she didn't startle Pauline or inadvertently offend her.

More mysterious to me is what must have been going through Mrs. J's mind. She had made it clear that she would not stand for the prostitutes being humiliated in front of the foreign journalists. At the same time, she had no patience for people who felt sorry for themselves. She was a poised woman who never broke a sweat; she would counsel her clerical staff on routes to professional success but she refrained from bestowing special favors. I had heard her say more than once that the future was no less than what you made of it.

Why, then, did she go out of her way to help Pauline? Why did she single out the streetwalker in the tin tiara and leave the others to their fate? I put myself in her place, and this is what I come up with.

This woman, who was charged with captivating the public so the Port Authority could pay its bills, who did not believe in luck, who liked to see recognition of her dominance registering in the eyes of her staff and who cowed even her superiors into doing her bidding, had a secret: for a while now, she had been looking for someone to save. She told herself that it would have to be someone in need but not needy by habit, someone who was suffering, someone with good judgment who had followed bad advice, someone who would benefit from a helping hand. And so, after the scene with the prostitutes, she had pondered their predicament, trying to understand what would compel a girl to choose to earn her living in that oldest and most taxing of professions. Probably some of them had been abandoned in their childhood, some had been abused, some were derelicts by nature; all were deserving of assistance. In a small way, Mrs. J had used her influence and helped them. She was still looking, however, for the one who would take full advantage of a fresh start.

Mrs. J continued to lead the journalists through the neighborhood, describing the plans for the World Trade Towers without offering a clue that she was thinking of something else entirely. Though the girls had scattered, Mrs. J guessed at their aptitudes, wondering if there was one she could retrieve and set straight. And then her shadow fell across Pauline.

The dark shape resulting from light being blocked by an opaque object is often cause for suspicion or distress. We talk about the shadows of war and doubt and death. In the case of Mrs. J's shadow, however, it might be helpful to consider the effect on a beautiful clear summer day when you are trying to see the bird that is the source of the warbling you've been hearing. Looking up, you have to squint against the blinding sun, but if you position yourself in the shadow of a branch, it is easier to find what you've been looking for. The shadow gives your vision new clarity.

From within the darkness of Mrs. J's shadow, the girl on the doorstep emerged with special vividness, fixed in place and time, enabling Mrs. J to register both her frailty and her strength, her bruises and her beauty. Mrs. J scrutinized Pauline, taking in evidence that was in plain sight—her wet hair a taunting reminder of humiliation, her tin tiara a pathetic echo of childish vanity—along with more subtle clues, like the forceful way she squeezed her fists and knocked the heel of one shoe repeatedly against the step. Where others saw a whore who made her living pleasuring men, Mrs. J saw a feisty soul laid low by exhaustion. Where others saw the same repugnant helplessness they'd seen a dozen times already that day in the form of dirty, crumpled addicts sleeping on flattened cardboard boxes or wild-eyed schizophrenics wheeling their few possessions around in shopping carts, Mrs. J saw someone who could use a break. In a matter of seconds, Pauline had become newly visible, emerging from her anonymity for just long enough to rouse the interest of a benefactor.

I caught the moment only at a glance: I saw Mrs. J extend the card and, to accept it, a hand reach out from the huddled shape on the doorstep. I wasn't close enough to hear what Mrs. J said to Pauline, but I expect it was something along the lines of *If you would like to try out a different career, give me a call.*

REALLY SORRY

In the Port Authority building on Eighth Avenue, in the Department of Public Relations, a little girl drifted between the desks, tugging one metal knob after another, pulling open drawers just for the fun of it. What would she find inside? Why, there were all sorts of treasures, including pencils and pens, hair bands and labels and lipstick, gum wrappers, napkins, ticket stubs, eraser wheels, notecards, and pictures. Here was a Polaroid of a boy in a bathing suit perched on the end of a diving board. And here, a set of coupons clipped from the newspaper. Now what was in this drawer? Let's see—a tube of mascara, ink cartridges, more pencils and pens. What else? To get a better look, the little girl pulled out the drawer farther, so far that it came right out of its slot and dropped to the floor with a clatter. Oh my! She knew enough to be sorry and would have said so, but a small cardboard box tempted with its mysteries. Before anyone could stop her, the little girl opened the lid and tipped the box upside down. Out came all the pushpins, scattering. The whole room fell silent in response. Well, now she was really sorry!

I took the little girl's hand, the one she kept balled in a fist, and led her away while Brenda Dowdle cleaned up the pins. The child's skin was surprisingly warm to my touch, soft over her bony knuckles. Her eyes bulged behind the thick lenses of her glasses, giving her a startled look. Frizzy strands had come loose from her braids. Without thinking, I grabbed a tissue from a box on a nearby desk and dried the girl's chin, damp from perpetual drool. I had little experience with children and none with those who needed extra care. I was surprised by her willingness to trust me. In truth, I was secretly flattered.

I looked around the room, calculating what I might give to the child to occupy her so all of us could get back to work. Brenda was on her knees, collecting the pushpins. Through the glass partition separating the offices, I saw the child's mother in conversation with Mrs. J, probably receiving instructions about her duties for the day. Ringing phones were being fielded by Jessie and Trudy. The other secretaries had returned to their typing, and the fast, efficient patter gave me an idea.

I stacked the white and yellow phone books on my chair and sat the little girl on top so she could reach my typewriter. I held her open hand and steered it toward the machine. At first, I pressed my forefinger on top of hers, teaching her how to depress the keys to make the letters appear on the paper. Soon she could type on her own. With her forefinger, she typed and typed, clearly more delighted with the rattling sounds she made than with the print, which she wouldn't have been able to read even if she'd managed to produce words. The girl's mother, back at her own desk, signaled her gratitude to me with an uncharacteristically regal nod, as if she'd been trained in etiquette by Mrs. J herself. For hours, the whole department hummed the steady, calming tune of uninterrupted work.

An Excerpt from a Page Typed by Sonia Moreau, Age Five and a Half

```
W R O # $ I G L J
P H F L E L B C N
J K O B N . W K J
P D K I M S K D L
M L # T S L S D K
R Y U N K P V B N
D M B N D X A L P
, C K D J $ I P F
Y T I ! ? O % Q A
```

A GOOD FRIEND

"Miss Gleason, could you come into my office?"

Mrs. J stood in front of me; she was a tall woman, and her stylish pink-velvet ring hat propped on the sturdy dark waves of hair added to her imposing presence, making her seem even taller and grander. I felt like I belonged to a different species, a smaller and weaker one. Mrs. J was a predator by nature; I was doomed to be the prey and survived only because I was quick, furtive, quiet.

Pauline had been working in our department for less than six months. Some of the other girls already resented her for the obvious preferential treatment she got from Mrs. J, but I'd come to accept her, especially since I'd seen how determined she was to make a good life for her daughter.

The previous week, the public schools had been closed for their April break, and Pauline had brought Sonia into work. At some point Pauline had left her desk, so she was unaware of the disruption the girl was causing. That's when I'd stepped in and given Sonia something to do to keep her busy. She loved typing, it turned out. She wanted to do nothing else and was happily occupied at my typewriter for hours.

Sonia was not there the day that Mrs. J invited me into her office. I wasn't thinking about Sonia. I was worrying that I had overlooked a mistake when I proofread some recent copy. Or I had messed up numbers in a report. I was thinking I must have done something wrong, and Mrs. J was going to call me on it.

Mrs. J was already back at her desk and on the phone by the time I entered her office. I knew by then that the cigarette smoldering between her fingers was only for show—she wasn't interested in smoking it. She gestured for me to sit across from her as she announced to whoever was on the other end of the phone: "It's true! I am mad, absolutely mad about clothes!"

After she hung up, she said, "Miss Gleason, I called you in today because I wanted to ask a favor of you."

A favor? I couldn't imagine what I could do for Mrs. J that a more powerful person couldn't do better.

"I'm happy to help out, ma'am, in...in any way."

"You see that girl out there." She motioned with her cigarette toward the interior window that gave a view of the corridor leading to the reception area. The back of Pauline was visible as she sat at her desk.

"You mean Pauline Moreau?"

"Yes. Pauline. You're friendly with her?"

"I...well...sort of..."

"I saw you helping her out last week when she brought her child to the office."

"I'm sorry if it was an inconvenience," I said, as if Sonia had been my own child. "I hope I didn't neglect my work."

"Maggie, dear, you are incapable of neglecting anything."

It was the most direct compliment I would ever receive from Lee Jaffe. I felt the pleasant burn of pride on my cheeks.

"That's why I've called you in here. I'm asking you for your assurance that you will watch out for Pauline. She needs a good friend. Will you be that for her?"

I couldn't answer right away, though not out of reluctance. I just found the question so odd, I needed a moment to consider it.

I blinked beneath the feather weight of Mrs. J's patient gaze. "Yes," I finally replied.

"If she needs help, you'll help her."

"Of course."

The intercom buzzed. Through the speaker came Pauline's

voice announcing a Mr. Lindsay. As Mrs. J moved to answer, she waved me away. "That's all for now, Miss Gleason. Thank you." On my way out of the office, I passed a man I didn't recognize. He swept off his hat as he greeted Mrs. J. He had an excited, nervous expression, as if he were meeting royalty. I learned later that he was John Lindsay, the man who would be elected New York's mayor that fall, and he had come to talk with Lee Jaffe about the Port Authority's ambitious plans for a new world trade center.

A Very Important Job

Among the clerical girls, Pauline was the only one ever invited out to Mrs. J's house on Long Island. I don't recall why Mrs. J chose to work at home that day, but I do know that she had business to conduct and needed a secretary for a few hours. Pauline brought Sonia with her, unannounced.

It was a fine May afternoon, sunny, and the sturdy blossoms affixed to the magnolia tree rippled like silk in the breeze. Pauline had never seen a home as grand as Mrs. Jaffe's, and she felt the nervousness of a foreigner who didn't share the language of her host. I imagine that as she approached the house, she hesitated, for she must have partly regretted having accepted the invitation to come out to Long Island, but mostly she felt the curiosity shared by everyone in our department. She'd chosen a smoky-gray cotton dress that fell tastefully to just below her knees and black pumps with kitten heels, an outfit she was sure would meet with Mrs. J's approval. Her self-appraisal gave her a surge of confidence, and she proceeded to the front door. She let Sonia ring the bell. Instead of the expected brassy notes reverberating from inside the house, there was a loud squawk from Pretty Boy, the mynah bird, causing Sonia to shriek in delight and begin a jumping dance that had her tumbling harmlessly off the front step when Mrs. J's husband opened the door.

Mr. J picked up the girl, set her back on her feet, and dusted her off. Mrs. J appeared in the doorway. She took Sonia by the hand and, with Pauline following, led the way into the glassed-in porch adjacent to her office, where a small white dog lay curled on the plush cushion of a glider. There, Mrs. J offered Sonia a very important job: brushing Giuseppe, the princely Maltese who had recently joined the family. Giuseppe was less than a year old and could be impatient at times; he didn't like to have his paws touched, and he might not sit still, Mrs. J warned. She wanted to be sure that Sonia was ready for such difficult work. Sonia nodded solemnly, clearly aiming to approach the task with the right amount of caution, struggling to contain her eagerness to begin.

While Pauline typed notices fed to her by Mrs. J, Sonia went to work. She began by carefully unknotting the bow tied to Giuseppe's forelock. After setting the ribbon aside, she picked a soft brush out of the box Mrs. J had placed next to her and gave the dog a slow once-over, somewhat fumbling in her efforts to smooth him from crown to tail. Following Mrs. J's warning about the dog's paws, Sonia carefully tested him by tapping one paw and then the other with her fingertip. The dog looked at her in puzzlement and accepted it when she caught his paw in her good hand. "Glad to meet you, mister," she said, "my name is Sonia."

From his perch in Mrs. J's office, hidden behind the door, Pretty Boy answered for the dog—"Hello, cutie"—drawing from the girl a two-beat braying that was her version of a giggle.

After brushing Giuseppe, she applied a fine-tooth comb, unraveling every tangle with a gentleness that so soothed the dog he fell into a contented trance and lay there gazing with adoring eyes at the new object of his love. When Sonia was finished combing him, she bundled his forelock and wrapped it in the ribbon. Unable to tie a bow, she tied it in a knot. Satisfied with the result, she curled herself around the dog and fell asleep.

The next day, all the girls in the office wanted to hear about Pauline's afternoon at the Jaffe mansion. Were the dishes really bone china rimmed in gold? Was she served champagne in a crystal goblet? Was there a butler in a white tuxedo? Did Mr. J walk around the house in a blue silk smoking jacket decorated with dragons? Did Pauline see the bronze medal Mrs. J had been given at a ceremony earlier in the month in recognition of her success in public relations? Did Mrs. J gossip about her superiors at the P.A.? Was she upset that her idea for the trade center had been delayed by red tape? Did she talk about her years as a journalist? There was a rumor circulating around the department that Mrs. J was planning to retire; was it true? Was she angry that she had never been considered for the directorship of the agency?

There was more I secretly wanted to ask: *Did Mrs. J explain why you are so special to her, Pauline? Did she list her expectations for you? Did she tell you the same stories she told us about herself in hopes that in you she had found the one girl who would really hear what she was saying and take her advice to heart? Did she give any sign that she was worried for you? Did she explain that a girl with your history should stay away from men with long memories? Did she instruct you in the art of pretending to be someone you're not?*

I kept my questions to myself, and Pauline had little to disclose when we gathered around her as soon as she arrived at the office the next day. She seemed changed by her visit, though the difference was barely perceptible and difficult to describe. I don't know if I am being accurate when I say that she seemed more quietly contented with herself, as if her self-worth had been raised in her own estimation. At any rate, she was reluctant to respond to our general nosiness and tell us about Mrs. J's home. Instead, all she wanted to talk about was the pup named Giuseppe and how handsome he'd looked when Sonia was through with him.

A COUPLE OF WORDS

"It is no secret that I am earning the highest salary in the country for someone of my level," Mrs. J said in a tone that was entirely matter-of-fact. This was back at our first luncheon at the Golden Door, long before Pauline joined the clerical staff of the Public Relations Department. I remember we were served lobster Thermidor for our main course that day. It was the first time I'd ever tasted lobster. The restaurant was bustling, gleaming, modern, intimidating. I was sitting there dazzled equally by the splendor of the surroundings and the eminence of Mrs. J.

"This for a girl from Wichita," Mrs. J added. "Actually, I was born in Pennsylvania, but that's beside the point. I began my real life in Kansas when I was hired to work in the office of Henry J. Allen."

"The congressman?" Trudy, who hailed from Chicago, knew more than the rest of us about politics.

"He was a newspaperman by the time I came along. He'd lost his bid for a seat in the Senate. I handled his correspondence. I read all the letters that came through the office, and I wrote replies to strangers who had asked Mr. Allen to use his influence on their behalf. I found the work unexciting, I admit. I wanted to get out of Wichita. So when I learned that a reporter who'd been assigned to cover a veterans' march in Washington had left for a job on another paper, I applied to take his place.

"I arrived in Washington in my high heels and percale suit and ordered the taxi driver to take me straight to Anacostia Flats, where the veterans were camped. When we got within a half a mile of the camp, the driver refused to go any farther. He said that was no place for a woman. I told him it was a good place for a reporter and paid my fare and jumped out of the taxi. I took off my shoes and ran in my bare feet all the way to Pennsylvania Avenue, where the veterans were already being pushed back by the police.

"Most of you girls probably hadn't even been born then. You might not know that these were veterans who had been awarded bonuses for their service in the First World War. All they were asking was to redeem the certificates for their cash value. When the police tried to evict them, they resisted. Two veterans were killed in the scuffling, and President Hoover sent in the infantry under the command of General McCarthy to break up the camp.

"From where I was standing," she continued, "I could see the last of the tanks rolling down the avenue, flanked by cavalry, with infantry troops bringing up the rear. I confess I had a moment when I saw the flash of a bayonet and was afraid for my life. But there were people around me who were too disgusted by the actions of their own nation's army to be afraid. 'Shame, shame!' they shouted. Smoke was rising across the river, where the veterans had set up their tents. I heard the popping sounds of gunfire coming from the distance. The crowds kept hooting, 'Shame, shame!' I watched the faces of the soldiers as they marched past. Some looked as young as boys who still had some growing to do. I wondered if any were the sons of the veterans involved in the march. In the midst of it, I thought I was witnessing the beginning of a new civil war."

She gave us a moment to digest what she'd said before she resumed. "I longed to be back in Wichita. Washington was more terrible than I had ever imagined. But I had a job to do and a story to write. I followed the crowd that followed the tanks that rolled down Pennsylvania Avenue, pushing back the veterans. At the time, there were more than three thousand men squatting in those shacks across the river. The army was ready to slaughter them all. Fortunately for our country's history, the veterans scattered ahead of the tanks, fleeing into the crowds that closed protectively around them.

"Hoover declared victory. 'It is a matter of satisfaction that the mobs which were defying the government have been dispersed without the firing of a single shot,' he announced. Or some lie to that effect.

"The shacks were burned. The troops returned to the temporary quartermaster depot set up near the White House. The veterans left Washington and went home. I must say, I was entirely sympathetic to their cause, though I tried to stay neutral in my chronicle of the event. The article appeared in the paper almost exactly as I'd written it except for the addition of two words. Before *bonus men* in the article, the word *radical* had been added. And in the headline, the veterans were referred to as Reds."

She tipped her glass to coat the inside with the remnants of gin, then rolled the toothpick between her fingers, examining the speared olive. "That was my introduction to the communication field," she said. "I learned what a difference a couple of words can make." She grabbed the olive between her teeth and closed her lips around it.

IV

Up in the North Country, in the fertile region of the St. Lawrence River Valley, a farmer exited his barn and surveyed his pasture. The morning sunlight had a sharp coolness, and the dew was still lingering on the seed heads. Scattered clouds moved slowly, low in the sky, their undersides tinged gray from the smoke that was carried by prevailing winds from the aluminum plant. Here and there, a fine silver dust covered the grass in patches, like old snow.

The herd had slowly scattered across the hill after the morning milking. Some of the cows were grazing near the pond; others had moved up the slope. One scrawny cow halfway up the hill was already lying down. That young cow, the farmer told himself, had been born lazy. He continued to watch her, pulling his cap lower to shade his eyes against the bright sun. He saw two robins in a skirmish for some sort of morsel in the mud beside the barn. The other cows had moved over the ridge. The skinny one still had yet to stand. Usually, a cow lying down does not graze, yet this one was resting on her belly as she tore at the grass.

The farmer climbed up the hill, breaking off a switch along the way. "Get up," he called as he approached the cow. "Up, up!" He pushed at her with his boot and flicked the switch against her haunches. What would it take to make her stand? "You, girl!" As the cow blinked sluggishly at him, the farmer ran his hand down her foreleg and felt the ominous throbbing of heat. An experienced farmer, he guessed immediately that the distal bone was broken. Stroking the animal's flank, he eyed the chalky ground around him but failed to find the gopher hole he figured had caused his cow to stumble.

Tom Finney Takes Charge

Take the time to notice it, and you'll see aluminum everywhere—in cans, of course, and doorknobs, window frames, kettles, trays, foils, railway carriages, power lines, candy wrappers, license plates, golf clubs, and baseball bats. Aluminum is used by the automotive industry to make cars lighter and more fuel-efficient. Seventy-five percent of the last plane you rode in was probably made of aluminum. Brush a sheet of glass with a protective coat of aluminum, and you'll turn it into a mirror. There is aluminum in antacids and aspirin, in siding, roofing, gutters, and paint. It is a versatile element, strong and light, more ductile than copper, with a melting point as high as its density is low. It is nonsparking and resistant to corrosion and will last intact in landfill for five hundred years. Although it is the most abundant metal in the earth's crust, it is never found free and wouldn't be so widely available if it weren't for clever extraction processes developed by chemists in the late nineteenth century that are still in use today.

In the production process used by Alumacore at the time the Visby plant was in operation, bauxite ore was heated in sodium hydroxide to extract the white powder called alumina. Petroleum coke was then mixed with alumina, and pitch was added as a binder. A hot green paste came out of the mixer and eventually went into a reduction cell, commonly known as a pot. The next main additive was cryolite, a double fluoride of aluminum and sodium. The final ingredient was aluminum fluoride, a chemical compound made from fluorspar. The fluoride was emitted as gas when heated, leaving behind liquid aluminum, which could then be cooled and cast as rods and ingots.

Getting the plant in Visby up and running was no easy task. Along with overseeing the design and construction and monitoring the budget, Bob Whittaker had to hire workers to operate the damn place. He had assumed that a provincial pit like Visby would have a high unemployment rate, that men would be begging for jobs with Alumacore. But GM and Reynolds, already firmly rooted in the area, had sucked up all the able bodies. Trying to persuade their workers, especially reliable supervisors, to come over to Bob's side was proving next to impossible.

Bob set up a booth at a job fair in Lake Placid, with little success. He sent out notices to newspapers within a sixty-mile radius. He grabbed a few men who had been terminated by the other plants because of some breach of protocol. During interviews, they would try to explain what they'd done and express remorse. With a wave of his hand, Bob shut them up. He didn't want to hear about what they had done wrong as long as they did things right when they were on his payroll.

After five months in Visby, with the foundation set and the walls rising, Bob still hadn't found a production supervisor. Watching the construction from the trailer office on the property, he was beginning to think he'd have to don a hard hat and do the job himself. And then Tom Finney appeared at his door.

"Hello, anybody home?"

Tom Finney had a reputation for being too amiable to bother much with the hierarchies of business. Men below him, men above—they were all worthy of Tom Finney's respect.

"Who are you?" Bob was in a foul mood that day. There was a hard sleet falling when he'd woken up. In the fog, he'd almost hit a stupid deer that had been crossing the highway as if she owned it. By the time Bob had arrived at the plant site, the sky had begun to clear, so why were none of the construction workers there? Because they used any hint of bad weather as an excuse to take the day off. *Lazy bastards,* Bob was thinking when Tom Finney entered the trailer and doffed his houndstooth cap.

"Name is Finney. Tom. You're Bob Whittaker, I take it." Bob reluctantly shook Tom's hand. "I hear you are accepting applications. If it's all right with you, I'd like to add my name to the pool."

Tom, who was from nearby Massena, had been working at GM for eight years on an hourly salary. His wife was pregnant with their second child, and he figured it was time to move up into a more senior position. Bob didn't tell Tom that he was the first and only man he'd interviewed for the job of supervisor. The arrangement went on to work perfectly for both of them. Tom, trained as a maintenance technician, lacked the know-how to ask disruptive questions about waste management. But when it came to organization, he was like an expert choreographer, assessing the abilities of the men under his supervision, assigning tasks as if they were dance moves, and achieving intended results. Bob rarely found a need to make an appearance at the plant and instead could set up a fine office downtown and get to know the handful of executives who made Visby their home. Soon they were inviting him to join them at the country club for golf. For a good decade, he enjoyed a relatively carefree life as director of the plant. As long as Tom Finney was around, the potline ran smooth as melted butter.

THE BENEFITS OF RECYCLING

It was true that during his tenure with Alumacore, Tom Finney did not pry into the secrets of the plant's waste-disposal system. However, he liked to translate common sense into practical applications, and he took it upon himself to recommend improvements for the Visby operation. Most notably, he was an early advocate of introducing recycled aluminum into the production process and swore it would save money in the long run. Bob Whittaker, however, was resistant, insisting that any change to the factory's original design would be too costly. He was forced to give in only after the order came from Alumacore headquarters to modify the potline. As it turned out, by mixing scrap aluminum with the pure alumina, the Visby plant needed less heat for the blended metal. There was no difference in quality between Alumacore's primary aluminum products and the aluminum produced with recyclables, and the company enjoyed increased efficiency. Unfortunately, Tom Finney had fallen ill and died before it was proved that he'd been right about recycling.

With or without recycled metal, the smelting required to

produce aluminum must be continuous. To keep the aluminum from hardening before it fully formed, the potline had to remain in production twenty-four hours a day year-round, a grueling necessity for the employees. It was one thing to give up forty-five hours every week to a miserable factory job. But who wanted to labor through the night in a hot, reeking, clamorous foundry in a remote town so far north it might as well have been inside the Arctic Circle? The night crew was inevitably a motley group made up of ex-cons, old men, and high-school dropouts, a bunch of fools who could not be trusted once Tom Finney wasn't around to train them.

In the immediate aftermath of the Visby fire, investigators tried to pin it on the carelessness of the crew, saying they had failed to monitor the new instruments that had been installed in the potline when recyclables were introduced. The workers themselves figured they must have done something wrong, but they couldn't say what. It would take some time before the real cause was understood.

SAVING UP

"Hey, Joe, you go out with Wanda Saturday?"

"Wanda and I are kaput."

"You and Wanda?"

"Wanda's up for grabs?"

"How much she charge?"

"You shits."

"Walt, numbers!"

"Five hundred and ninety."

"Billy, pump it up a notch. Fucking Visby. Sweet Jesus, what am I doing here."

"There's some famous picture of sinners in hell, and it looks just like this. I mean, really, like us on the potline in Visby."

"Hear the Injuns are trying to shut us down."

"They been trying for years."

"Hear their chickens stopped laying, and their cows all keeled over."

"That's what they get for setting up downwind."

"They were here first."

"So what. They coulda moved. Walt, gauge!"

"Six hundred and three."

"My sister-in-law had a preemie last week. Size of a white-hot."

"Air's poison. That's a fact."

"You sound like you're rooting for the Mohawks."

"I'm just saying no one should stick around here for long."

"He's right. Ask Tom Finney."

"Who's Tom Finney?"

"He's dead."

"That's the point."

"He got a tumor in his head. First he couldn't walk. Then he couldn't talk. Then he went blind. Then he died."

"Air's poison."

"Shut up."

"What are we doing here..."

"Me, I'm saving up for Florida."

"He's saving up for Flor-ee-da."

"Saving up his money."

"Saving, saving, saving up."

"Saving up for Flor-ee-da."

"Saving up his money."

"Oh yeah."

"Oh, man."

"Saving up his money for Flor-ee-da."

THE HOO-HA OF HISTORY

Robbie put down his pen and sipped his egg cream through the long straw. After rereading what he'd just written, he came to the conclusion that it was sheer drivel. He was twenty-five years old and his own harshest critic. His ambition was to write about Tammany Hall—in particular, the influence of William Randolph Hearst, who ran for Congress backed by Tammany, was defeated in his run for mayor when Tammany withdrew its support, then was put up by Tammany as a candidate for the governor's office and lost. There was already a fair amount written on the subject, and Robbie thought he knew what he wanted to say. He had limited his portrait to a precise period of New York City politics, but the threads kept getting tangled, and the more he wrote, the blurrier his focus became until he had lost track of the argument he had set out to make.

It was early autumn of 1982, five and a half years before he called his mother on the day of the Visby fire and told her he and Brigid were engaged. He was as in love with Brigid Finney as ever, though he would have to wait to ask her to marry him. She was younger than Robbie and, after delaying school to help her family, was only in her junior year at Barnard. Robbie had followed her to New York. It was fate that he had been accepted into the graduate program at Columbia, a sure sign that he and Brigid were meant to stay together. Everything was falling into place. He was on his way to becoming the kind of intellectual he most admired, making a name for himself in a corner of the world where ideas were more valuable than material goods. He thrived on the serendipitous discoveries that came from research and was as captivated by the stacks of the library as his peers were by the downtown clubs. But unable to get started on the dissertation that was supposed to stand as the culmination of his studies, he figured his plan was doomed.

He reminded himself that, unlike most people his age, he had a fallback. Bob Whittaker had assured Robbie that there was a job waiting for him with Alumacore if he ever wanted it. He could return to Visby with Brigid and build an aluminum house overlooking the golf course. He could make millions telling other people what to do and give his children all the luxuries money could buy. Robbie moving back to Visby would please his parents more than anything. His mother didn't hide the fact that she longed to have her son nearby, and his father was just waiting for him to come to his senses and give up all that intellectual hoo-ha.

Well, they would have to keep waiting. Brigid would never let him abandon his studies. Just yesterday Robbie and Brigid had been walking together up Broadway, talking breathlessly about the *being* part of Sartre's *Being and Nothingness,* arguing their way into agreement that a girl who chooses to hold her boyfriend's hand could not be said to be acting in bad faith, as Sartre maintained, because her willful affection in itself was a testimony of her own *facticité.* Bouncing between them like a ball of Silly Putty, the French word took new shape: *facticité-hey-hee-hee.* How the two of them loved to dissolve into hilarity together. They loved each other and shared their interests, along with their skepticism, as if they were one person. Everything was worthwhile when they were in each other's company.

They spent their weekends together in the room Robbie rented on 103rd Street. It was a dingy space with a view of the air shaft, but the bed was comfortable, and the old wallpaper smelled like wheat. He always woke first and would wait for Brigid to roll into his arms and sleepily caress his chest. They would welcome the day with their mouths latched together. He would dip his fingers into her and feel the warm pulsing of her body. The whole act of making love never failed to seem magically fresh, as if each time were the first time.

Lord, what a lucky guy he was. He picked up his pen and reminded himself that he must use his luck to good advantage and get to work. He must figure out something meaningful to say about William Randolph Hearst.

He turned his pen upside down and clicked the ratchet repeatedly against the counter, as if to free a word that was stuck in the cartridge. It occurred to him that he might organize the story in a different way, in accordance with the force of association rather than in obedience to the order of time. It seemed a novel idea right then. He drew an X over the paragraph he'd written.

To start over, he needed to review his most recent set of notes. As he reached for the folder in his messenger bag, a movement outside caught his eye. He looked out the front window at the streams of pedestrians passing in opposite directions. Among them was a small individual, around five feet tall, a dark-haired girl who walked with a staggered gait, jerking leftward with every other step, which caused her thick ponytail to swing wildly. She wore navy high-tops, jeans, and a denim jacket that was too big for her. That she managed to stay upright surprised Robbie, for her lurching movement seemed severe enough to throw her off balance. Wondering vaguely what was wrong with her, he pulled the folder from his bag and opened his notes.

THANKSGIVING

"Compliments to the chef, Kay. Bob, could you pass around that delicious cranberry sauce?"

"Here you go, Jenny."

Twelve Whittakers had assembled for the feast: Aunt Jenny, who had never married; Uncle Charlie; his wife and their twin six-year-old girls; Uncle Frank and his wife, Donna; Kay Whittaker; Grandma Whittaker; and the three generations of Roberts—though to some at the table, it was only two generations, since Robbie didn't have any real Whittaker blood in him.

The family fell into a happy silence as they went at their food. The storm outside increased the feeling of contentment. The china and silverware added to the sense of splendor. The reflections from the candles burned like liquid gold deep inside the aluminum panels on either side of the room.

"Robbie got a very prestigious fellowship at Columbia," announced Kay, breaking the spell, offering the boast without a prompt.

"Isn't that nice," said Grandma.

"They turned you into a Communist yet?" This wasn't the first time Uncle Charlie had tried out the question on him. Robbie knew to expect it.

"Not quite yet. But soon," he replied.

"I'm coming into the city next month," Aunt Jenny said. "Can I take you to lunch?"

She was a high-school teacher in Albany. Of all the uncles and aunts, she was the only one Robbie felt he could speak to honestly.

"Robbie would love that!" Kay announced on her son's behalf.

"Sure, I look forward to it."

There was another lull, punctuated by the clatter of silverware and a heavy sleet falling on the aluminum roof.

"Nasty weather," Uncle Frank observed.

The twin girls kicked at each other under the table, and one exclaimed in pain. From the other room, Robbie could hear sportscasters on the television that had been left on announcing that the football game was about to start.

"The bird is perfect," Grandpa Whittaker declared.

"It comes straight from the reservation," Kay told them. "They have the best turkeys for miles."

"This turkey is from the reservation?" Bob asked, abruptly pushing away his plate. Robbie was puzzled by the look his mother and father exchanged. Kay's expression mixed hurt at the insult with a warning she didn't dare speak aloud. With obvious embarrassment, his father pulled his plate back and resumed eating.

"What's wrong with the reservation?" Aunt Jenny asked.

No one replied, so Robbie chimed in. "Yeah, what's wrong with the reservation?" Met with silence, he kept pressing. "Dad?"

"You worried that the bird is toxic, Bob?" Uncle Charlie followed his question with a gruff laugh. "We all gonna die of cancer because of this bird?" He kept laughing to prove his joke was funny.

Robbie turned in confusion from his father to his mother. "Mom?"

"There's talk," Kay said. "Just talk. People are always talking. They've been talking about the pollution for years. They want money, that's it. Isn't that right, Bob? They want the EPA to fine you so they can start a civil suit. But the EPA won't levy fines if there's not an issue. And there's not an issue."

"It's the best bird I've had in years," said Robert Senior.

"It's nice," said Grandma.

"Thank you," said Kay. "I'm so glad we could all be together today."

"Hey, Frank," said Robert Junior to his brother. "Don't hog the stuffing."

PARADISE

Robert Whittaker III was an idiot, by his own admission. Even though he went away for boarding school and college and had not lived in Visby for more than a month at a time since the age of eight, he thought of himself as a native. He had spent his vacations roaming the periphery of the golf course near his house, collecting arrowheads and shards of pottery. Once he even found a figure of a woman carved out of stone. Feathery lines had been made in the stone to show her long hair; she had a round torso with a bump the size of a pinhead for her belly button; her eye sockets were hollow, perhaps an indication that they had been filled with glass beads.

The figure was on display in Robbie's bedroom along with the rest of his collection. He'd set up the whole exhibit on one of those built-in aluminum shelves his mother had requested that the builders install throughout the house. Even as an adult, Robbie took the time to pick up different items and examine them. He would be reminded of the pride he felt whenever he had found something to add to his collection. As a young boy, he had fancied himself a bold explorer, at home in the land of the Haudenosaunee.

He understood too late that he had missed a crucial part of the story. It had never occurred to him to ask about the impact of aluminum production on the region. He didn't bother to read the local newspaper and so failed to learn that the Mohawks were demanding financial reparation for the damage done by Alumacore. Mr. and Mrs. Whittaker had avoided the subject in Robbie's presence. The whole town had avoided the subject. If conversation ever turned in that direction, there was always someone around to steer it elsewhere. And after Tom Finney passed away, Mrs. Finney had kept her suspicions about Alumacore to herself, refusing to complain about a company that had set up a charity fund for her children. Robbie first heard it mentioned in an offhand remark when he was home for Thanksgiving in 1983, and he had to search for months to discover the whole truth.

He would learn that shortly after the Alumacore plant was up and running, the farmers on the St. Regis Mohawk Reservation started to notice that the legs of their cattle were swelling. Soon the cattle became so lame that they couldn't stand up and had to drag themselves across the fields to graze. They had trouble swallowing water. Their teeth rotted, and masticating was painful. Eventually they stopped eating altogether and died of starvation. Soon after, the honeybees swarmed from their hives and never returned. Migrating songbirds failed to return in the spring, the deer moved deeper into the wilderness, and the white pines turned brown.

The Mohawks accused Alumacore of poisoning their tribal lands. Conceding that there could be a problem, the company sent a team of scientists to collect data. But the scientists concluded that parasites were to blame for the cattle die-off and that other environmental changes were impossible to document. The Mohawks hired their own researcher from Cornell, who identified illegal disposal areas—secret landfills and an industrial lagoon. He found poisons on off-site soil along the riverbanks. Prevailing winds carried fluoride emissions from the foundry onto the reservation. Deadly cyanide was detected in the wetlands. In a series of reports, he referred to Turtle Cove as "Contaminant Bay." In an interview, he was quoted as saying,

"Boy, it was like child's play up there as a scientist!" He couldn't contain his astonishment as he described his research in the field: "You would go up to the pipes—coming out was yellow water, foam, dead fish, and you would find PCBs right away, in the fish, the snapping turtles, the shrews."

All the while, Robert Whittaker III had been oblivious. As a boy home from school on summer vacation, he would look out the bedroom window of his aluminum house and believe that he was back in paradise.

IN THE BEGINNING

Imagine the St. Lawrence River Valley on a summer's day, before there was even a state of New York, before the Jesuits built their missions and the Mohawks of the region were designated the Keepers of the Eastern Door:

The hardwoods, undisturbed for centuries, are thick at their base and so tall that the crowning clouds skim the forest canopy. Here and there, a conifer drips gluey, resonant sap. Tall grasses sport seed heads in meadows where the bedrock blocks a deeper root. Ravines that gushed with snowmelt in the spring are now dotted with vernal pools. By the end of June, the bitter cherries are already raked clean by bears. In the shade, bedded fawns wait for the does to return. Red squirrels claw their way up the trunks of slender oaks and sail from branch to branch. Mosquitoes buzz, warblers warble, and when a grouse hidden in a web of sumac drums its wings in a crescendo, a boy wrapping a string to bind flowering catkins to the top of a snare stops to listen.

All is peaceful. All is as it was designed to be—

—Until, beyond the ordinary music of the natural world, a

splashing is heard upriver, faintly at first, a bubbling of surging water, a gust of wind, then a growl that rises to a roar, resounding like thunder through the valley. The fawns clamber to their feet, desperate, confused. Terrified birds rise in flocks and race southward. The boy drops his knife and runs ahead of the fate he already knows will consume him as out of the great river rises a beast the size of a mountain, its green scales wet and glistening in the sun, its fangs dripping slime, its single horn as sharp as a spear. The beast bellows in rage, in hunger, in warning. It has been born only to kill.

Fury of evil unfettered. The beast swishes its tail, and the river swirls in a whirlpool. The beast roars. The dark caves of its nostrils flare, spewing gray cords of poisonous smoke that fill the air and spread across the valley, blackening the sky, enveloping the world. Day turns to night in an instant. Stars fall out of the sky, setting the land ablaze. Smoke is everywhere.

The beast twists and screams. The swelling river explodes, sending huge walls of water over the banks, drowning the earth.

All is death. All is lost.

The beast roars in triumph and sinks back into the river, then swims in the direction of the sea to disappear into its lightless eternity, where it will live forever, ready to return, at its own summons, in search of something new to destroy.

Tom Finney's Advice

"Pumpkin, are you there?"

"I'm right here, Dad."

"How ya doing? How's school?"

Her father was back from the hospital, lying in a new bed in the living room with the sheets tucked up to his chin so Brigid could not see his emaciated body, only his face with the gaunt cheeks and the few listless gray strands sprouting from his splotched skull.

"School's good, Dad."

"You're a smart girl. Promise me you'll go to college. Pumpkin, promise me. College is your ticket out of Visby. If you go, your brothers and sisters will follow. Brigid, honey, give me your hand."

The skin around his fingerbones was waxy and cold. Brigid Finney told herself she was glad he was blind. A blind man can't see the tears oozing from his daughter's eyes, the glistening snot on her upper lip, the grief in her heart. She could fool him into thinking that she was strong. She could tell him that school was good, everything was fine. He would never know what she really felt as long as she did not cry aloud.

He held her hand against his face. Where there used to be fine stubble that escaped his razor, now the surface had a smooth, doughy texture.

"How did you get so beautiful?" he asked feebly. His pupils were like specks of dust inside the watery blue of his irises. He stared, unseeing, at something beyond Brigid's shoulder. "You like that Whittaker boy, don't you?"

"Daddy, please—"

"Do you love him?"

"I don't know."

"Well, if you don't know, then you don't love him."

"I do love him! I love him more than I can say, and he loves me, but I don't see why any of that matters right now, with you...oh, Daddy!"

"He's a good man. He'll make a fine husband. But don't let him keep you in Visby. Go out and explore the world, Pumpkin. Don't be afraid to raise your hand and ask a question. Don't ever stop learning, do you hear me? Choose new adventures over old habits." He emitted a series of brittle, unproductive coughs. "Stay alert," he continued when he'd caught his breath. "Be kind, Pumpkin, and give aid where it's needed. What else . . . Trust your instincts about people but stay open to surprise. Take care of your mother—will you do that for me? Be sure to take care of yourself. Eat your spinach, young lady! Sing loudly. What else . . . Keep your boots polished. Memorize three jokes. Kiss the Blarney Stone for me. Light a candle in St. Peter's. Thank God for His mercy every day. Don't drive more than seven miles over the speed limit, and watch out for deer. Dig a spade's depth and turn the soil as you go. What else . . . Face traffic when you walk along the shoulder of the road. Do the kind of work that can't be done by machines. And wipe those tears away, Pumpkin. It's no good crying over what can't be helped."

A CORRECTION

Tom Finney liked to give advice, that's a fact, though whether Brigid had an accurate memory of what would be one of her last conversations with him is unclear. That she might have invented as much as she remembered is understandable. Her father was sick, after all. She had a right to be rattled. She was seventeen years old, the eldest of five children. Tom Finney's savings were used up on medical bills. He would be dead by June.

If it had been Brigid's choice, she would have quit school forever and found a job to help support her family. Her father had cut her off at the pass, she liked to say with a bitter laugh. He made her promise that she would go to college. She kept her promise, eventually. She devoted a year after high school to helping care for her younger siblings while her mother took the necessary courses to get her teaching certificate, and then Brigid went to college for her father's sake, in his memory. She was in her junior year at Barnard when Robbie Whittaker finally told her about the lawsuits pending against Alumacore.

Robbie had put off telling Brigid until he had assembled all the information he could find. Stupidly, he presented his research to her all at once, laying out the facts over lunch at Charlie's Diner. He'd thought she would share his indignation. He'd failed to foresee the scope of her outrage.

Three years after her husband's death, Mrs. Finney had taken her younger children to live in Schenectady, where she had found a job teaching fifth grade. She put the Visby house on the market. But no one wanted to buy a run-down American Foursquare in such a dump of a region, so the house remained unsold, providing Brigid with a place to stay after she learned about the ongoing study commissioned by the Mohawks. She insisted on moving back to Visby as soon as she finished the semester, and through the summer she made herself available to the Mohawks as an advocate, organizing locals and petitioning state and federal legislatures for stricter emissions standards. She conducted her own research, taking water and soil samples in the area, and studied the data regarding health effects of industrial toxins. And though she would return to New York in the fall and fulfill her promise to finish school, she remained so obsessed with punishing Alumacore that she could think of nothing else.

How It Will End

"Brigid, please, open the door!"

It was early May 1984, four years before the fire at the

Alumacore plant. The blossoms on the dogwood in front of the Finneys' house had already turned brown. Even as Robbie stood on the front porch, the petals blew off in handfuls.

"Brigid, I know you're in there." Robbie opened the screen and pounded on the wooden door. He tried to peer through the vertical sidelight window, but the interior was dark. Maybe Brigid wasn't home. Yet her car was in the driveway—she must be inside, and she was choosing to ignore him. He had considered his plan to ask her to marry him one day. It was too late. His world had collapsed under the knowledge that the land he loved had been poisoned by Alumacore. The fish in the St. Lawrence were infused with toxic chemicals. The beehives were empty. Tom Finney was dead from a brain tumor, and his eldest daughter had locked her door to keep out the son of the man who was responsible for it all.

The dogwood petals made a whispery sound as they fell. It was unseasonably warm, already eighty degrees and humid. The sky was hidden behind a rubbery skin of clouds. The only birds around were crows that perched like buzzards on nearby trees. The neighborhood had the empty feeling of a ghost town. Half of the houses had been abandoned once Alumacore had built an apartment building closer to the foundry. The only people who remained were too old to go looking for work or too young to have a choice about their lives. Across the valley, the Mohawks continued to fish and hunt and work their poisoned farms. And then there was Brigid, who had swooped into town with the fury of Hera.

"Brigid, please, open the door."

The earth gave off the grassy smell of midsummer. Robbie could hear the churning of train wheels in the distance, and then the long whistle.

"Please, I beg you." He beat on the door until his arm was

weak. No sound came from the interior. Across the street, an old man emerged beside the garage and looked suspiciously at Robbie before scuttling away again, probably to call 911 and announce the presence of an intruder in the neighborhood.

Robbie contemplated slamming the window with his fist, then decided against it. He pressed his lips against the door. Desperation made him pathetic. He couldn't live without Brigid. Saturated with the passionate certainty born of devotion, he told himself that he had been put on this cruel earth only to love Brigid. He had no other real purpose. If Brigid left him for good, she would take with her his reason for getting up in the morning. He wouldn't have to kill himself. His body would voluntarily shut down. He imagined curling up right there on the front steps, closing his eyes, and drifting into the darkness of eternity.

"Brigid, don't leave me."

Still there was no answer. The neighborhood remained silent but for the soft whispers of the falling blossoms. Robbie sank down onto the porch, his hands braced on the crusty surface of the boards. *This is how it ends,* he told himself. He would die simply because he had lost the will to live.

With his eyes closed, his head buried beneath the wedge of his folded arms, he couldn't see her when she came out of the woods holding the handle of the test-tube kit she'd been using to monitor water quality in a nearby creek. He heard her, though, as she crossed the lawn and mounted the steps of the porch. Without looking up, he knew whose shadow fell across him.

INCENTIVES

Up in Visby, two old women sat in plastic deck chairs outside the Cumberland Farms convenience store, keeping dry under the overhang, its edge still dripping from the refreshing morning rain.

"I told you we was gonna get our comeuppance, didn't I, Gladdy?"

"You sure did, Lorna."

"Didn't I say those Brylcreemed company men landing in town was up to no good, and we'd be fools to trust 'em?"

"We can always count on you to spot a roper, Lorna."

"Wasn't it long before the first bulldozer started bulldozing at the factory site that I said for sure those company men was throwing loaded dice? But you know government folk, always one brick short of a load, never thinking about cons'quence, ready to sell their souls for the price of a steaming hot dog covered with fried peppers and onions."

"Yum."

"Just saying, Gladdy."

"I hear you, Lorna."

Gladys Moss was a retired elementary-school music teacher remembered among the children for the bags of flesh that swung from her upper arm as she conducted the student choirs. Her best friend was Lorna Ducourt, former proprietress of the Salon de Beauté, a local source of wisdom and, in her old age, as knowing as ever, as loquacious and sparkling and indignant as she used to be when she chopped at her clients' hair with dull shears, her own mop of hair dyed jet-black, violet lipstick framing her yellow teeth, a hole in the place of her right cuspid, gold wire reading glasses propped on the bulb of her peach-colored nose as she held forth.

"Like GM and Reynolds wasn't enough, the county uncaps the honeypot and in comes a swarm of pitch flies buzzing with promises 'bout how they gonna raise the standards round here and put two cars in everybody's driveway, color TVs in every home, promising jobs like the weatherman promises sunshine on your wedding day. It's all good news, Gladdy, long as we don't say that dirty word, the one sends the rich folk running, rhymes with *ax* . . ."

"*Tax?*"

"Oh, Gladdy, you know better than to say that word. We got finer words to offer, remember, fancy words, like, ahem, rrrrrebate, *exemption, déduction,* ah, *mon dieu,* you name it, those company men got every handout in the book and in return they took our land, they took our water—for crying out loud, they took our sky!"

"You saw right through them, Lorna, you warned us."

"But no one believed me."

"I believed you. I believed you then and I believe you now."

"The strange thing is, we made a deal with the devil, and—"

"I know what you're going to say, Lorna."

"What am I gonna say?"

"You're going to say, 'Lo and behold, we made that deal, and we survived.'"

"That's right, the devil's hightailed it back where he belongs, and here we still are."

"Here we still are."

V

"Ladies, look around you," Mrs. J directed. This was at our first annual luncheon at the Golden Door, when I was still getting used to the full-time career girl who was my new self. We had moved on to our sherbet course, but we put down our spoons and obligingly looked around, then fixed our attention on Mrs. J.

"The ceiling, the floor, the windows, the airplanes— everything manufactured begins as an idea, and every idea has to be sold," she continued. "We sell the ideas of the Port Authority to America. If we were in charge of a political campaign, we would be selling the integrity of our candidate. For both occupations, we must foster the slow development of sentiment in our favor. Simply put, in the fields of public relations and politics, we aim to drum up votes."

Right then, as if in emphasis, the table began vibrating from a plane taking off on the nearest runway. The whole activity of the airport, inside and out, seemed orchestrated to move in sync with Mrs. J's speech. I remember thinking that her manner combined natural elegance with almost miraculous command. To me, the newest member of the clerical staff, the director of the Public Relations Department had the bearing more of a magician than an executive.

"It's important for you girls to know about the national campaign of 1928. Who can tell us something about it?"

Trudy was quick to answer. "Al Smith ran on the Democratic ticket against Hoover."

"Correct. What you might not realize is that this campaign was different from previous campaigns for one reason: women. Suddenly, women got involved in politics. Businesswomen, farm women, shop women, factory women, housewives, and teachers. Women had influence. Women had power. You know the old joke about how to get important news out into the world—telegraph, telephone, or tell a woman? Well, the women were telling, and women were listening."

Jessie Putnam couldn't help herself. "And the result was President Hoover!" she blurted out, adding, "Maybe women should stay out of politics!"

Jessie was clearly drunk by then. But Jessie Putnam didn't need to be drunk to say the things that the rest of us were thinking.

"Women are as apt to make mistakes as men," Mrs. J said curtly. She was as unflustered by Jessie's candor as she'd been by my earlier disrespectful comment about pretending to be someone you weren't. "But when women believe in a cause, they will figure out how to sell it to the public. If any of you girls were ever to manage a political campaign, you would sell the ideas of your party. The same is true for public relations. First, in both arenas, you must do a comprehensive study of the public mind." She withdrew another cigarette from her case and lit it. "Know your audience," she said, articulating each word for emphasis. "Talk to a cop on the beat, to the taxi driver, to the newspaper boy. Find out what interests them. Let them tell you their worries. Listen in on conversations when you're at a coffee shop or in a waiting room. Find a crowd and mingle. And then go to the drawing board. Say what your company needs you to say in the style that the public wants to hear it."

Her nails were painted the color of blood that oozes from a deep puncture wound. Her hair rippled sleekly below her hat. I thought to myself how contradictory it was to admire her and yet know that I never wanted to be like her. I struggled to put it all in perspective.

"Women," she said, "are natural supersalesmen when they want to be. If the business world didn't know the truth of this when I first came on board, they know it now. I rallied support for every project on the books. The P.A. wanted to build a bridge, so I convinced the public they needed a bridge. The P.A. decided it was time to build a tunnel? The public agreed to pay for it, thanks to me. I sold blueprints and ambitions. Everything that can be conceived of needs to be sold, but not everyone has the disposition it takes to persuade people to hand over their money.

"You all have the potential to be supersalesmen," she said, looking forcefully around the group. "You can convince anyone of anything if you set your mind to it. And when the chairman thanks you by pinching your derriere, you smile and blow smoke in his face." She demonstrated, using Jessie Putnam as her victim. It was the only time I ever saw Mrs. J, who typically used cigarettes as accessories, actually take a drag. Jessie coughed and waved her hand to disperse the cloud.

"It hasn't all been easy. Sometimes I get tired. Sometimes I get tongue-tied. There have been occasions when I'm supposed to write a speech and I can't get it right. I stay up all night writing and then crossing out what I've just written. I begin to fear that I will never write another word. I can't think of a thing to say. But a notion always comes to me at around four in the morning, that magic hour that is both very late and very early, when the world is still dark but the dawn is just beginning to press against the barrier of night." Mrs. J had grown uncharacteristically animated. "I'm not sure exactly how to explain the sensation," she said. "It is a time that's so quiet," she went on in a lowered voice, as if speaking to us in confidence, "my mind has to fill the space. The darkness seems to come alive with gabble, laughter, whispers, roars. Do you girls know what I'm talking about?"

We poked with our spoons at our sherbet. I reflected on my own recent bouts of insomnia. I was twenty-one years old at the time, unused to New York. I shared a room with a girl from San Antonio who worked at Macy's during the day and was taking a bartending course at night. She stayed out late and inevitably woke me when she returned. I would lie in bed watching the sliding patterns of dappled light on the wall from the cars on the East River Drive. When I heard a siren, my imagination would spin scenarios of accidents and crimes that played out on nearby streets.

In the silence that followed Mrs. J's speech, I turned the edge of my spoon in my sherbet, creating a little hole in what was left of the scoop. I waited for someone to say something. The pause went on so long it began to seem awkward, until Mrs. J beckoned to the waiter for more coffee. Lifting her cup, she gazed over the rim from girl to girl and finally to me. "One thing is certain," Mrs. J concluded. "You can't have good public relations unless you put on a good show." And then she gave the kind of wink a person might use as a reminder to keep a secret safe.

Joanna Scott

AT THE TRACK

When Pauline Moreau went away for a weekend in the summer of 1974, she left her daughter, Sonia, with me. This in itself wasn't unusual. There must have been half a dozen other occasions when Pauline asked me to watch Sonia. Pauline liked to bet on horses, and she would go up to Saratoga every August for three or four days at a time. She refused company—she said she needed to be alone to concentrate on the races. I gladly took charge of Sonia.

Pauline's sojourn at the Port Authority had lasted five years. After she quit, she didn't bother trying to hold down another job. She reported mysteriously that she had come into a small fortune after the death of a benevolent distant relative. I wanted to believe her and appreciated how happy she was to be able to spend money on Sonia. I worried that Pauline would lose everything at the track and was relieved when she had good results.

On that August Saturday, Sonia and I went to the Central Park Zoo. It was a hot day, and the air reeked from manure and the garbage overflowing the bins along the path. In the heavy warmth, many of the animals were lethargic. Sonia and I made a game of trying to coax Gus, the polar bear, to come out from his concrete den, but he wouldn't budge. We finally gave up on him and walked on. We bought a pretzel from a vendor, and large orange sodas. Sonia spent a long time chewing on the ice.

I was steering us around the shorter loop to the exit when we passed the elephant pen. The elephant was lying on its side, with several men gathered around it. I assumed the elephant was deathly ill; I worried that the men were preparing to euthanize it in front of the spectators. We soon learned from a guide, however, that the elephant was feeling just fine and was merely being given a manicure. The elephant lay peacefully, seeming to enjoy itself, while two of the zookeepers scraped a nail file across its foot, back and forth like a crosscut saw.

Sonia was enthralled. She turned to a girl standing near her and said, too loudly, "I never saw an elephant get a manicure." Sonia's giggle ended in a hiccup, and her chin was suddenly wet with drool tinged orange from the soda. The girl she had addressed retreated to the other side of her mother and shielded herself behind the woman's wide hips. Sonia, who was used to such snubs, turned to me and repeated, "I never saw an elephant get a manicure."

"Neither had I, until now," I replied, taking the hand she kept balled in a fist and pulling her close to me.

Sonia's muscle impairment was limited to her left side. She had difficulty bending her left leg and walked with a listing gait. Her left arm hung crookedly, and the fingers of that hand were always curled. She had trouble closing her lips and long ago had learned to widen her smile by moving her jaw to the right. Her thick glasses only partially corrected her severe myopia. In terms of intelligence, she made up for any deficit with her hunger for knowledge. She might have been slower than average in picking up skills, but once she learned something, she didn't forget it.

In the summer of 1974, she was almost fifteen years old, small for her age and reading at a second-grade level. She had a native optimism and lacked any awareness of cruelty. I don't think she knew it existed. Other children could taunt her, push her, pour her milk over her food in the school cafeteria, and she still believed they were her friends. She explained away a bloody nose by saying that a boy had "bumped" her with his hand. When children were laughing at her, she laughed with them. When children ran from her, she ran after them. When they told her to go away, she obeyed and promised to meet them the next day. She still hadn't entered puberty.

Pauline tried to teach Sonia to stand up for herself. She demonstrated how to knee a boy in the balls and pull a girl's hair. Pauline even bought her a pocketknife, which Sonia promptly gave as a gift to one of her so-called friends.

When I was in charge of Sonia, I did my best to keep her away from anyone who might hurt her, and then I tried to distract her if she was treated unkindly. The zoo had plenty of distractions, and Sonia was enthralled with them all on that hot day in early August 1974. After watching the elephant's manicure, we wandered over just in time to see the sea lion being fed. Inside the monkey house, we watched capuchin monkeys swing from rope to rope. Sonia tried to imitate them, grasping at the air and taking an awkward skip. She loved the colorful peacocks and was amazed when we stopped in front of the lion's cage and it opened its mouth in a huge yawn.

After the zoo, I took Sonia for an early dinner at the Auto Pub on the corner of Fifth Avenue and Fifty-Ninth Street. We sat in a Shelby convertible and ate chili dogs and fries. The waitress took a liking to Sonia and brought her a free Shirley Temple.

"Guess what I saw today," Sonia said to the waitress.

"Um...a fire engine with its lights on?" The waitress was about twenty or so, with the slender, muscular body of a gymnast. I pictured her popping into the air and doing a backflip for us.

"I saw an elephant get a manicure!"

"No! Really?"

"Cross my heart!"

"Wow, that is so cool," said the waitress with conviction.

"I can't believe I saw an elephant get a manicure!" Sonia kept repeating to me after the waitress had gone into the kitchen. "It was so funny!" To make sure I knew how funny it was, she crossed her eyes and wobbled her head. I burst out laughing.

The next day was drizzly, so we stayed inside. We had a late breakfast of blueberry pancakes and then played simple games—checkers, go fish, dominoes. While Sonia took a long nap in the afternoon, I read through the Sunday paper. I prepared a dinner of fried chicken and applesauce, and then we watched TV and waited for the arrival of Pauline, who had promised to pick up Sonia no later than nine.

By eight we were watching *The Wonderful World of Disney*. As I recall, the movie that night was about a duck that accidentally gets irradiated in a laboratory and, as a result, starts laying eggs that contain gold nuggets, producing a new egg whenever it hears a barking dog. The duck, of course, creates all kinds of havoc, and Sonia shook in fits of contagious giggles through most of the movie. She laughed at the duck, I laughed at Sonia, Sonia laughed at me.

It was so easy to enjoy the simplest kinds of fun with Sonia. Her good nature had purity and strength, and there was a radiance to her crooked, freckled face. I remember that as we laughed together, I promised myself that I would do anything to protect the child.

Even before the movie ended, I began to feel a worrisome premonition, attributable, I thought at first, to my awareness that my apartment would seem so quiet and empty after Pauline took Sonia home. I lived downtown, in an apartment on Jane Street in the East Village. Pauline and Sonia lived in Morningside Heights. My work at the P.A. kept me too busy to visit them more than once every couple of months.

Pauline hadn't arrived by ten o'clock, so I tucked Sonia into the guest bed and went on waiting. Sonia slept soundly after our long, tiring day. I made myself coffee and turned on the local news.

Pauline had been late before, but she had always called to let me know where she was. When she still hadn't arrived by two in the morning, I dialed the number she'd given me of the hotel where she was staying. I was greeted by a recorded message informing me that the number I had dialed was not in service.

I took Sonia uptown to her summer program the next morning and then called the police. They advised me to check with all the hotels in and around Saratoga Springs, so that's what I did, calling them one by one from my desk at work.

I missed the strengthening presence of Mrs. J, who had long since retired. I wished I could have gone to her straightaway to share my worries. Instead, Mr. Quipley occupied her office. It was Mr. Quipley I had to tell that I had failed to finish proofreading a report. It was Mr. Quipley who warned me that my pay would be docked if there were any more delays.

On the bus uptown to pick up Sonia, I found myself remembering something Mrs. J liked to say about herself. I had heard her announce more than once that when she was young she was known as "the Deadline Girl" because she always finished every assignment just ahead of the deadline. The thought filled me with an urgency that I knew had nothing to do with falling behind in my work but was born of the sense that I had to find Pauline before it was too late.

By then Sonia was attuned to my worry, and back in my apartment she kept asking when her mother would return. All I could tell her was "Soon." I don't know how many times I said it over the subsequent days. "Soon, Sonia, she'll be here soon." I said it that day, and the next. I kept saying it through the weeks that followed. "Soon, she's coming soon, as soon as she can. She'll be here soon. Soon, I promise. Very soon."

...When You Are Up

When the World Trade Center opened for business in December of 1970, it had only two tenants, on the tenth and eleventh floors of the North Tower. The rest of the floors in both buildings remained empty for months. The towers weren't officially dedicated until April 1973. In August 1974, the summer that Pauline Moreau disappeared, the huge buildings were still not even half occupied, and the World Trade Center was operating at an enormous yearly deficit.

Under the direction of Raymond Quipley, Public Relations was asked to devise attractive lures to stir interest among potential tenants. The pressure made for a tense atmosphere, especially for the writers assigned to come up with ads. I don't remember who was responsible for the slogan It's Hard to Be Down When You Are Up, but it provoked Mr. Quipley into berating three young copywriters.

We could see Mr. Quipley through the interior window of his office, cradling his chin in the curve of his thumb and smoothing his silver beard with his fingers. He stood in front of the copywriters in silence for a minute, then roared, "We are losing thirty million dollars a year, boys! Thirty. Million. Dollars. These towers weren't erected just to be admired. If we don't fill the real estate, we . . . you . . . the P.A., yes, the Port Authority will go on asking for subsidies. And then what? Surcharges will be levied on tolls. The public will blame us, and rightly so. The governor will respond and cut our budget. So what are we going to do to prevent that from happening? 'It's Hard to Be Down When You Are Up'? If that's the best you can offer, lads, I'll have to start looking for your replacements."

He motioned the copywriters to return to their desks. We all worked quietly and avoided discussion. We clerical girls glanced at one another in suspicion, as if the threat to our jobs was hiding in our midst.

The next morning, I remember, I went to wake Sonia and paused for a moment before saying her name. She lay on her side under the flowered sheet, her mouth slightly open, her thumb pressed against the beak of her upper lip. Asleep, she resembled her mother more than I had realized, with the line of her jaw following the same graceful curve around the chin as Pauline's, her eyelashes naturally thick and dark, the skin smooth and plump above her cheekbone. Perceiving Pauline so present in her daughter's face, I felt her absence with a sharpness that caused me to murmur aloud, to say, faintly, "Oh," jolted by the surprise of recognition.

I took the subway back downtown after escorting Sonia to her program. I stopped in the lobby to purchase coffee and a buttered hard roll, and then I headed up to the twenty-eighth floor. When I exited the elevator, I was surprised to find the department deserted. I was a few minutes late, and my first panicked thought was that I'd missed a notice for a meeting called by Mr. Quipley. I learned only later from someone in the department across the hall that everyone had gone up to the penthouse dining room to watch a man walk on a tightrope between the two towers. I hurried up the elevator, but by the time I arrived, Philippe Petit had finished the performance that would make him famous.

Mr. Quipley thought the stunt would reflect poorly on the Port Authority. But Guy Tozzoli, who by then was in charge of the whole World Trade operation, saw it as an opportunity. "This is really something," he was overheard saying that morning as he watched Philippe Petit lie down on the wire on his back. "It'll be on the front page of every newspaper in the world. We couldn't have asked for better publicity." Mr. T paused, then added, "As long as he doesn't fall off."

GLORIOUSLY HUMAN

"What's that?"

"My God!"

"Is it . . ."

"A man!"

"Way up!"

"Look there!"

"A man on a tightrope!"

A man dressed all in black, holding a long, thin, curved pole as he steps gingerly along a cable rigged between the Twin Towers. A Frenchman who has rehearsed the feat for three years in the streets of Paris near Saint-Germain-des-Prés. A man—twenty-four years old—who has come to New York to realize his dream.

A man high up in the air. A man lying down on the wire. A man running. A man bending on one knee. A man so far above the street that to spectators he is a speck the size of an ant.

New York, wake up! he calls out in his mind, keeping his lips sealed tight in concentration.

New York is awake. New York is cheering in the street below. Traffic has come to a standstill.

A man who might plummet to his death at any moment. A man risking everything to do what he does best. A man enjoying himself.

"Philippe's motives were unusual, but gloriously human," wrote a reporter for the *Wall Street Journal.* "This expression of the virtuoso spirit deserves our applause, and we can be proud that it was in America that Mr. Petit raised his art to such heights."

"I did just what I felt," he told the reporters who greeted him after he had been released from the police station. "It was a show for me. I was happy. I was dying of happiness. I was not scared because it was a precise thing," he said as he signed an autograph for a policeman.

"But why take such a risk?" someone called out from the crowd.

"If I see three oranges," the Frenchman explained, "I have to juggle. And if I see two towers, I have to walk."

A NEW LOGIC

It is difficult to describe my state during this period. The world seemed so powerfully illogical, I felt as if the old rules of cause and effect had become obsolete. According to the new rules, a man walked on a tightrope thirteen hundred and fifty feet above the street, and a woman went away for the weekend and never returned. Where there had been a body of flesh and blood named Pauline Moreau, there was only an emptiness, and memory. Pauline had no family other than Sonia. Sonia herself didn't really grasp the significance of her mother's absence. She had to repeat the eighth grade, and she was preoccupied with the challenge of her remedial studies. The grief she was not allowed to feel was passed to me, yet to accept it would have meant giving up on Pauline. Even though I guessed that she was gone forever, I could not allow myself to fully mourn my friend. And so I existed in a state of torturous paralysis, aware of the truth yet unwilling to act on my belief.

I went to work, I scrambled to meet the deadlines for every assignment, I shopped and cooked and tended to Sonia. But as I think back to those months, I picture myself moving about the city in a daze, shocked into an incoherence that feels, in retrospect, like a sickness. The only event that could have kept

Pauline from returning for Sonia or sending word of her where-abouts was her death, yet death wasn't a reality without any official confirmation. Even after I'd given up hoping for her return, grief seemed premature, even disrespectful.

If Pauline had disappeared twenty years later, there would have been cell phone records to trace and computer services to help locate credit card activity. But this was 1974, remember. The first product bar code had just been stamped, on a pack of Wrigley's chewing gum. I'd recently bought my first pocket calculator. I didn't have an answering machine.

I kept thinking of Mrs. J's words: *If she needs help, you'll help her.*

Of course, I'd said.

It was an easy promise to make but not to keep, as it turned out. How could I help her if I didn't know where she was? The fact that Pauline had given me the number of a nonexistent hotel convinced the detective on the case that she had run away voluntarily. When he learned that Sonia was—in the language of the report—retarded, he identified her as the object from which her mother had obviously fled.

A police officer was finally assigned to accompany me to Pauline's apartment. When the building's super unlocked the door, we were greeted by the noxious smell of decay. I thought for a terrible moment that it was the smell of a rotting human corpse. We soon discovered, however, that the utilities had been turned off, and the stench came from milk and raw hamburger that had been putrefying for days in the warm refrigerator.

I pointed out to the officer that a woman who left food in the refrigerator must have been planning to return. He said he knew next to nothing about the case, and I should direct all questions to the detective in charge of the investigation.

The apartment was a small one-bedroom; the main room served as Sonia's bedroom, and her artwork was taped to the walls. I remember there was a drawing of a roller coaster, and in the front carriage were two smiling figures I took to be Sonia and her mother. Sonia's hair was in braids that stuck out comically above her ears. Pauline's thick black hair was unbound and streaming wildly in the wind.

The sound of a passing siren jolted me. The officer was conferring with the building's super outside the open door of the apartment. The police radio crackled softly.

I packed a suitcase with Sonia's clothes and cleaned out the refrigerator. The super locked the door behind us. I picked up Sonia at her program and we took a taxi back to Jane Street.

All we could do at that point was go on waiting. We waited for so long that Sonia stopped asking me when her mother was coming home, and I no longer had to lie and say, "Soon."

THE MIDDLE OF NOWHERE

It is three months after Pauline left for her weekend in Saratoga, and Sonia and I have come to the edge of a canyon. As I understand it, we are there to admire the view. While I am fiddling with my camera, Sonia steps forward to the edge of the cliff. Suddenly the lip of ground gives way beneath her feet, and I look up just in time to see her fall. I scream out her name, driven by the terrible premonition that she is already lost to me. I drop to my hands and knees and crawl to the rim, dreading the sight of the child's body crumpled on the rocks far below.

I am surprised to discover that no more than three or four feet below the rim is a second overlook terrace. There, in the grass, is the crumpled body I'd been expecting to see, lying facedown, but now I have hope that she has survived the short fall. I lower myself to the terrace and gently turn her, discovering only then that the person lying in the grass is not Sonia. The body belongs to Pauline; her eyes are black and lifeless.

The vision keeps throbbing in my mind after I wake, yet its implication is so foreign to my bleary consciousness that I have trouble relating it to reality. Through the subsequent hours, I try to lose myself in my routines and throw off the dream's tyranny, but the vision keeps pressing itself on me, forcing me to acknowledge it until I comprehend the unfathomable meaning as a physical sensation. To keep from suffocating, I have to let myself feel the full impact of agony, which is why I close myself in the women's room at work later that morning and flush the toilet to drown out the sound of my sobs.

VI

If Only I Could Have Asked Him a Few Questions

Mr. Whittaker, please take a seat. I have called you here in the hopes that you can shed some light on a mystery in which you yourself played a significant part. I will go so far as to point out that there would not even be a mystery without you, Mr. Whittaker. Without a mystery to unravel, there would be no story to tell, and I would not need you to fill in the blanks created by your own silence.

Speak to me, Mr. Whittaker, so I can lay it all out on the page in front of us. Tell me, first off, how many times did you take advantage of Pauline Moreau. Six? Twenty? Fifty? I know about the first time, when you leaned over her chair after everyone else in the office had gone home. She was seventeen years old, hoping to get her GED someday but at the time boasting one marketable talent: she was a whiz at typing, thanks to a teacher in her secretarial-skills class who wouldn't tolerate any slacking. Pauline typed her way into the job at Alumacore; it wasn't long before she had caught your attention.

Did she tell you what she told me? That it wasn't much fun to make love to Bobo, but she sucked it up because she had been led to believe that *no* wasn't an option? You wanted her to do things for you. *Things*—yes, that's how she put it, leaving me to guess. You took to staying late at the office so Pauline Moreau could thing you. It worked out for a while, didn't it? Pauline earned herself a few nice pieces of jewelry—a Carrington and Company silver orchid pin, a top-of-the-line Timex watch, a double-stranded necklace of freshwater pearls. You looked forward to going to the office. Kay was oblivious, and Pauline never gave you any trouble. Your special arrangement could have gone on for years if only you hadn't gotten careless one of those times when Pauline was thinging you.

Maybe you are one of those men who love the thrill of knowing that they have the power to create life. Even if you weren't looking to father a child at the moment, maybe you were tempted by the gamble. You did not pause to consider that your perfectly managed life could be undone with a single lively spermatozoon. It's a good feeling, isn't it, when you're risking everything for pleasure? Maybe you said to yourself, *I don't need the rubber...just this once.*

"Bobo, I gotta talk to you."

"What's that, sweetheart?"

"I'm late."

"Aw, don't worry, I got you covered. You're under my protection. Anyone tries to give you trouble for being late, you come to me."

"No, I mean I'm *late*-late, by two whole weeks, not even a spot."

"'Oh, the sun shines bright in my old Kentucky home,'" sang

the maid in the adjacent office as she ran the carpet sweeper over the floor.

Your office door was locked. You were in the midst of unbuttoning Pauline's blouse when she announced that she was *late*-late. Your first response was a stab of pride at the proof of your virility. Your next response was terror mixed with disgust. This girl...this whore...she had the power to ruin your life.

Your thoughts careened, crashed, exploded, blew off in pieces. You, the son of a farmer who went bust in the Depression. You knew the gnawing pain of an empty stomach. Your sisters made their skirts out of old bedsheets. Your mother filled your shoes with beans and water and set them on the windowsill to stretch them out. But you were no dummy. You left home and never looked back. You had the wherewithal to take care of yourself. You married up. Kay's father had a friend at Alumacore willing to give you a chance. You made yourself essential. By 1959, you were a rich man by your father's standards. But you could lose it all. You—Robert Whittaker Jr.—could not afford scandal.

Among the fragments of ideas that must have flown through your mind after Pauline told you she was pregnant were, in no particular order:

(1) You wanted to wrap your hands around her throat and squeeze with all your strength. Maybe you would have done it if the housekeeper hadn't been in the next room.

(2) You'd heard of a doctor who had a basement practice.

(3) There wasn't any problem money couldn't fix.

CLICK

Pauline received the money in cash—bundles of tens and twenties packed neatly into a frog-green vinyl Royal Traveller suitcase. She hid the suitcase under her bed in the attic room she shared with her uncle's two young daughters. The next day, she stayed in bed, pretending to be sick. Her uncle's third wife, now his widow and matron of the house, graciously brought her a cup of tea, took her temperature, and reminded her that she'd be eighteen in three months, ready to be an independent young woman.

Pauline wasn't about to wait to be kicked out onto the street. While her aunt was at the grocery store with the children, Pauline slid the frog suitcase out from under her bed, clicked open the buckles, and raised the lid.

She had looked at the money once already, in Bobo's office. He showed it off to her like a jeweler displaying his inventory, lifting the cardboard lid as if he were peeling velvet off a box of diamonds. His face was mottled with the blush of strong emotion he was straining to repress. He had hardly spoken to her all month. It was easy for management to hide behind a locked door at Alumacore. Soon, though, his young mistress would begin to show; just in time, he was ready to speak to her. He said something about his wife. He said something about the president of the company and *perfidy*. It was clear he blamed Pauline for letting herself get knocked up. Now he just wanted her out of his sight. To speed her on her way, here was a thousand dollars. She trusted that he was being honest about the amount and didn't try to count it there in front of him. But before he handed it over, he made her promise that she would go away for good and never, ever try to contact him.

I promise, Bobo.

In her attic room, under the light from the single bulb

screwed into a rusty socket in the ceiling, Pauline surveyed her prize. Many of the bills were old and worn. She set an Alexander Hamilton beside an Andrew Jackson to compare them. Their faces were chalky and wrinkled. They looked like brothers. Pauline wondered what they would think if they knew they were associated with a girl who had gotten herself knocked up at the age of seventeen. Studying their faces, she thought Andrew Jackson was more likely to disapprove. Alexander Hamilton, she decided, would have a more sympathetic response. *Take it in stride,* she could imagine him saying. She had a vague memory of someone once saying that to her.

Most of Pauline's memories were vague. She liked it that way. She might even have willed it to be so. The memory of finding her mother passed out on the kitchen floor, for instance, was shrouded in a misty darkness. The fog did a good job of blurring the blue of her mother's lips, the gray of her skin, the weird whites of her rolled-back eyes. Pauline hardly remembered. And regarding her uncle's friend who came over to listen to ball games on the radio and liked to slip his hand inside Pauline's panties when no one was looking—she couldn't even remember whether he had a beard or not. As for her own father, she didn't remember his name; she wasn't sure if she had ever known it in the first place.

Out of this fog emerged a girl in the present who was enjoying looking at her stash of Andrew Jacksons and Alexander Hamiltons, the faces multiplied over and over again, as if in a hall of mirrors.

One thousand dollars. That was a lot of money. Actually, she discovered after counting that it came to eight hundred and forty. She counted again. This time she got eight hundred and fifty. She counted once more and got the same number as the previous time. She felt a little cheated because it was less than the thousand Bobo had said was in the suitcase. He had lied to her. Or maybe he had just made a mistake. She resolved to shrug off the discrepancy. Eight hundred and fifty wasn't nothing. All of a sudden, Pauline Moreau was rich!

She told herself that she should be *late*-late more often. Now she didn't have to worry about how she would support herself when she turned eighteen. Why, thanks to Alexander Hamilton and Andrew Jackson, she could support herself plus the child she would welcome into the world round about October.

She couldn't wait to have her child. Once she was a mother, she would have a family of her own and would no longer have to pretend to belong to a substitute family that didn't want her, nor would she have to share her baby with anyone, not even the father. Especially not the father. She was glad to be through with him and would have left of her own accord with or without a sendoff. A suitcase full of cash was much appreciated, thank you very much, but it did not earn Bobo a role in shaping the future for the child growing inside her. Pauline's baby would belong only to Pauline! Just feeling the hard bulge low down in her belly was enough to make her want to kick up her heels. She would never be alone again. She just needed to decide where she wanted to not be alone. She asked herself if she would rather be in Albany, where she'd gone to school, or Schenectady, where she was born. She had promised Bobo that she would go away for good. The truth was, she wanted to get so far away from him that he could never touch her again.

Far away but still eminently possible was New York City, where, to the amazement of everyone she'd told, she had never been. New York City. Where else should a girl go when she wants to start living? She was free to leave, just like that. A train ticket would hardly make a dent in her fortune.

And so Pauline Moreau went down the Hudson Line, clutching her frog suitcase on her lap, afraid to let it out of her sight. She wore a brown serge skirt, knee-length, a striped cotton blouse, and a scarf tied over her head. Even before she made it to Grand Central, she knew she had to get some fashion tips. How drab she was in contrast to the woman in the mustard-yellow suit seated across from her. The woman probably thought Pauline was a servant girl who had just arrived from the Old Country. Pauline felt stupid and provincial beneath the haughty gaze. She wanted to open her suitcase to show the woman what was hidden inside. In fact, she did click the buckles open, but in the next breath she pressed them closed—then popped them open again, and closed them, opened and closed them as she thought about the import of her two secrets, one inside her, the other in the suitcase.

Click.

Click.

Click.

There are few things more annoying to some people than an irritating noise that shows no sign of abating.

"Will you stop!" This from the woman in the mustard suit, who seethed the supposed question as a command. But Pauline was already in the midst of the action and couldn't prevent the buckles from opening one more time.

Click.

And then, of course, she had to lock the suitcase back up.

Click.

It was a satisfying *click,* perfectly calibrated to annoy the kind of woman who aspired to be all the qualities associated with the color she was wearing: harsh, burning, oily. The lady in the mustard suit on the Hudson Line train was used to being the dominant flavor in life. But with almost one thousand dollars to her name, Pauline Moreau was done being a pushover.

FAIR PRICE

Back then, Bob had a thick black mustache he'd laugh at years later when he looked at pictures of himself as a young man. He brushed his fedora free of lint and polished his loafers every morning before work. He was as eager as he was obedient, absolute in his resolve never to fall back into poverty. He did what he was told to do. *Just make a few changes in the books, son. That's all they asked of him. Elevate production costs a notch or two. Go on, Bob, no one will notice.*

Here, you mean? In this column?

That's right. And on the next page, if you can add a zero to fifty? Will you do that for us, Bob?

This was back in the good old days, before cell phones and computers, before anyone thought to worry about fluoride in the air, when contractors in America were making a fortune building bomb shelters, when Eisenhower was playing golf to avoid coming face to face with Fidel Castro, when everything was clear and simple, and accounts were kept in big leather books the color of burgundy.

Bob wrote in pencil. Kept the tip sharpened at all times. Crossed his sevens. Double-checked everything. And once a year he took his burgundy books with their carefully recorded numbers to Washington for a meeting to set the coming year's price for aluminum.

He never much liked long train rides. Little things would bother him: the roughness beneath his collar from the laundry's starch, the smell of another man's aftershave. He worried that he would leave the books behind when he got off the train in Washington. He would try to anticipate every question he would have to answer at the meeting.

On the trip back to Albany, he could relax. He would treat

himself to a leisurely lunch in the dining car. Between Philadelphia and New York, he would make up for the sleep he'd lost the previous nights. From New York to Albany, he would enjoy gazing out at the expanse of the muddy Hudson and the steep wooded hills across the river. When he saw fishermen bobbing in a rowboat in a cove adjacent to the track, he'd feel a pleasant envy. He would observe the shadows of clouds floating weightlessly on the surface of the water. Everything seemed worthy of his appreciation: a barge making its way downriver, sunlight glistening on the current's ripples, yachts in a boatyard, even graffiti painted on the concrete of an underpass. After Poughkeepsie, he would head to the bar car, where he would drink Manhattans and smoke through the remaining stub of a cigar and trade jokes with the other drunks on board. All along the way, he would congratulate himself on a job well done.

This went on for some time, long after Pauline's departure. Bob grew so used to the price-fixing scheme that he forgot to question his own role in it.

Then Bob's superiors learned that the authorities were launching an investigation, and they scrambled to destroy all evidence. New burgundy account books suddenly appeared to replace the old ones, and Bob was given a formula for recording a different set of numbers. There was an urgency to the work, he was told. He had to finish the books before the week was over.

He stayed late every day, writing until his hand ached and his eyes burned from squinting. He would work deep into the night, long after everyone else had left. Alone in his office, he would stiffen at the memory of bedding Pauline. By then she had been gone for three years, yet sometimes he imagined that he could still smell the perfume he'd given her for Valentine's Day.

Then came Bob Whittaker's annual performance review. Bob

dreaded these meetings. They were awkward and humiliating, with the boss disguising his criticisms with avuncular jocularity. Year after year it had been the same; always, the review would tilt ever so slightly in a negative direction, just enough to reduce Bob to a servile promise to do better in the future, to work more quickly and protect the company's reputation at all costs.

On this occasion, however, the boss had a different agenda. Bob had barely settled in his seat when he learned that he was being given a fancy new title in recognition of his excellent service. Robert Whittaker Jr. was going to join the ranks of Alumacore's managing directors. No kidding, a promotion out of the blue! It came with a substantial raise along with a stock option and a bonus to cover the cost of moving.

Moving?

That's right, Bob—Alumacore had to get you out of its headquarters, and fast! Pack your bags and go. Up north, Visby was waiting with open arms, ready to claim you as one of its own, you and your young family.

"And if anyone ever asks for Bob Whittaker," said the boss to the receptionist in the lobby after Bob was gone, "you say, 'Bob who?' You say you never heard the name Bob Whittaker in your life. You say no one named Bob Whittaker has ever worked here."

PAULINE FINDS A NEW HOME

The mercury had topped ninety degrees when an elderly widow named Mrs. Clayborne removed three plastic plates from a small table in her apartment overlooking Second Avenue. One of the plates, she noticed, had a hairline crack, so she threw it away. Blotting her perspiring forehead with a tissue, she made a mental note to buy a pack of new plates, hoping to get them at a discount from the five-and-ten.

Mrs. Clayborne was always low on cash these days because the parents of the children in her care were low on cash. For years, she'd had a thriving home day care in East Harlem, where she was appreciated for her ability to convince even the most indifferent children that the hard work involved in learning was worth the effort. She would march her young charges down to the library on Ninety-Sixth Street, and they would look for books that would help them figure out why the wind blows and how electricity works and what dreams mean. Even before they learned to read, the children were encouraged by Mrs. Clayborne to come up with possible solutions to the world's most intractable problems. To keep people from going hungry, one small girl who wasn't yet four suggested that every building should have a garden on the roof. To keep people from being cold in the winter, a little boy offered a diagram showing how mirrors could reflect the warmth of the sun. To entertain the group on a rainy day, a precocious five-year-old girl wrote a play based on Hansel and Gretel and performed all the parts herself.

At her busiest period, back in the mid-1950s, Mrs. Clayborne had had eleven children in her care. With their own parents, they might have pitched tantrums and refused to do what they were told; with Mrs. Clayborne, they were too proud of their importance to misbehave. Choosing the right crayon to draw a picture of the sky, for instance, required a great deal of concentration, as did eating a peanut butter sandwich. Mrs. Clayborne expected them to think hard about everything they did. Someday they would grow up to become leaders in their families, in their communities, in government and business and education. Until then, they learned from Mrs. Clayborne how to consider all the mysteries life presented them with and not to worry if their guesses were wrong. "There's a lot of figuring out to do in the world," she liked to say, "and plenty of time to get it right."

By 1961, most of Mrs. Clayborne's students had moved on to public school, and the parents of the three children left on her roster were poorer than ever. The father of the boy named Ishmael had recently lost his job as a doorman, and the mother was sick with a tumor in her breast. The parents of the twin girls were recent immigrants from Jamaica and were unemployed. How could parents pay for child care if they did not have jobs? How could they look for jobs if they did not have child care? Mrs. Clayborne stopped asking for payment; the company of the children was payment enough, she assured the strapped parents, neglecting to mention that to cover her own expenses, she had to borrow from her nephew.

Now, as she rinsed off the two remaining plates, she told herself she could not bring herself to ask her nephew for more money. She would have to sell the white-gold necklace with the cross pendant that her godparents had given her back when she was married, in 1923. With her hopeful nature, she figured she could get enough for it to cover this month's bills.

She was still hopeful when the mother named Pauline arrived at her door later that day and asked if Mrs. Clayborne had room for a little girl who toddled with a limp and could not keep from drooling. No matter that Pauline was penniless; Mrs. Clayborne was glad to add gentle Sonia to her charges and ready to help this young mother get back on her feet.

STOCK PHOTO

"Name?"

"Pauline Moreau."

"Mr. Hopley will be right with you."

"Thanks...Nice day, huh? Well...too bad there's no elevator."

The woman looked coldly over the rims of her glasses. Pauline shrugged. She didn't wait for the inhospitable receptionist to invite her to sit. She collapsed into a chair with dingy bark-cloth upholstery. The springs squeaked as she shifted her weight.

She was out of breath after climbing the dark stairs to the fourth-story office in a deteriorating building on West Twenty-Second Street. Along the way, she had passed a door for a company that identified itself as a wholesale cutlery vendor and another door with only the faded outline of stenciled letters spelling out PRIVATE INVESTIGATOR remaining on clouded glass.

Her appointment was with Photomat, a stock-photo supplier that, according to the brochure Pauline paged through while waiting for her interview, served companies around the country. The brochure included hundreds of photographs with labels like *smiling businessman, negro girl with large afro, dentist chair, sexy aviator woman, interior bedroom, teenagers by swimming pool.* If a company wanted to produce an ad showing a middle-aged Northern European–looking woman, Photomat could supply the image, for a small fee. If for some odd reason a company needed a picture of a little boy holding a pet mouse, Photomat could provide it.

By the fall of 1961, Pauline was broke. All the money from Bobo had been gone for a while, and Pauline had been relying on the largesse of friends she'd made around the city, sharing their apartments, eating their food. One by one, her friends had stopped answering her phone calls. The only one willing to help was Mrs. Clayborne.

Thanks to Mrs. Clayborne, Pauline and Sonia never had to go to a public shelter. The old woman had offered her and Sonia a room in her apartment in East Harlem, and she graciously watched Sonia while Pauline was out on interviews. She said Pauline just needed a break. She didn't ask for payment. But Pauline looked forward to paying Mrs. Clayborne everything owed to her, plus some. Pauline would give Mrs. Clayborne money as soon as she had money to spare. She was as hopeful as Mrs. Clayborne about the future. The Photomat listing in the classifieds was for a typist, and no references were required.

"Mr. Hopley will see you now." The receptionist had not moved from her desk. No buzzer had sounded, no phone had rung. Pauline could only wonder how Mr. Hopley had communicated that he was ready for her.

"Um . . ."

"Through that door."

Pauline followed the receptionist's pointing finger, expecting to enter an office. Instead, she found herself in a huge room, mostly empty but for file cabinets lining the walls and a small desk at the far end, behind which sat a little gray-haired man wearing glasses with thick Coke-bottle lenses.

Pauline hesitated and cleared her throat, waiting for directions. The man called out, "Approach."

She crossed the room tentatively, as if testing the boards beneath her feet, her eyes fixed on the man as he watched her. "Mr. Hopley?"

"Have a seat."

She waited while he scribbled something on a notepad.

"Age?" he finally asked without looking up.

"Twenty. Well, really, I'm nineteen. I'll be twenty on Monday. So I'm already starting to say I'm twenty, you know, to get used—"

"Height?"

"Why do you need to know my height?"

Mr. Hopley finally looked up at her, gazing mildly from behind his thick lenses.

"To see if you'll fit."

A rustling sound near the ceiling caught Pauline's attention. She looked up just as a pigeon flew across the room and landed on the sill of one of the high windows. What a strange place this was, Pauline thought. Yet somehow this Mr. Hopley, gruff as he appeared, put her at ease. She liked that he wasn't trying to impress her or flirt with her. He was just a little man at a little metal desk in a cavernous room. A harmless little man with a form he needed to fill out.

"Height?"

"I'm maybe five four, give or take a quarter of an inch. I don't know, I haven't been measured in a while, it could be I've grown."

"Weight?"

"I thought you needed a typist."

"I assume you can type."

"Sixty-eight words a minute! Though I may be a little rusty..."

"Is that your real hair color?"

"Of course!"

"Ever tried life as a blonde?"

"The ad didn't specify a blond typist."

"I can offer you seventy-five dollars a week. You'll get two weeks' paid vacation, plus holidays. Some days you can go home early. Other days I might ask you to stay late. I expect you to be able to work on weekends when necessary."

"I got the job?"

Mr. Hopley stood and extended his hand across the desk. "Welcome to Photomat, Miss Moreau. Pauline. May I call you Pauline?"

"I can't believe I got the job! You won't be disappointed in me. You'll see, I'm a fast typist. I'm not so good at spelling, though, just to warn you. When do I start?"

"How about now?"

"Today?"

She turned at the sharp sound of heels on wood. The receptionist was crossing the room, summoned by some mysterious means. She wore a tight-fitting floral dress that accentuated the curves of her body. She had removed her glasses. Her eyeliner was brown and extended like wires from her upper lids.

"Ann, you'll show Pauline around?"

"Sure, Mr. Hopley." To Pauline, she ordered, "Come with me."

"I can't believe I got the job!" Pauline repeated as she followed the receptionist she now knew as Ann back across the immense room. Ann shut the door carefully behind her. "He doesn't like the sound of the latch" was her curt explanation.

Pauline followed her down the hall to a windowless alcove that was packed with more file cabinets. Some of the cabinets were pushed together to free up space. In the center of the alcove was a card table crowned by a Royal manual typewriter.

"You'll be doing the labels. You can start at the *B*s, here." She pulled open a file drawer. She dropped a folder on the table. "You're supposed to look at the picture and type a description of it on the labels here. Make sure you begin with the letter the photo is filed under. A picture in the *B* file should begin with *B*. Keep it short. He doesn't like lots of words." With that, she prepared to leave.

"Hey," Pauline called to stop her.

The woman turned, her face hardened in grim impatience. "Yes?"

Pauline had opened the folder and was examining the first picture. "Why is this picture filed under *B*? I mean, it's a flower. Shouldn't it be under *F*?" She received no response, so she continued jabbering. "I guess what you're saying is I need to name the kind of flower. A kind of flower that begins with the letter *B*. I don't recognize this flower. Do you?"

"You're not very good at this."

"I was just asking."

The woman ignored her and clattered down the hall.

Pauline studied the flower. Its petals were white, edged with a rosy tint, and bound by a circlet of green. She wondered if it was a lily. She tried to think of the names of other flowers before remembering that she was working with photographs filed under the letter *B*. She couldn't think of any kind of flower that began with *B*.

B flower.

Grim Ann had told her to keep it short.

She sat at the card table and rolled a label around on the carriage. *Beautiful flower,* she typed. She turned to the next photo. She continued working, typing labels, photo after photo. And if she couldn't figure out what to name a picture, she simply put it in her pocketbook and moved on to the next.

THE ALCOVE GIRLS

Pauline had plump red lips, big eyes topped by crescent lids she tinted purple, and full hair that took the shape of every curler she put in. She was trailed by the fragrance of the rose water she splashed herself with every morning. She had the kind of beauty it didn't occur to me to envy. I just liked to admire it and giggle with her at the men who turned their heads to watch as she passed by. When I knew her, she liked to recall the days when she'd had success as a model—a career that unfolded from her job as a typist at the stock-photo company. She said modeling was the best work she'd ever done, and she wouldn't mind trying it again someday.

Pauline worked for a week or so in the alcove of the filing area, dutifully typing labels for photos. Then the time came when Mr. Hopley asked her to come into the office on a Saturday.

Mr. Hopley needed cheap models, so he chose young girls who didn't know what they were worth. As long as he told them they were more beautiful than any of the women in the photos they had spent the week labeling, they trusted him. They were like lambs he fattened with compliments. They would have their pick from the wardrobe Mr. Hopley accumulated just for them: dolly-bird dresses that showed their skin through the crochet, silk dresses with cleavage cutouts, strapless evening gowns, minidresses decorated with brocade. A girl would choose a dress to wear, and then Mr. Hopley would bring her out to prance along the street while he walked backward with his camera.

Getting paid for looking gorgeous and having your picture taken was a better gig than typing labels, in Pauline's opinion. She had fun that day walking up Sixth Avenue in the sunshine, following Mr. Hopley, calling a warning to him when he was about to back into a signpost.

At the end of the day he gave her twenty dollars and sent her home. He didn't try to make a move on her. He didn't dirty the work by asking for a kiss. He just paid her, and that was that.

Pauline couldn't have been happier. She'd made twenty dollars just by being herself!

The routine continued for several months. She would type labels in the alcove through the week and on Saturdays earn extra cash modeling for Mr. Hopley. It was a good deal, and timely, since Mrs. Clayborne had been threatened with eviction, and now Pauline could save the day and pay her for rent and child care.

I don't blame Pauline for thinking of herself as the heroine of her own life, but I do wish she'd had better judgment. Later, she would say she loved that job with Mr. Hopley more than any other. She would say she wished it had lasted forever.

BEAUTIFUL

She smiles. *Click.* She loosens her ponytail and lets her long hair blow in the breeze from the fan. *Click.* She turns and looks over her shoulder. *Click.* She purses her lips and kisses the air. *Click.*

She does everything the photographer tells her to do.

She rests one foot upon the edge of the chair, drapes her fingers over her knee. She lifts her skirt to show the seam of her pantyhose. She lifts her skirt higher.

The photographer walks backward, ahead of her, down the sidewalk. People stare at her in awe, thrilled to be witnesses, convinced that the woman being photographed is some kind of celebrity.

Back in the office, the photographer follows her into the dressing room, his camera still clicking. He pauses long enough to affix an umbrella to a light stand and push a garment rack aside, revealing a wall of white canvas. He motions to the empty space he wants filled.

She moves forward tentatively, unsure of her task. She fails to interpret his gesture when he tugs at his own shirt, so he has to make his expectation explicit by reaching forward and undoing the top buttons on her blouse. Now she understands. She undoes another button; his nod indicates approval and anticipation; she undoes another button, and then another. She stands in nervous docility as he helps her slip her arms out of her sleeves. With an expert maneuver, he reaches behind her and pops open the clasp of her bra, then he gently pries apart her arms, which she is using to shield her breasts.

Once he is hidden behind his camera again, she does not mind the exposure. Spotting her own miniature reflection on the lens pointed at her, she feels like she is performing in front of a mirror. She might as well be alone in the room. She feels free and naughty, absorbed by impropriety that will have no consequence. She flaunts, struts, twists, throws back her head, lifts up her breasts. Remembering a poster that once caught her attention in Times Square, she goes so far as to pinch her nipples before bursting into coarse guffaws at the absurdity of it all.

BOTTOMS UP

Then the Saturday came when the shoot lasted longer than usual. Mr. Hopley had wanted her to take off all her clothes. She said that she drew the line at her panties. She had meant it as an idle joke, but Mr. Hopley registered her resistance as an inconvenience he did not have the time to suffer. Either she stripped for him or they were done for the day, he said, so she stripped. As she stood entirely naked before him, she felt nothing—not fear, not shame, not even the thrill, familiar by then, of being in possession of her own beautiful body. She was ready to do what she was told to do. He had her sit on a stool and open her legs. He had her face away from the camera. He had her squeeze her bare feet into pointy, brocaded pumps, but when she tried to walk to her position in front of the canvas, she turned her ankle, and the heel of the right shoe snapped off. Mr. Hopley barked at Pauline, angrily denouncing her for being, in his word, a klutz. Pauline, out of habit when people were impatient with her, pretended to cry, causing the photographer's brown eyes to narrow as he surveyed his newest model. He told her to get dressed.

He must have known already what he would do with Pauline. It was the same with all the alcove girls. Each would model for him for weeks or months, and then one day he would take her out to dinner, to a gentlemen's club on East Sixtieth, where the girl would be fawned over by Mr. Hopley's friends; they would go on to offer the girl a job, promising tips that would bring her ten times what she was earning at Photomat. Mr. Hopley would protest—the girl was too valuable to lose, he'd say. The friends would suggest a payment. The men would barter, money would be exchanged, and eventually Mr. Hopley would leave, abandoning his model to her new line of work. Girls who protested were persuaded that they had stumbled into a rare opportunity. Girls who kept protesting found themselves out of a job. Girls willing to wear nothing but thongs did all right. Girls who agreed to go into a back room with gentlemen clients did even better.

As for Pauline...did she object to being traded by Mr. Hopley for an undisclosed sum? She didn't like to dwell on the subject. Still, she couldn't help but welcome the prospect of making more money. Nothing scared her more than being out of work. She had a child to support, a child who needed a brace on her leg, asthma medicine, prescription glasses. Mrs.

Clayborne did all she could—she was like a grandmother to Sonia—but her tenants couldn't expect to live there for free. The old woman had come to depend on Pauline's income. Without money, everything would fall apart.

At the gentlemen's club on East Sixtieth, Pauline saw two paths for herself. One led into the dark chasm of poverty, while the other was lit with electric candles and included free glasses of champagne.

Bottoms up, darling. Here's to you, sweetheart.

Pauline avoided talking about this period in her life, so it is left to me to make up a story about the first time she was paid to have sexual intercourse with a stranger.

Did I put that too clinically? I can't think of a better way to say it. I don't trust myself when I imagine an unnamed man pulling Pauline by her wrist and leading her between the tables and down a long hallway. When I try to see the stranger, I keep thinking of Mr. Hopley walking backward up Sixth Avenue, clicking the button on his camera.

Click.

Click.

Click.

DING-DONG

Up in Albany, Kay Whittaker felt her heart skip a beat; she would never get used to the sound of the doorbell! And now here it was after seven, and Bob still wasn't back from the office. He worked so hard to prove himself. His insecurity went deep—that was one of the things she loved about him, for it made him appreciate her support. That he came home late most days showed that he was fighting for a foothold in a corporation where he was surrounded by men who had launched themselves into business with the help of trust funds. They had the advantage over a poor farm boy like Bob. Kay had used her father's connections to get her husband placed in Alumacore, but now it was up to him to work his way up, rung by rung.

Little Robbie was asleep in his bedroom. On the television, Judy Garland sat with legs crossed on a platform on a railroad track singing "Nothing could be finer than to be in Carolina" to Tony Bennett. Judy looked angry, Kay was thinking—angry, and too thin. Maybe Judy was irritable because she was hungry.

And then came the ding-dong of the doorbell.

Kay peeked through the peephole, but the view was blocked. She couldn't identify the visitor through the tiny hole, so she unbolted the lock but opened the door no more than a crack, trying to see more clearly.

"Hello?"

A big bouquet of flowers was thrust in front of her nose as she heard her husband's voice: "Celebration time!"

She threw open the door. In a moment, she and the bouquet were being squeezed together inside the embrace of her husband's arms. He was so giddy, he had difficulty speaking. She shared his joy without knowing why. It hardly mattered why. Something wonderful had happened to him, and they were celebrating together, waltzing around the front hall, scattering rose petals.

"Oh, Bob, they're beautiful, but..." She felt a vague presentiment of an intrusion that was about to disrupt their lives.

"Meet one of Alumacore's new managing directors!"

Kay heard Tony Bennett singing back to Judy Garland in the other room.

"You've been promoted? Bob, I am so proud of you! How wonderful! What happy news!"

She had been waiting for him so they could eat dinner together. Now she would have to wait a little longer while he washed up and changed his shirt before she would hear all about Bob's promotion—first, the hefty raise he'd be getting; second, the number of employees who would be reporting to him; and third, the little detail that they would be moving to Visby.

HOOKED

"You got to realize," explained Eleanor Rickman, champion fisherwoman and wife of Walter Rickman, former mayor of Visby, "we used to ship five tons of caviar to New York City. You know—"

"Wasn't it ten tons, sweetie?" interrupted her husband. They were sitting together at the overlook park above the power dam, sharing a cheese sandwich, when the journalist from Watertown happened upon them. "That's what I recall."

"New York City will always love caviar," said Eleanor with a shrug. She passed the sandwich back to her husband. "We had sturgeon grow to six feet and more. The last one I caught weighed ninety-eight pounds."

"And was something near one hundred and twenty years old."

"I snagged her with a piece of sucker fish on a troll line. I kept her long enough to take a picture, and then I threw her back."

"Ellie can catch anything once she sets her mind to it. Perch, carp..."

"Bullhead eel..."

"Handsome young bachelors..."

"You were easy, lovey. You practically jumped out of the water into my hands."

"Hooked like that sturgeon. Except you didn't throw me back."

"I never did catch another sturgeon, though not for lack of trying."

"They disappeared for a long while. We thought they were gone for good."

"Like everything else around here, they suffered from the effects of pollution."

"And human greed."

"Plus the dam blocked their spawning routes."

"But they're coming back. I hear they're plentiful again on the west side of Wolf Island."

"They're still babies, mind you. Nothing like that ninety-eight-pounder."

"Nothing like it. They'll need time to grow and spawn."

"New York will have to wait to get its premium caviar."

"A hundred years or longer."

"And then it will be all right."

MUDPUPPIES

Visby: Where Alumacore followed GM and Reynolds and capitalized on the shipping channel of the St. Lawrence and the power generated by the system of locks and dams that had taken half a century to build. Once home to lumberjacks and, before that and still, the Mohawks. Where the Alumacore plant began operation early in 1964, sending its waste into Turtle Creek and its emissions into the sky to be blown southeast by the prevailing winds onto the reservation.

Within two years, farmers began to notice changes in the leg bones of their cattle. At the same time, the children growing up on the reservation were making their own discoveries.

Picture this: Two boys, Max and Jimmy, are pedaling furiously, racing each other along the lumber road. Max, the older by a year, is ahead, but Jimmy gains on him on the downhill portion. They whoop as they bump over potholes and rocks, the plastic pails in their baskets bumping with them.

They throw their bikes aside at a trailhead and scoot down the slope. The stones are slippery with moss, yet they are surefooted boys, as agile as goats, and they move easily along the trail, each carrying one of the pails. At the creek, they station themselves about ten yards apart. Max chooses a place where an indentation in the bank forms a little cove and the water is still, with a cloudy surface like fogged glass. Jimmy lies on his belly, draped across a flat rock. The two set to work, studying the water beneath them, occasionally dragging their hands through the sediment. A soft breeze rustles the leaves overhead. Hidden in the trees, two wood thrushes on opposite banks pipe back and forth to each other. From half a mile away, the boys can hear trucks rumbling along Route 41.

"Got one!" It is Jimmy who calls first. In his fist he squeezes a small mudpuppy, nearly as skinny as a snake. Jimmy turns it on its back, and Max approaches to examine it with him. The mudpuppy is a common color—a brownish gray with blue spots—the tail is wide, the gills fringed with the usual red. But where there should have been two stubby legs, there are none.

For several years, legless mudpuppies were considered prize bounty among the schoolchildren of the St. Lawrence River Valley. No one could remember which of the children of Akwesasne had first come up with an explanation for them, but it was said that these mutant amphibians were the offspring of the great horned monster that had once risen out of the river and destroyed the village of the children's ancestors. Legless mudpuppies would grow into monsters if left alone, so the children hunted them, brought them home in their buckets, and tried to keep them as pets, feeding them worms and slugs in an effort to win their trust and convince them that humans were not their enemies. The mudpuppies never survived in captivity for more than a couple of days, but this didn't bother the children much; they knew there would always be more legless mudpuppies to catch in the creeks and rivers that threaded through the valley.

VII

At the Ballet

About the time Mr. Hopley was walking backward down the street in front of Pauline, I was, most likely, sitting at my desk. Perhaps I was addressing an envelope or gazing idly out the window at the sky. Maybe Jessie Putnam, across the office, was surreptitiously filing her nails. There would have been phones ringing and typewriters rattling and the surging sounds of buses picking up speed on Eighth Avenue. And then Mrs. J appeared, going from desk to desk, handing out complimentary tickets as if they were gumdrops, inviting us all to a public forum on the local housing shortage.

Mrs. J apologized for the last-minute notice, and she assured us that she understood if we had other plans. In truth, most of the girls simply weren't interested in the topic and made up excuses about previous commitments. Only Trudy and I bothered to attend the event. We shared a cab to the clubhouse on West Fourth Street, and by the time we arrived, Mrs. J was already planted in the front row, pen in hand, as if she were the reporter she used to be.

We took seats in the back of the hall. Soon the speakers filed onstage. We waited expectantly as they opened their folders and cleared their throats. We listened attentively to all they had to say.

The speaker I remember best was Jane Jacobs. While others made ominous predictions about the future of the city, she spoke in a spirited manner about the present. Mostly, she told us about the people who lived and worked in her neighborhood. There was the man behind the counter at the corner deli who made the finest meatball wedges in the city, and the elderly owner of the penny-candy store who abandoned his counter to guide small children across the street and had been known to threaten shoplifters with a water pistol. We heard about a locksmith who broke up fights between gangs and reported delinquents to their parents before the police could get to them. The neighborhood tailor was famous for rushing to the church to fix a bride's train after her ring bearer stepped on it by accident. The grocer's wife gave health advice, and the laundry girl always had something to say about politics.

Jane Jacobs compared her block to an intricate ballet in which every individual had a featured part. On the colorful stage that was Jane Jacobs's neighborhood, adults watched over the children playing in the street, and the economy hummed along, its system of exchange fair and square.

Let people live where they work, she said. Bring them in droves, the more the better. Let the block bustle with vendors and pedestrians. Give the residents a sense of community.

She was such a charismatic woman that her performance on that September evening still resonates in my memory all these years later. But even more vivid to me than Jane Jacobs's lecture is the question Lee Jaffe asked afterward, during the reception.

"Mrs. Jacobs, you are a remarkable woman," said Mrs. J, extending a hand adorned with several rings, rose gold and silver, set with rubies and amethysts.

"Thank you for coming, Mrs. Jaffe. I know you're very busy."

"I wouldn't have missed it. Now, if I may call on your expertise, Mrs. Jacobs: Do you believe there's a neighborhood in our city that has room for the tallest building in the world?"

WHISPERS AND SHOUTS

To fully understand Mrs. J's influence at the Port Authority, it is necessary to go way back to June of 1943, the year before she was hired, when the agency issued a statement outlining its future ambitions, identifying two main components of its long-term plan: one, a new program would be charged with modernizing airports and other transportation terminals, and, two, the P.A. would hire a skilled practitioner in the field of public relations to nurture contacts with newspaper reporters.

The executive director at the P.A. was Austin Tobin; he had won his leadership position after heading up the legal department. He had ambitious plans, and he made it known that he was eager to expand the agency's influence through a public relations campaign. As it happened, the chairman of the board of commissioners at the time was a man named Frank Ferguson, who was more financially conservative than Tobin and objected to every project study that threatened large deficits. He didn't want to pay the cost of hiring extra staff, and he certainly didn't think the P.A. needed a director of Public Relations.

Controversy over the issue divided the board. But Tobin was

a persuasive man, and he eventually convinced several members of the board that the P.A. could not function without someone in charge of publicity. For the position of director of Public Relations, he nominated a woman named Marion K. Sanders who was already employed by the P.A. in another department. She was known for being a hard worker who never complained. She was liked by everyone—except Frank Ferguson.

By all accounts, Frank Ferguson was good at hatching plots. As I imagine it, he leaned over to his friend Frank Dorsey after a board meeting and said something along the lines of "Give Tobin an inch, and he'll put every member of his family on the payroll."

"What's that you say?" Frank Dorsey, a decade older than Frank Ferguson, was beginning to lose his hearing.

"Tobin and Sanders. They might as well be cousins."

"Tobin and Sanders are cousins?"

"Jesus, Frank, not real cousins! I'm talking about Tobin's tribal loyalty. He makes Edelstein his assistant, he cozies up to Cullman, and now he's nominating Marion Sanders."

"Sanders is a Jew?"

"Of course she's a Jew. Leave it to Tobin, and he'll pack the agency with his own kind."

The two Franks were still sitting at the boardroom table, their briefcases closed in front of them. Frank Ferguson tapped the eraser of his pencil on the wood. Frank Dorsey shivered visibly. The pause in their conversation lasted for a minute or more, until Frank Ferguson finally said, "I got an idea, Frank, but I need your help."

"What's that, Frank?"

"I need your help getting to Edelstein."

"Edelstein, you say?"

"We bring down Edelstein, and we block the Sanders nomination."

"And you need me—"

"To help me go after Edelstein."

"What did Edelstein do wrong?"

"It's what we're going to say he did. Listen to me, Frank. There's a pretty little number named Betty who works for Edelstein. Edelstein and Betty...some of the staff have been whispering, you know. I've been hearing those whispers."

"What am I supposed to do with whispering, Frank? You gotta shout if you want me to help you."

"That's just what I intend, Frank. I'm going to shout it to the world. Edelstein and Betty. Put the pressure on Edelstein, and we weaken Tobin. It's like cutting off Samson's hair. We'll force Edelstein out, and we'll start repairing all the damage Tobin has wrought during his misbegotten reign."

"I'm not sure I follow you, Frank, but just tell me what to say. You're a good man, a good leader. I'll always stand with you."

In January, Frank Ferguson asked Edelstein to come to his office at his bank in Jersey City. There, Ferguson confronted Edelstein with supposed evidence of his affair with Betty. Edelstein denied it, but Ferguson, with Dorsey's help, had already spread the word through the board of commissioners: Edelstein was a scoundrel, not to be trusted. The word Bob Whittaker would come to fear fifteen years later, *perfidy,* was used in connection with Edelstein. The board threatened to investigate. Before the scandal could go public, Edelstein resigned, and the Sanders nomination was tabled.

While the two Franks celebrated with drinks at the Biltmore, Austin Tobin devised a backup plan. He drew up an advertisement for the job of director of Public Relations and sent it to everyone he knew outside the P.A. Applications rolled in, and one in particular caught his eye thanks to an endorsement from Bob Wagner, a senator from New York. The candidate was a woman known for her reports from Washington. Her name was Lee K. Jaffe.

"That operator," Frank Ferguson would later say of Tobin during a board meeting. "It's always all in the family with Tobin. Howard, aren't you related to this Jaffe lady?" Ferguson was directing his question to Howard Cullman, the vice chairman of the board, who didn't bother to reply. Everyone knew what Ferguson was implying: Lee Jaffe, like Howard Cullman, was a Jew.

Imagine how brittle the emotions were in the P.A.'s boardroom during the silence that followed Frank Ferguson's question. This was in April 1944. One of the board members had just lost a nephew in the Slapton Sands debacle in England. American patriotism was a stronger force than ever and was expected to cross religious boundaries. Yet there were men in the room who belonged to country clubs that excluded Jews. The commissioners didn't know how to react to Ferguson. Was he blocking Jaffe's nomination because she was Jewish? Cullman was Jewish, and he was respected enough to have been elected vice chairman. Tobin was Jewish. Could that be why Ferguson despised him?

It would take a phone call from Senator Wagner to the Port Authority commissioner Arthur Walsh for Lee Jaffe's nomination to go forward. The senator threatened to alert the press to Ferguson's resistance to Jaffe. Ferguson had no choice but to allow Mrs. J to be hired. His only victory was making sure she came in at a lower position, as assistant director, even though there was no director to assist.

Mrs. J didn't wait to cast her spell. She met weekly with Frank Ferguson to *pick his brain*, as she liked to tell him. She asked him what he wanted the world to know about the

P.A., about Ferguson's Jersey Bank, and about Frank Ferguson himself. She wrote flattering articles to feed to editors. Ferguson forgot his initial resistance to Mrs. J. Maybe he even forgot she was Jewish. In October of 1944, he was the first to advocate her promotion to director of the Public Relations Department.

Within a year, Frank Dorsey had died and the rest of the commissioners had rebelled against Ferguson and were supporting Tobin. Frank Ferguson didn't bother to attend the P.A.'s annual garden party—a good thing, in the opinion of the P.A. staff, since Ferguson had a way of spoiling the fun. Everyone else was ready to celebrate. Thanks to Mrs. J, the future had never looked more promising. The guests ate and drank away the hours in Howard Cullman's Long Island backyard. Word got out that it was Austin Tobin's birthday. Fireworks were set off in his honor, filling the sky over the lawn with a dazzling display. Someone pulled out a harmonica, and the guests started to sing.

A JOLLY GOOD FELLOW

"'For he's a jolly good fellow, for he's a jolly good fellow!'"

"Old Frank Dorsey must be rolling over in his grave right now!"

"Aw, he never cared much about anything. He did what Ferguson told him to do."

"If it were up to Ferguson, I would never have been hired."

"Me either!"

"Tobin's a sly one. You think he has given it up, and then he does an end run and makes a touchdown every time. The way he got that Jaffe broad on the books—that was something."

"He sure is clever."

"He'll do some good for New York."

"He has big dreams."

"God knows the city needs a man who can dream."

TOWARD CLEAR SKIES

"Maggie, Mrs. J wants to see you in her office."

I remember it was Brenda Dowdle who summoned me. Brenda Dowdle—the one who, back at that first luncheon at the Golden Door in 1958, had speculated that the most difficult and simultaneously easiest part of Mrs. J's position as director of Public Relations was dictating letters. Now she was delivering the message from Mrs. J: I was wanted in her office—to take dictation, as it turned out. Usually, she called on someone else for the task. She knew I was slow and had never learned shorthand properly. Why she wanted me for this particular job, I'll never understand.

"How are you, Maggie?"

"I'm fine, Mrs. J."

"You're liking the city?"

"Oh yes, there's always something new to explore."

This was in June of 1960. I'd moved from the boardinghouse on the East Side to my own little apartment down on Jane Street. I had met Tammis by then. She had grown up in the Bronx, though she could trace part of her ancestry to a great-grandmother who had been born into slavery in Virginia. She saw me as a country bumpkin who needed training in city life, so she took me on as her project and made sure to introduce me to all the eligible males she knew. Thanks to Tammis, I went on my fair share of dates and even had a sweetheart named Gerard for a while, until he moved to Chicago for a new job. After Gerard left, I kept busy on my own, and I would meet Tammis and other girls for a night out now and then. I was beginning to get used to New York. I was being honest when I told Mrs. J that I liked the city.

"That's good," she said mildly, somewhat distracted by a paper she'd glanced at on her desk. She shuffled through folders, rearranging their contents for a few minutes. I sat down and looked out the window at the cars on Eighth Avenue.

"Ready to take a memo?" Mrs. J finally asked.

"Sure, I just need . . . I'm sorry, I forgot a pencil."

"Here you go."

I thanked her and sat forward, pencil tip touching the pad. "Ready when you are."

"Relax, Maggie." Mrs. J leaned back in her chair and lit a cigarette. She studied the glowing end thoughtfully, then set it in the ashtray. "There was a feasibility study done the year after I got here. There was talk of need for a trade center. Planning came up with a proposal. They even got as far as conceptual drawings—twenty-one buildings covering ten blocks, mostly exhibition halls. But then they decided there was not enough demand. The proposal was shelved."

It had been a long time since I'd made the map of the Radio Row neighborhood, but I still hadn't heard anything about the P.A.'s intentions in the area.

"Are they rethinking the idea? Of a trade center, I mean?"

Instead of answering my question, she said, "Have you ever been to the top of the Empire State Building?"

"Well, yes, once."

"What did you think?"

"It was a nice view."

"Rockefeller won't stop until New York gets a trade center.

They're all fighting about it. The Clee report was buried after recommending that further study should be discontinued."

I wasn't sure what she was referring to but I didn't want to interrupt.

"At the meetings, they keep saying that whatever they build, it must be spectacular in proportion. That's the phrase I hear over and over: *spectacular in proportion.* They know it will be a hard pull, and there's no assurance of success, even with Rockefeller at the helm. They won't give up, though. You know men. They don't like to lose." She fixed her eyes on her cigarette, seeming to let her thoughts wander for a moment before continuing.

"We need to coach Austin on how to talk to the press. He's too used to speaking off the cuff."

"He always sounds educated to me."

"He says things he shouldn't." She ground out her cigarette. "'High growth of iron, slender, strong, light, splendidly uprising toward clear skies.' Walt Whitman. He knew how to make himself heard. Now it's my turn. When they get around to asking years from now who thought up the idea for the World Trade Center, you can tell them Walt Whitman. Ready to take a memo, Maggie?"

"Ready."

"To Guy. Let's make it short and sweet."

I wrote, *Let's make it short and sweet.*

Mrs. J saw me writing. "Maggie, I'm talking about the memo—that's not part of the memo."

"Oh." I crossed out what I'd written.

"Ready?"

"Ready."

"'If you want to build a great project'..."

If you want to build a great project...

" 'You should' . . ."
you should . . .
" 'Build the world's' . . ."
build the world's . . .
" 'Tallest' . . ."
tallest . . .
" 'Building.' "
building.

ANOTHER JOLLY GOOD FELLOW

Twenty years after Mrs. J attended her first P.A. garden party as director of Public Relations, the employees of the P.A. were ready to sing again, though by late summer of 1965, Howard Cullman had moved away, the annual event was held at a different home on Long Island, and the mistress of ceremonies was the newest clerical girl in the department, one Pauline Moreau, self-appointed life of the party, who showed up with a megaphone after being delegated by her coworkers to present Mrs. J, who had recently announced her intention to retire, with a gift on behalf of the staff of the Department of Public Relations.

I stood in the front row holding Sonia's hand. As I watched Mrs. J unwrap the gift, peeling off the tape so as not to rip the paper, I felt a stab of sadness provoked by the certainty that for the clerical girls, our days were about to become far less pleasant.

Mrs. J held up the gift for everyone to admire. It was a painting showing Pretty Boy, Mrs. J's mynah bird, together with Giuseppe the Maltese. The two pets stared out from the canvas, their bright eyes glistening. In the background of the picture, reflected in a mirror on the wall behind them, was Mrs. J.

The idea for the painting had been Pauline's. She had located an artist and collected donations from the rest of us. Mrs. J was obviously delighted. Everyone applauded. Beside me, little Sonia squealed with excitement.

"Speech, speech!" people yelled. Mrs. J gave a dismissive wave and tried to ignore the demand. She set the painting on a nearby table. While she concentrated on folding the wrapping paper into a neat square, Pauline called through the megaphone, "Mrs. J, you are the best speechwriter in the country—of course you gotta give us a speech."

"Speech, speech!" we all chanted.

I couldn't believe how vulnerable and meek Mrs. J looked, now that she was being celebrated. I was reminded of the luncheon years earlier when I had said something along the lines of how it must be both easy and difficult to have to pretend to be someone you're not in front of a crowd.

She cleared her throat. "I want to thank..." She shifted from one foot to the other as if to rebalance herself. "I want to thank Austin Tobin..." Pauline handed her the megaphone. Mrs. J examined it as if she'd never seen one before, then held it to her mouth. "Austin, where are you?" she called.

Mr. Tobin waved from the back of the crowd. "I wouldn't be here without you," she said. The megaphone gave her voice a tinny echo. Everyone applauded for Mr. Tobin. "And Guy... Guy?" He waved from his place. "Guy Tozzoli, you're the best rival any girl could have." The crowd laughed. "My staff, all of you, you always did more than I asked. Girls, don't let these big boys walk all over you." There was scattered laughter in response. Pauline shouted merrily, "That's right!" and some of the younger men hooted.

"Most of all," Mrs. J continued, "I want to thank Izzy, my husband. Izzy?" He was standing on the patio with a drink in his hand. He raised the glass in a toast to his wife. She paused and looked over the crowd. After lowering the megaphone to her side, she asked Sonia directly, "Do you like stories?"

Sonia's eager nodding sent her braids bouncing.

"I want to tell you one last story," she said to Sonia in her own strong voice, as if she were having a private conversation with Pauline's little girl rather than giving the final speech of her professional career.

THE HAZEL KIRK DISASTER

When Mrs. J said, "I want to tell you one last story," at the P.A. garden party, it was the second time I'd heard those exact words from her. The first time was in 1958 after our luncheon at the Golden Door. We'd been driven back to the office in a limousine, and we eleven clerical girls had shared the seats meant for ten while Mrs. J rode up front. The girls were fidgeting and gossiping the whole way, so I wasn't able to catch any of Mrs. J's conversation with the chauffeur. My hunch is that she learned from him that he was from the same town outside Pittsburgh where she had been born. At the very least, something he said must have stirred her to think about her hometown. She had told us earlier that day that her being born in Pennsylvania was "beside the point." It *was* the point by the time the limousine dropped us off at the P.A. headquarters.

We were hanging up our coats when Mrs. J said to us, "Girls, I want to tell you one last story." Happy to put off returning to work, we followed her into her office and gathered around her desk.

She began, I recall, by telling us about her parents, who were Hungarian Jews. She told us that, shortly after they were married, they immigrated to America and joined relatives in Pittsburgh. Her father found a job as a foreman with the Westmoreland Coal Company, and when he arrived at his post he discovered that the conditions in the mine he was supervising were dangerously unregulated. I could hear the indignation rising in Mrs. J's voice as she reported that her father repeatedly filed official complaints with the company, but nothing was changed. He kept on with the work; he had no other choice.

"Every evening when the clock struck six," said Mrs. J, "my mother would stand at the front window to watch anxiously for my father. I remember that when he came home, he would go straight to the kitchen and wash the coal dust off his hands and face, and then he would pause to inspect the pot on the stove and taste whatever was simmering. Sometimes he would add another heaping spoonful of paprika before my mother could stop him. He believed paprika was an aphrodisiac."

I was not the only girl who, feeling the effects of the liquor from lunch, gave an approving giggle. Mrs. J seemed not to notice.

"My earliest memory," she continued, "is of the night my sisters and I were woken by a loud sound coming from the house next door. It was warm, I recall, and I was sleeping with my window open. I thought I was hearing music, but then one of my sisters explained that the woman next door was crying. All the lights were on in the house, and I could see people milling about in a downstairs room. Only years later did I learn what had happened that day at the mine."

In the pause that followed, I could hear the honking of impatient drivers on Eighth Avenue, the sounds faint, as if coming from a great distance.

"You see, the housewife next door had two babies," Mrs. J continued, "one just a month old, the other not yet three. Her husband, a fire boss at the mine known as Hazel Kirk Two, had been among a contingent assigned to open a bulkhead built to contain a fire burning deep inside a tunnel. The fire had been burning for over a week. The mine inspector had warned that the area was still unsafe, but the supervisor didn't want to hear it. He didn't want to wait any longer." Mrs. J paused to clear her throat. "He believed that the fire had burned itself out, and at midnight he led the party of five fire bosses to tear down the bulkhead. They'd opened one brattice and were at work on the second when the gas behind the bulkhead exploded. The six men were hurled a great distance. Five were fatally injured. One man escaped and made it to the surface and was able to tell what happened. The next day my father was part of the team that went down to recover the bodies.

"My family moved to Kansas shortly after the accident. None of the children were told our father's reason for leaving Pennsylvania. Not until I was a grown woman and about to take a job in Wichita did I learn the truth from my mother. She told me that my father had been ordered by the supervisor to lead the fire bosses into the mine that night. He'd refused and reminded the supervisor of the inspector's warning. The supervisor responded with those particular invectives designed to humiliate a Jewish man and then told my father to empty his locker and get off the premises. No one else but my mother knew about this conversation, since the supervisor died in the accident. But my father believed that his only honorable option was to quit Hazel Kirk. And my father was an honorable man.

"When I asked him about the accident, my father confessed to me that he had always felt ashamed for refusing the supervisor's order to lead the men into the mine," Mrs. J said. "He apologized to me for being such a coward. Do you think he was a coward?" she asked, directing her question, unfortunately, at shy Eugenia, who froze with embarrassment and confusion.

Jessie Putnam, emboldened by the several martinis she had gulped at lunch, piped up, saving Eugenia. "Seems to me he was one of the few men there with any courage."

"Thank you, Jessie. His refusal to go into the mine was the opposite of cowardice. It would have been easier to do as he was told. Yes, it took courage to defy the supervisor, and after I moved to Wichita, I wrote my father a letter to tell him so. This is how I got started in a career in public relations. You see, girls," she said, glancing toward the open window just as a sparrow alighted outside on the sill. "Let me try to make myself clear. It's difficult, sometimes, to be clear. In order to write that letter to my father, I had to put myself in his place. I had to let myself be haunted by the same thing that was haunting him—and so I tried to imagine the terror those men deep in that Hazel Kirk mine must have felt in the fraction of the second while they were still conscious and were being hurtled across the space of the dark tunnel by the force of the explosion. I sat in my room and pictured the accident as best I could. That was the only way I was able to understand my father's shame at having refused to join the miners on a job that proved fatal. I know I came up short in imagining the reality of the tragedy, but my effort made it possible to propose a different version of the past, a better, truer version. I wrote my father a long letter to soothe his conscience. That letter remains, in my personal estimation, the most important document I ever authored."

She turned back to us. "It is because of that letter I wrote to my father that I came to realize I wanted to spend my life using my pen as a weapon of persuasion. And so I jumped at the opportunity to work as a reporter in Washington. Remember

I told you about covering the Bonus Men's March in Washington?" I was not the only one who was nodding. "My future husband, Izzy, employed as a lawyer in New York, was visiting Washington at the time, and we were introduced by mutual friends later in the week. You know how it goes—it was love at first sight! If my father had not needed to be persuaded that he had done the right thing, I wouldn't have gone to Washington, and Izzy and I might never have met. If I'd never met Izzy, I wouldn't have wanted to move to New York to be near him, and I wouldn't have applied for the job at the Port Authority. Trace it backward, girls," she said in conclusion, "and you can blame the Westmoreland Coal Company for setting me on the roundabout path that led to this desk."

THE OTHER STORY

But that was not the story Mrs. J told at her retirement party in 1965. The story she told that day was a far less personal one about meeting with Mayor Lindsay to inform him that the Port Authority was going to build not just one but *two* of the world's tallest skyscrapers in downtown Manhattan. She recounted his demand for better financial terms for the city, and she gave her audience suggestions for winning him over. She said she was leaving the blueprints for her "twins" in the hands of her successors. "A great city deserves great buildings. There will be nothing like those towers anywhere on earth when they are finally built," she said with passion. She ended her story by saying she *loved, loved, loved* a job that allowed her to spend her time turning dreams into reality!

The party lights around the patio jingled softly in the breeze. A moment later, a solitary clapping, slow and determined, could be heard. It was Pauline who was clapping, and soon the audience followed her cue.

Mrs. J handed the megaphone back to Pauline, then picked up the painting of Pretty Boy and Giuseppe and moved through the guests to join her husband on the patio.

"Mrs. J!" Pauline said through the megaphone. In contrast to Mrs. J that evening, Pauline seemed at ease with the device, happy to be in front of a crowd. Sonia cried out cheerfully, "Hi, Mommy!" "Hey there, hon!" Pauline yelled back. Pauline could never get enough attention. "We want to thank *you*, Mrs. J . . ." she called, but the crowd was clapping so vigorously that it was hard to hear her. "Mrs. J," Pauline shouted through the megaphone. "Mrs. J."

The crowd picked up the chant, Sonia included.

"Mrs. J! Mrs. J!"

Mrs. J's husband had taken the painting from her and set it to the side. They stood with linked arms, looking like a king and queen gazing at their subjects from the balcony of their palace. Mrs. J appeared confident and happy, though there was a redness in her cheeks that might have come from blushing.

"Mrs. J! Mrs. J!"

I thought we would all exhaust ourselves with cheering. We were saying good-bye to a woman who had earned our loyalty by sharpening our sense of possibility. We would never again have a boss like Lee K. Jaffe.

From somewhere in the crowd, a harmonica could be heard.

"'For she's a jolly good fellow,'" Pauline sang through the megaphone. "'For she's a jolly good fellow . . .'" The crowd joined in, and couples skipped drunkenly, elbows linked, around and around in circles.

Hours later, on the train back to the city, Pauline held her daughter on her lap. Sonia was fast asleep, snoring lightly.

Pauline stared out the window, softly stroking Sonia's hair. The train whistled forlornly as we passed through a station without stopping. I heard Pauline murmuring.

"Did you say something?" I asked.

"She saved our lives," Pauline replied.

She looked drawn, spent, like a lead actress might look back-stage after a raucous show. I didn't think Pauline wanted to continue the conversation, so I didn't ask her if she meant that Mrs. J had saved her and Sonia or if, with *our*, she was including me.

VIII

The Wrong Direction

If you had happened to be strolling through lower Manhattan on a late summer's day back in 1963, a striking young woman in a pink-and-white polka-dot shift dress, her hair pinned on the side with a barrette, might have caught your eye. This was Pauline, age twenty-one, and in her arms she carried little Sonia. They had come downtown to visit Mrs. Clayborne, who had been transferred to Bellevue because there was no room in the uptown hospital. Pauline had brought Sonia to visit Mrs. Clayborne every day that week. But that day when they had gone to the room where Mrs. Clayborne was supposed to be, she wasn't there. Her bed had been stripped, and the card with her name was gone from the door.

Pauline walked west and then turned downtown, with no destination in mind. Sonia, her head resting on her mother's shoulder, was giving the gurgling sound that came out when she couldn't find the words to express her distress. She was slow in learning to form full sentences, but Pauline knew what she'd wanted to ask ever since they left the hospital:

Where is Mrs. Clayborne, Mommy?

"I expect Mrs. Clayborne was off getting some tests, honey. You know, like what the doctor does when he looks down your throat. That's why she wasn't in her room."

Sonia grew heavy in her mother's arms, and Pauline set her down. She walked on in a daze, holding her daughter by the elbow, confounded by her predicament. With Mrs. Clayborne in the hospital, there was no one to watch Sonia while Pauline was at the club, so Pauline had called in sick for three days in a row. When she called on the fourth day, her boss told her that she'd better get down to the club right away or he would turn her pretty little ass black-and-blue. After that, she didn't bother calling. She knew she could never go back. She didn't want to go back. But now Mrs. Clayborne was gone, and Pauline couldn't leave Sonia alone. What would she do? If she didn't work, she couldn't pay the rent on Mrs. Clayborne's apartment. She couldn't afford to pay a babysitter plus buy their food and Sonia's prescriptions. If she didn't have a babysitter, she couldn't find a new job. They would be evicted...and then what? Pauline believed that her recent line of work servicing gentlemen was visible to everyone, and she was forever tainted. And what do the authorities do with the children of tainted women? Why, they take them away, of course.

Walking along, Sonia whimpered, tugging on her mother's hand. She pointed to the soda bottles on display on a street vendor's cart. Without thinking, Pauline used all her change to buy her daughter a Coke.

It was a hot, muggy day. As if doomed always to head in the wrong direction, Pauline kept walking downtown. Though it was Saturday, traffic was backed up on Broadway. With Sonia in tow, she turned down Fulton Street, and then, hearing drumming, turned onto Cortlandt Street in search of what Pauline assumed was a parade.

There is nothing like a parade to lift a girl up when she's down. The drumming grew louder, and the crowds thickened. To Pauline, the drumming was the sound made by the heart of humanity, beating strong and steady, its rhythm shared by all people, *ta-dum, ta-dum.* It was the sound of faith, community, perseverance, *ta-dum, ta-dum.* It was just what Pauline Moreau needed to hear right then, and she scooped Sonia into her arms so she could walk faster, in the direction of the parade.

MR. SMALL BUSINESSMAN

Let's imagine it from little Sonia's point of view. Sonia, who was too young to understand what she was witnessing. Who would never learn the multiplication tables. Who then and for the rest of her life would lack the cognitive ability to register cruelty. Who could only be gentle. Gentle little Sonia, who made sense of the world in her own way.

Tell me my portrait of Sonia is falsely sentimental. I dare you. You, who never knew her.

I choose to be indignant on her behalf, voluntarily doubling the anger she didn't know to feel. She who was Pauline's beloved daughter, and then mine. I would do anything to protect her. Before I go on, it is important to acknowledge the power of her goodness.

Okay. So there she was, a small child perceiving the chaotic world through a foggy innocence.

Ta-dum.
Ta-dum.

"Look, sweetie, a parade."

There was stickiness on her tongue from the soda. Mmm.
The sun was too hot. They had gone to say hello to Mrs.
Clayborne, but Mrs. Clayborne wasn't there. The doctor was
looking down her throat. Once Sonia had looked down Mrs.
Clayborne's throat when Mrs. Clayborne yawned, and at the
back, to one side, was gold.

Gold!

Mrs. Clayborne had gold in her mouth! Sonia thought the
gold looked pretty beside Mrs. Clayborne's red tongue, and she
told Mrs. Clayborne so, and Mrs. Clayborne took Sonia into her
arms and laughed until tears poured from her eyes and filled
her wrinkles. Mrs. Clayborne was always nice.

Now Mrs. Clayborne was showing off the gold in her throat
to a doctor, and Sonia was going to watch a parade with her
mother.

Parades were fun. People clapped and waved. Bells rang.
Drummers drummed.

Ta-dum.
Ta-dum.

Sonia's mother always pushed to the front of the crowd no
matter what. Once there, she set Sonia on her feet and held her
hand tight. The parade was approaching. Sonia couldn't wait!
What were people shouting?

"The Port Authority has no authority to take away our livelihoods!"

"Stop the demolition!"

"Stop the trade center!"

"Stand up for the little guys!"

"Save our neighborhood!"

"Save our shops!"

Remember the photograph of the funeral for Mr. Small Businessman? Well, here was Mr. Small Businessman himself, smartly dressed and laid to rest against the satin cushions of a very fine oak casket on loan for the day.

A man in a box. What did it mean? Sonia thought he looked like a girl. Maybe he was a girl. A wide-eyed girl dressed up as a man, lying in a box. Boxes were for funerals. Funerals were for dying. What was dying? It was not coming back again—everyone knew that, even Sonia. The girl-man in the box was not coming back again. As soon as people said good-bye, she-he would be taken away and put in the ground. There would be dirt over the box. This was a parade for saying good-bye.

Ta-dum meant "good-bye."

Good-bye meant forever.

Sonia, not quite four and with obvious developmental impairment, wasn't stupid. Far from it. She had an active brain and could make leaps impossible for other children her age. With a running start, her thoughts jumped and flew from the casket containing Mr. Small Businessman to the empty bed where Mrs. Clayborne wasn't. Right then, she fathomed the eternity of Mrs. Clayborne's absence, felt in her heart the truth of death and understood within the fuzzy sphere of her consciousness the sadness of life.

Poor Mr. Small Businessman.

Poor Mrs. Clayborne.

Little Sonia shivered, though her mother didn't notice. Little Sonia gripped her mother's hand, determined never to let go.

Remember those two shadows, one bigger than the other, in the photograph of the funeral on Radio Row?

SPINSTERS

Among the crowd of onlookers at the funeral of Mr. Small Businessman was an architect visiting from Detroit. He listened to the speeches. He registered the protests. But he didn't linger. He wandered on through the side streets, Vesey to West to Liberty, up Washington to Barclay, over to Church, down to Cedar, back up Greenwich. He observed the crumbling brick walkups, the graffiti on the plywood nailed over the entrances to the old finger piers. He passed through empty lots and stood across the street from the blank gray Hudson Terminal buildings.

From there, the architect headed uptown in a zigzagging fashion. He studied the shape of the new Chase building. He observed the colored accents on the terra-cotta of the Woolworth Building. He walked to Thirty-Fourth Street and by foot traced the square around the Empire State Building—the highest skyscraper in New York, and the least successful aesthetically, in the opinion of the architect. The building looked like a squat crate, its magnificence hidden by its stocky base. If the architect from Detroit had designed the Empire State Building, he would have made sure that its height would be visible from the street.

He had a bigger job than the Empire State Building. His commission was clear: he had been charged to design the tallest building in the world. He, best known for his small-scale, jewel-box buildings, had won the competition, to the surprise of all, including himself. Now he had to give his clients what they had requested.

Joanna Scott

*   *   *

Back in Michigan, the architect got to work. Initially, he scorned the very project he'd been assigned. He thought it foolish to make a building unreasonably tall simply for the sake of the record books. With his associates, he tried out models in different arrangements—a cluster of four small towers in a tight square; two long, low slabs of buildings running parallel to the harbor. But nothing looked right to the architect. He went off by himself and drew new sketches. He drew a pair of towers, each eighty stories high. He thought they were ugly. They reminded him of sisters who were so tall, no one would marry them. And at eighty stories, they still wouldn't be tall enough. *Fine,* he thought angrily. He would give his clients what they wanted. He drew a new sketch and added thirty stories to each tower. There they were, two sisters who would be the tallest in the world. Spinsters forever.

When the models for the towers were delivered to the architect's drafting room, they were too tall to stand upright. One of the draftsmen carried in a ladder and removed tiles from the dropped ceiling. Now the models would fit. They were pushed to a standing position and secured on the plywood base.

The architect and his associates gathered around the display. From any side, each man saw the same thing: identical towers with vertical slits for windows and square, flat tops. Like dolls, these miniature versions stood proudly, inviting admiration. They were sleek and shiny and lightweight enough to be easily shipped. They were made of aluminum.

GOOD FOR ONE FARE

Have you ever seen those old subway tokens with the Y punched out? Well, Pauline did not have one when she needed it that day on Radio Row, having spent the last of her change to buy Sonia a soda. Without subway fare, Pauline had no way to get back uptown. On her own, she would have walked, but she couldn't make her little daughter walk, nor could she carry the girl the whole distance.

Standing with other spectators at the funeral for Mr. Small Businessman, Pauline watched as a woman nearby opened her purse and took out her compact. Pauline knew something about purses, and she recognized that one as an Evans original. With the purse's clasp open, Pauline could see inside. She spotted a lipstick holder and the corner of a wallet. The purse remained open, dangling from the woman's wrist while she used her free hand to powder her nose and forehead. Pauline imagined sneaking her fingers inside and furtively taking the wallet. She might have done it if Sonia hadn't been holding on to her, her presence a silent reminder to avoid the kind of risk that would separate mother and daughter. Pickpocketing, Pauline reflected, was a crime worse than prostitution in the eyes of the police. No question; if they caught her lifting a wallet, they would book her for certain. From her jail cell, she'd be writing letters to Sonia that Sonia couldn't read, sending them to her care of some foster home far away.

Sonia and Pauline moved on from the protest. They walked slowly, hand in hand. When they came to a subway station, Pauline stopped. She and Sonia stood to the side as people hurried down the steps or came huffing up, soaked in sweat.

"Mommy?"

"It's fine, sweetie, just a minute," Pauline said without

looking down at her daughter. She kept watching people pass into and out of the station—mostly men wearing sport shirts without jackets because it was Saturday. One man's shirt was gold with red stripes. Another man wore a simple white shirt with two patch pockets. She saw one in a tan shirt with a loop collar that buttoned—he was her favorite, she decided. She flashed a quick smile at him as he passed her on his way down to the train. He looked at her in surprise and kept on going.

"Mommy?"

"Honey, please, be patient."

A couple came out of the subway carrying an umbrella stroller with a baby strapped in. The man came up first, holding the rod at the bottom of the stroller, while the woman held the handles behind. Pauline was reminded of the carriage for Sonia that Mrs. Clayborne had given her. She had left it behind that day because she had no one to help her carry it up the subway steps.

Two older men, maybe from the Radio Row protest, brushed past her. She went on waiting. Sonia's hand was damp with sweat inside her own.

A younger man approached wearing a green-and-yellow-striped oxford shirt. With his round glasses, he looked like a student. He was carrying a briefcase under his arm.

"Spare some change?" Pauline whispered.

He hurried past without hearing, or else pretending not to hear.

She forced another smile even as she felt the heaviness of Sonia's hand—not tugging, just heavy with exhaustion.

Here were two men approaching at the same time. One had a stocky Germanic look, the other a face that reminded her of Pat Boone's. She said just loudly enough for both to hear, "Spare some change?" The German continued into the station, but Pat Boone hesitated. His gaze moved from Pauline's face to Sonia and back to Pauline. He dug in his pockets and pulled out all his change—dimes and nickels, pennies, even a quarter; enough for a token, plus some. He gave it all to Pauline and then, as if embarrassed on her behalf, fled down the stairs.

THE SOUND OF SHAME

At the corner of 115th Street and Second Avenue, Pauline stopped in a liquor store and used the extra money she had earned from begging for a bottle of Old Taylor. She couldn't wait to get into the apartment. She took a swig as soon as they were inside the door of the building, and another swig on the stairs. The only thing that quieted the clamor in Pauline's head back in those days was the good burn of Old Taylor. She hated the taste but loved the effect and consoled herself with the awareness that she could have had worse habits.

Up in the apartment, Sonia disappeared into Mrs. Clayborne's bedroom. When Pauline peeked in on her, the child was looking at herself in the old woman's hand mirror, opening her mouth wide and trying to see down her throat. Pauline thought her daughter so amusing she laughed aloud, startling Sonia. "Sweet pea," Pauline said, kissing her on the cheek. Then she went into the kitchen and resumed drinking. Soon she felt better, calmer. She could think more clearly.

She had to consider the fact that she was broke. There were three weeks left in the month. She wouldn't be able to pay the whole month's rent for Mrs. Clayborne's apartment without a job. She had made good money at the club, but she couldn't just go out on the street and solicit passing strangers. In her appraisal of herself, she wasn't the kind of girl who called obscenities from corners. Even lower, though, the lowest of lows, was begging.

Spare some change.

As far as she knew, Mrs. Clayborne had no family. Maybe she had drawn up a will at some point, though Pauline doubted it. Poor people didn't have wills. Pauline wandered around the apartment, looking for anything she might be able to pawn. The pearls of Mrs. Clayborne's earrings were plastic, and the clothes in the closet were faded and stained. Mrs. Clayborne hadn't bothered much with housekeeping in her old age. Grease was cooked so thick on the kitchen pans that no steel wool could remove it. All in all, there was little of value in the apartment except a necklace with a white-gold cross hall-marked *18K*.

Pauline would do anything to avoid the humiliation of ever begging for money again. Almost anything. No way was she going to show herself at Social Services and start answering questions to prove that she took proper care of her daughter just so she could get a loaf of bread.

She would have to find a job. Employers would wonder about her experience. They would want references. She almost laughed aloud at the ridiculous thought of asking Mr. Hopley from Photomat for a reference.

Her thoughts turned to the father of her child: Bobo, who had paid her to go away and never come back. *I promise I won't pester you again,* she'd said in return for the money. She liked to think of herself as a girl who kept her promises.

Gulp.

Old Taylor made her feel better.

She remembered a time long ago, when she was a schoolgirl, she and a couple of friends had gone to a flea market. Amid the clutter on a table was a dusty old bottle set inside copper mesh with a windup key on the bottom. She turned the key, and the bottle played a jingle.

I'm tired and I want to go to bed.

She giggled again. Then the room darkened, maybe from a cloud passing in front of the sun or maybe from Mrs. Clayborne's ghost.

You'll always hear me singing this song.

Gulp, gulp.

She thought of the other girls she'd met at the club, decent girls, but none of them were much better off than Pauline. She thought of the nice young couple across the hall. They were from Puerto Rico. Pauline didn't speak Spanish, and they didn't speak English, so that was that.

The bells of Mount Olivet began to chime. Pauline looked toward the window that she'd left open that morning. On the sill was one of those round double A batteries. No, it wasn't a battery—it was a cockroach sunning itself. Pauline crossed the room and with a flick of her finger sent it sailing off the sill into the open air. She watched it fall until she couldn't see it anymore, then she went back to the sofa, into the shadow cast by the ghost of Mrs. Clayborne.

Pauline, you have a problem.

There was that horrible word again.

Don't talk to me about problems.

But it was true, she couldn't deny it. For a single mother in New York City in 1963, having no money was definitely a problem.

She tried to re-create every step that had led to the depletion of the money from Bobo, but she soon gave up. Where had it all gone? She remembered a scene in a movie from years back, when a thief is trying to sneak a suitcase full of cash onto a plane. Suddenly a dog jumps from the arms of a woman who's waiting for her husband on the runway. The driver of the luggage cart veers to the side to avoid hitting the dog, and the thief's suitcase goes flying, splits open, and all the cash scatters in the wind. Millions, blown away like dust.

Bobo hadn't given her millions. But a thousand dollars wasn't nothing. What had she done with all of it? One thousand dollars. Well, not quite. Remembering that the suitcase had contained only eight hundred and fifty dollars, Pauline felt newly cheated. What she'd accepted as a mistake now struck her as a flat-out lie. When a man says one thousand, he'd better mean it, she thought with a satisfying rush of indignation! Not Bobo. He said things that weren't true. He had broken his promise to her. Then why couldn't Pauline break her promise to him?

This was the reasoning that led Pauline to make arrangements to go to Albany. The next day, she pawned Mrs. Clayborne's necklace. With difficulty and lots of hand gestures, she communicated to the wife across the hall that she needed a babysitter. The wife kindly agreed to watch Sonia for the day. On Wednesday morning, Pauline went to Grand Central to board the Albany-bound train, intending to confront Bobo in his office at Alumacore and demand that he give her at least the one hundred and fifty dollars he owed her.

By the time she was on the train, she was focused, even optimistic. Her task seemed so completely logical to her that she believed the outcome was guaranteed. She felt almost lighthearted, as if she were going on vacation.

SCUM

I picture the gleaming scaffold of the new Visby plant rising from the foundation, and I think of Pauline's last visit to the Alumacore headquarters in Albany. I think of Pauline walking in her high heels three-quarters of a mile from the bus stop as the sky darkens and the rain begins to fall.

The revolving door is already turning, pushed by a businessman exiting the building, before Pauline has fully inserted herself between the glass partitions. Squeezed against the edge, she knocks urgently on the glass. The door stops revolving just long enough for her to free herself. She hurries to keep up with the fast motion of the door, taking little steps on her tiptoes, and lurches forward when she is spit out into the lobby.

She rights herself, straightens her skirt, attempts to smooth her wet, bedraggled hair. She looks around. On the far side of the space, where the lobby narrows into a hallway with elevators on each side, is the receptionist at her desk. Pauline is surprised that she doesn't recognize her. In the six months she worked at Alumacore, she thought she'd met all the girls. This one must be new. She hadn't considered the prospect of confronting a new receptionist.

She takes a deep breath and heads toward the desk. It is midafternoon, between the lunch break and the day's end, and now that the one businessman who trapped Pauline in the revolving door is gone, the lobby is empty except for Pauline and the receptionist.

"Hi," Pauline says pertly to the girl.

"Can I help you?" The girl's jaw moves busily, prompting Pauline to wonder pointlessly which flavored gum she is chewing.

"You're new here."

The receptionist looks more annoyed than surprised by the statement. "Actually, I've been here six years."

"Odd that we never met."

The girl keeps chewing, her lips separating slightly each time her jaw jerks to one side. Pauline is reminded of Ann, the receptionist at Photomat—not because this girl is anything like Ann, but simply because receptionists have a gatekeeper's power that Pauline can't help but envy.

"I'd like to see Bob Whittaker."

The girl looks blankly at Pauline.

"Robert Whittaker Jr. He's expecting me," she lies.

"No one by that name works here," says the girl.

"You must be mistaken." Pauline gives a little snort to emphasize the ridiculousness of such an error.

"Ma'am, I'm sorry, but there is no one by that name employed here."

Pauline feels the first stirrings of panic. "Robert Whittaker... in Accounting?"

The girl shakes her head.

"Well, where did he go?" Pauline is angry at herself for displaying such desperation.

"I don't know."

"Where does he work?"

"I don't know."

"How can I reach him?"

"I don't know."

"What do you mean, you don't know!"

"Like I said, I don't know."

"He didn't just disappear into thin air. What happened to him?"

"I already told you."

"You don't know."

"That's right. I. Don't. Know."

"Excuse me, miss, what's the trouble here?" A man in a security uniform appears from around the corner and walks rapidly toward them. He is as unfamiliar to Pauline as the receptionist. The company didn't even have security on staff when Pauline worked there. Everything has changed so in the years since she's been in New York, she feels disoriented enough to wonder if she is confused about the past.

"I'm looking for someone," she says feebly to the security guard. "He used to work here."

"She won't leave," the receptionist announces.

"You didn't ask me to leave!"

"We're asking you now," says the guard, reaching to take her arm in a gentlemanly fashion.

Pauline shakes him off. She sees now that she has walked into a trap. She imagines that the mirror on the far wall is one-way glass, and Bobo is behind it in a darkened room, laughing at her. "You bastard," she cries in the direction where she imagines her antagonist is hiding. "Fuck you!" Pleased with the power of her bluster, she tells herself that she is glad not to have to confront the father of her child. She can manage just fine without him. "Scum!" she shouts on her way back out into the rain.

EIGHTEEN KARAT

Now you know how Pauline's trip to Albany turned out. But while she made plenty of mistakes in her life, you have to give her credit for being persistent. Once she'd decided to get that one hundred and fifty dollars owed to her, she wasn't going to give up. She would track down Robert Whittaker Jr. even if it took years.

When she returned in the early evening and put her key into the lock of Mrs. Clayborne's apartment door, she discovered that the chain across the door had been latched from within. Her first thought was that Elena from across the hall had brought Sonia to the apartment so the girl could sleep in her own bed. But that didn't make sense because Elena didn't have a key to Mrs. Clayborne's apartment. Someone else must have latched the chain.

Pauline knocked loudly and rang the buzzer at the same time. In a moment she heard the rattling of the chain. The door was opened, and there stood a man in military garb, a USMC cap on his head, peering through his glasses at Pauline with obvious irritation, as if her arrival had interrupted important work.

"What do you want?" he demanded.

"I live here," Pauline said with surprise.

"This is my aunt's apartment," the man replied.

"I'm her tenant."

"She passed away," the man announced.

"I know. I'm real sorry. She was a good woman, always wanting to help those in need."

"You been staying here alone?"

"I have my own key. I've paid rent."

"You been going through her personal possessions?"

"I . . . don't . . . know what you mean."

In fact, Pauline did have an idea of his meaning, a faint idea that became sharply, dangerously clear when he said, "Like her gold-cross necklace? You have some knowledge of its whereabouts?"

He was referring to the necklace with the eighteen-karat white-gold cross that was Mrs. Clayborne's only possession of real value and that Pauline had pawned the previous day for the cost of a round-trip train ticket to Albany, plus a sit-down lunch.

Sometimes silence conveys more than words possibly can. That's what happened when Mrs. Clayborne's nephew asked Pauline about the necklace: Pauline had nothing to say. And so the nephew told her to pack up her things and get out.

She spent that night with Elena and her husband in the apartment across the hall. The next day she strapped Sonia in the carriage that was almost too small for her, and with the suitcase balanced on the bars underneath the seat, Pauline and Sonia went off in search of shelter.

IX

BULLETS

Mrs. J had settled into the serenity of her retirement when the first piece of structural steel for the World Trade Center was hoisted into place in 1968. Not many people know how pivotal she was in creating those towers. But from the time she first proposed constructing a building that would be the tallest in the world until her retirement in 1965, she had steered the P.A.'s plan toward fruition. Though she made it clear, at least to her staff, that she disapproved when the commissioners decided that one huge skyscraper wasn't enough, it was easy to change the slogans she'd come up with to feed to the press; all she had to do was add *two* and an *s* to *building*.

TWO BIGGEST BUILDINGS IN WORLD TO RISE
AT TRADE CENTER!
GOING UP—WORLD'S TWO TALLEST BUILDINGS!

When concerns were raised about the stores on Radio Row being forced out of business, she gathered testimonies from city planners who approved of the development. One called the neighborhood a slum and claimed it was overrun with rats. She quoted from interviews with residents who welcomed the opportunity to be relocated. And when Lawrence Wien, a real estate magnate who had recently become owner of the Empire State Building, attacked the P.A. with the inadvertently prescient claims that the Twin Towers would be structurally unsound and "unsafe in an explosion or if hit by an airplane," Mrs. J refuted what she called the false allegations with a three-page telegram to the press informing them that independent engineers had investigated the plans for the buildings and found they would be safe even in the event of "a collision with a large jet airliner traveling at 600 miles per hour."

With the great and powerful Mrs. J shooting slogans from her office in the Department of Public Relations, the architect's design for the two towers was approved by all relevant boards, and development proceeded. Eviction notices were sent out to businesses I had listed on my map of the neighborhood years earlier. Protesters gave up. Signs were posted in store windows: PRICES SLASHED, EVERYTHING MUST GO!!! Only a handful of proprietors continued to hold out.

Still the prostitutes came looking for quick lunchtime money. Still the men unzipped their trousers. And there, joining the girls willing to sneak down alleys with strangers and take them into their mouths, was Pauline Moreau.

Well, it wasn't really Pauline. Pauline had learned at the gentlemen's club to stay separate from her work. And now, having fallen lower than she had thought she would ever go, she pretended that her real self was elsewhere. In her heart, she remained unsullied. Or at least that's what I'm left to imagine on my own because Pauline wouldn't tell me much.

"For Christ's sake, Maggie, quit asking me," Pauline finally burst out after we'd been friends for a couple of years and I'd been expressing curiosity about her past.

"I thought...maybe...you might want to talk about it," I said, already aware of my idiocy.

"I don't want to talk about it. Understand?"

"Sometimes it helps, you know, to talk—"

"And sometimes it doesn't help, you know, to talk."

TRASH

She needs a good friend. Will you be that for her?

When I remember Mrs. J asking me to be a friend to Pauline, I can't help but invest her with an impossible visionary power, as if from her office chair she could see into the past and future and grasped in that quick, voracious mind of hers the whole story I'm telling you now. But then I wonder whether Mrs. J had been mistaken to trust me, of all people, to help Pauline. If Mrs. J had been a true prophet, she would have foreseen my failure.

I was older than Pauline, a veteran of the P.A. by the time she came on board, and I took her under my wing. I explained the workings of the department. I helped keep Sonia busy when Pauline brought her into the office. I regularly asked Pauline over to dinner. Of course she'd bring Sonia. I usually invited Tammis, a neighbor in my building on Jane Street, to these little parties too. Over the years, our friendship deepened. The three of us, plus Sonia, took to spending holidays together, even after Pauline quit her job at the Port Authority.

Then Tammis fell in love with a medical student she'd met

at her cousin's wedding. She married him and moved to Brooklyn. Soon she was pregnant, and then put on bed rest because of preeclampsia. She'd been working as a bank teller, but she had to quit her job. After Tammis's baby was born, we saw her only a few times a year.

Pauline and I stayed close, and I would take care of Sonia whenever Pauline was out of town. As you know, I was in charge of Sonia when Pauline went away in 1974 and never returned. I've told you about how I waited for Pauline, how I kept waiting. Waiting and waiting. I haven't told you about Danny, though.

I met Danny Sullivan at Tammis's party for her son's first birthday. I was there without Pauline—Tammis was full of remorse because she'd forgotten to invite her.

Tammis had said that she wanted to set me up with Danny, a friend of her husband's from medical school; she'd told him the same thing. When we finally met at the party, we were ready to notice each other.

In the months that followed, Danny was enmeshed in the grueling hours of his surgical residency, so I saw him only sporadically, though we were in plain, honest agreement that we liked each other and looked forward to spending more time together when Danny finished his training. Until then, he didn't often have the opportunity for a leisurely dinner. That's why I couldn't introduce him to Pauline, I convinced myself. Later, when he had joined an orthopedic practice based in Montclair, I would take the bus out to New Jersey and stay there for the weekend. We began talking of our future together. I expected we would be engaged soon. I never got around to telling him about Pauline and Sonia.

Here's what I can say now that I couldn't admit back then: It was fine being friendly with Pauline, and I did my best to look out for her, but I never got over the feeling of being a little embarrassed around her when we were in public, a little reluctant to be seen associating with a woman who had an air of . . .

My guilt over this is unbearable. I am sorry, Pauline, for my arrogance. I am sorry for my selfishness, my stupidity.

. . . *Trash*, I was going to say. I associated Pauline with trash. She might as well have continued to sport that ridiculous tin tiara. I actually perceived some women subtly withdrawing in revulsion when she passed by, and men following her with a hungry gaze. For the sake of Mrs. J, I put up with being known at the P.A. as Pauline's best friend. Alone with Pauline, I was fascinated by her and admired her courage. In the privacy of my apartment, Pauline and I were at ease, anchored by our concern for Sonia. Yet I had a capacity for quiet contempt I hadn't even been aware of, a vacancy in my heart that should have been filled with compassion and respect.

Tammis will offer the same admission. With profound regret, we've talked with each other about this over the years, about how, most of all, we wanted to keep our men from meeting Pauline. Tammis didn't really "forget" to invite Pauline to her son's birthday party.

How blind we were to our own pettiness. How disappointed in me Mrs. J would have been if she'd known what I truly felt about Pauline Moreau. Or perhaps she did know, having quickly reached the obvious conclusion that Pauline was a much better person than I would ever be.

TWISTER

Yet I can't help imagining Pauline standing ready to correct me: *Aw, but Maggie, we had a blast together!* Get the girls together and watch out! While I mixed up Manhattans, I would feed Sonia maraschinos out of the jar as if she were a baby bird. We'd put on "Proud Mary" and dance until the neighbor downstairs rapped on the ceiling with a broomstick. "Quiet down, ladies," Tammis would scold, and we'd all burst into laughter.

With the chicken casserole bubbling in the oven, I'd roll out the mat for Twister, one of Sonia's favorite games. She made up for her lack of balance and hypomobility with her enthusiasm. The four of us would get so wrapped into knots, big limbs and little limbs crossing in a tangle, that we would have to go backward through the steps of the game in order to extract ourselves without breaking a bone.

Pauline, Tammis, and I were comfortable with one another, enjoying the kind of relaxed friendship that wasn't complicated by sexual intimacy. Sex we reserved for other relationships. Tammis and I were plotting futures that included husbands. Pauline liked to say that she was done with men, but that didn't keep her from flirting with them at every opportunity. Without men around, we were uninhibited, our behavior in concert with Sonia's. We told ourselves that we were allowing ourselves to be silly for Sonia's sake. Really, I think she was the most mature among us—and clearly the only sober one in the room. But she didn't judge us. No one judged us. During those parties, we were free to act like children. We could think of ourselves as carefree and innocent.

Always, though, the reality of our differences was with us, invisible, unspoken. I defined myself in relation to Pauline. I was a sensible woman, educated and reliable. I came from a good family.

Differences sometimes make knots harder to undo—that's the whole principle of weaving, isn't it, when the warp and the weft are threaded together? Looking back on those games of

Twister, I picture us from above; as different as we were, we would have looked like a single mass of flesh and bone with too many heads, so inextricably entangled that you'd think we'd never separate.

Why Tammis Wouldn't Ride in Elevators

At one of these little parties in my apartment on Jane Street, we got to talking about Mrs. J, and I told Pauline and Tammis about the memo she had dictated calling for the P.A. to build the tallest skyscraper in the world. Pauline pointed out that the building would need lots of elevators. In response, Tammis announced that she had never ridden in an elevator and never would.

Never? Pauline and I were incredulous. By then, Sonia had fallen asleep, and we'd tucked her under a blanket on my sofa. I had mixed up another round of drinks. We were glad to relax after a long week.

"I once overheard my aunt tell a story about a friend of hers named Mrs. Foss," Tammis began, signaling to the two of us to lean closer to her across the table. "Mrs. Foss, who hadn't married yet and so was still a *Miss*, though my aunt always referred to her as Mrs. Foss...anyway, when Mrs. Foss—"

"Who wasn't yet Mrs. Foss," pointed out Pauline.

"—when she was just sixteen, she was living in a little town in Maine," continued Tammis, ignoring her, "and she went to work at a nearby textile mill. Her first job was to put cones on the spinners, but after a year or so, the woman who operated the freight elevator retired, and Mrs. Foss was given the job."

"Not the elevator!" I said, meaning to make lighthearted fun of Tammis's fear of elevators, but she registered it as an insult and sat back in a sulk.

"You can't stop now," insisted Pauline, "not in the middle of your story!"

We had to make an exaggerated show of supplication, begging Tammis with clasped hands to finish the narrative, before she finally gave in.

"So anyway, Mrs. Foss went to work as usual one day in the winter of 1946, a snowy day, and the river below the mill was frozen solid." Tammis paused, apparently to admire her hands. She seemed to find a speck of dirt that bothered her and dug under the nail of her index finger with her thumbnail. Then she rummaged through her purse, extracted a cigarette, searched again for the lighter, succeeded in producing a flame after several failed attempts, and pulled an ashtray closer to her. Pauline and I forced ourselves to wait in silence.

"So Mrs. Foss went to work," Tammis eventually continued, "and the day passed like any other, without trouble. Mrs. Foss made dozens of trips on the elevator, carrying workers and equipment and stacks of boxes up and down, up and down. There was no sign that anything was amiss."

I couldn't help myself and blurted out, "I think I see what's coming!" Tammis shot me a look to warn me that her story would remain unfinished if there was one more interruption.

"Go on," Pauline urged.

"At the end of the day, the elevator was always packed. After long hours on their feet, the girls preferred to take the elevator instead of the stairs. A dozen girls had just walked into the elevator that day. They had all finished with their work and were eager to get home. They were chattering so loudly that no one but Mrs. Foss heard a far-off bang come from above the elevator. I should mention that Mrs. Foss was not a nervous girl in general, but that day she was a little jittery because she had read in the morning newspaper about a local woman who had suffered terrible burns on her face when her kerosene stove exploded. If there was one thing Mrs. Foss was afraid of, it was fire. She had been thinking all day about fire and that poor, burned woman. She was jittery, like I said, and when she heard the sudden, distant bang, she jumped off the elevator. The doors closed behind her, and the elevator, with the twelve girls trapped inside, plummeted three stories down the shaft. But that wasn't the worst of it. The assembly and cable and drum snapped free, fell on top of the elevator, and crashed through the roof. Two girls died instantly. The others survived with bruises and broken bones."

I observed the obvious: "But Mrs. Foss was unharmed."

"People wondered, naturally, why Mrs. Foss wasn't on the elevator when the cable snapped. An investigation cleared her of any wrongdoing, but still, there were rumors. It was whispered that she had been having an affair with the husband of one of the girls who was killed."

Tammis looked satisfied at our shocked expressions. She fished a cherry from her drink and dangled it before sucking it off the stem.

"Mrs. Foss maintained her innocence. But still she felt unwelcome at the mill after the accident, so she quit and moved from Maine to New York."

"And met Mr. Foss," Pauline filled in.

"And lived to tell the story to my aunt, who told the story to my mother one evening when I was lying awake in my bed on the other side of the door. I could hear every word. I even heard my aunt admit at the end that she couldn't help but think it fishy that Mrs. Foss jumped off the elevator in the nick of time. I heard her say, 'Those poor girls with their broken necks. And Mrs. Foss without a scratch.' I heard the water gushing as my mother filled the teakettle, and then I heard the bang as my mother set the kettle on the burner. I swear I popped ten feet straight up out of bed at that sound."

"So now you won't ride in an elevator," I said to sum up.

"Never have," she declared. "Never will."

A VITAL PUBLIC IMPROVEMENT

By January of 1965, most businesses on Radio Row had willingly relocated, warehouses had closed, and residents had packed up their apartments and moved out. But construction on what Mrs. J had labeled "this vital public improvement" couldn't begin because of the few businesses, including Oscar's, that refused to leave, so the Port Authority served notices: *Unless you remove from the premises on or before the termination date of March 11 of this year, appropriate proceedings will be taken by the Port of New York Authority to obtain possession of such premises.* When Mrs. J saw the notice the lawyers had drafted, she regretted that she hadn't been asked to compose it herself. She would have used more respectful language, she said.

After work one day, I made my way down to the neighborhood I'd mapped as one of my first assignments at the P.A. Although I knew that almost all of the businesses were shuttered by then, I was surprised by how deserted the area was. Along the stretch of Greenwich between Fulton and Dey, where I was used to seeing traffic jams, the street was empty of cars, mottled from patches of a light snow that had begun to fall. I saw only one other person on the opposite sidewalk, a man in a thin trench coat, his face hidden by the brim of an old-fashioned Stratoliner fedora. He was carrying a large cardboard box, struggling to support its weight. As I watched, he set the box down and took a few deep breaths. After a minute, he lifted the box and continued his awkward shuffling, disappearing around the corner.

I had forgotten to bring my boots, and now the needle-fine flakes were making the sidewalk slippery under my pumps. I regretted visiting in such poor weather and at the same time interpreted the bleakness as the inevitable fate of a neighborhood that had outlived its usefulness. I thought of Mrs. J, who could look at the desolate present and see a better future. Though some of the businesses remained resistant to change, I believed Mrs. J's promise to their proprietors, that they would all be better off in the long run.

It was then I noticed the woman farther down the sidewalk, peering into a Rolleiflex camera that hung from a cord around her neck. I was curious about her interest in such a desolate scene. She was pointing her camera at the building housing Oscar's Radio Shop. The snow, I assumed, would give the facade a blurry appearance in the photo, and with such thick cloud cover, even the windows that weren't boarded up would be dark and uninviting. I wondered if, in the final photograph, the signs on the upper floors would be legible enough for someone to see that they were advertising cabinets, tables, and radio and television parts. I wondered if the frame of the picture would include the whole top floor of the building, which was covered with plywood.

I wanted to ask the woman why she'd chosen that particular structure to photograph. If she'd wanted to document buildings scheduled for demolition, there was finer architecture in the area. Did she have a personal attachment to it, or maybe a family interest in Oscar's? Was she a professional photographer? She didn't look professional in her oversize nubby tan coat.

I thought it best not to disturb her and walked on toward the bus stop on Fulton. I wish now that at the very least I had learned her name—then I might be able to find out if she was the same photographer who'd captured the shadows of Pauline and Sonia during that funeral for Mr. Small Businessman.

DEMOLITION OF RADIO ROW

It's amazing how much noise our species can make; Monday morning rolls around, and suddenly there are jackhammers, bulldozers, explosions as a wrecking ball breaks through bricks, backhoes rumbling, clatter of rubble being dumped into trucks, engines growling, rollers rolling, foremen shouting, workers whistling, cranes lifting steel girders, and walls rising, sheathed in aluminum.

HEAVEN-BOUND

Rotten John: You do what I tell you to do, you fucker! Now get to work!

Martin the elevator operator: I am sorry, sir, but us elevator operators are on strike.

Rotten John: Then you're fired!

Martin the elevator operator: You can't fire strikers.

Ed the ironworker: It don't look right to me, without bar joists.

Fontes, a Cape Verdean: You really want me to hook it?

Chickenbone: Hook it!

Rotten John: That's bullshit. I can fire whoever I wanna fire.

Dick Brady, northeast corner foreman: If you want to move, Martin, you can come work for me in my new post.

Martin the elevator operator: You're leaving?

Jack, a journeyman, brother of George: I call Brady's job!

Ed the ironworker: It just don't look right to me.

Chickenbone [*to Fontes*]: Go ahead and hook it!

George, southwest corner foreman: Hey, Jack.

Jack, new northeast corner foreman: Hey what?

George, southwest corner foreman: Beat you to the top!

Willy the Penguin: Chickenbone's gonna beat you both.

Rotten John: What the hell?

Chickenbone: I'm flying!

Rotten John: Bring him down!

George, southwest corner foreman: It's too late.

Ed the ironworker: I already said, it don't look right to me.

Willy the Penguin: Leave it to Chickenbone.

Rotten John: Chickenbone, you motherfucker!

Chickenbone: Hey, Chief!

Rotten John: When I get my hands on you—

Willy the Penguin: There goes Chickenbone.

Louie the plasterer: Leave it to Chickenbone.

Hahdahn, another Cape Verdean: I told him it was unsafe.

Unnamed signalman: What's going on?

Willy the Penguin: Going up, you mean. Chickenbone's riding
    up to heaven on a floor panel!

Martin the elevator operator: Oh Jesus!

Louie the plasterer: If I was him, I'd never come down.

How to Build a Tower

First you collect a whole lot of grass clippings from the lawn.
Then you take a trowel and you dig a big hole. You dig straight
to the bottom of the sandbox, as deep as you can go. If you can
find some soil below the sand, that's good. Clay is even better.

Make a big pile of sand and clay. Then carve out the sides of the hole to make a square and line it with cardboard left over from your father's shirts after they've come back from the dry cleaner.

Done?

Good.

Now, remember that heap of old gravel behind the garage? Go back there and fill your bucket with gravel, then pour the gravel in the hole. Fill it right to the top, and cover it with a square piece of plywood. If you don't have plywood, make a big square out of four pieces of the cardboard.

Excellent.

That bucket, by the way, is very useful—just make sure it doesn't have a hole in it. Now go and fill it with water from the garden hose and put it on the rim of the sandbox. Perfect. See the big pile from the hole you just dug? Pour some water on the top of it to make a thick mush. Don't use too much water because you want it to be firm like Play-Doh, not runny like pancake batter. Okay. Now it's time to make the bricks. It would help if you had a ruler and a knife to shape the bricks, but you can use the side of your trowel if necessary.

To make the bricks, mix the wet sand, and clay if you have it, with the grass clippings. Experiment with different proportions to see which gives you the strongest brick. Make lots of bricks, and leave them in the sun to dry. Leave them there while you eat your bologna sandwich, and maybe longer. Remember, building a tower takes time.

Once the bricks are dry, you can start to stack them one on top of one another. If the bricks are strong, you can stack them really high. See how high you can go!

"Robbie, honey, Brigid is here to play."

Robbie doesn't have time to play. He is building a tower.

Joanna Scott

"He's in the backyard. You can go right on out, Brigid. Do you see him there?"

"Hi."

"Hi."

Robbie Whittaker is eight years old. He is more grown up than the other children his age, everyone says so. In the fall, he is going to school in a place so far away that he will have to live there. He is proud to be so brave.

Brigid Finney is five years old, way too young to build a tower. Robbie doesn't mind when she comes over, but today she will have to watch. He won't let her stack the bricks.

She doesn't want to stack the bricks. She is busy licking a raspberry Popsicle that Robbie's mother gave her after Mr. Finney and Robbie's father went off to talk about aluminum.

"What are you building?" Brigid asks Robbie.

"A tower."

"Oh."

Robbie stacks the bricks carefully, one by one. Secretly he is frustrated that the bricks are too small, and the walls aren't higher, and the tower reaches only to his knees.

"That's a really tall tower," Brigid says.

Robbie works hard to hide his gratitude. "Thanks," he says with bland indifference. From his kneeling position, he looks up at her. She is wearing overall shorts and a flowered blouse. With the sun shining on her head, the little fuzzy curls sticking out from her pigtails look like straw. He admires the way the freckles cross her nose to make a dotted line. When she licks her Popsicle, she starts from the bottom, right near the stick, and drags her tongue slowly up the side of the rectangle. Her tongue is the same color as the Popsicle. So are her lips.

"That's the tallest tower I ever saw," she says.

X

The Day It Rained Bread

Descending from the Adirondack dome, the land of northern New York State opens to the wide, flat expanse of the St. Lawrence Valley. Rivers and creeks swell and run muddy in the spring, lacing the soil with nutrients. In the peaty marshes, tiny sundews trap insects with their sticky tentacles. Beavers, once prized for the soft insulating pelts that were, for years, much in demand by the European millinery industry, drag branches across stream beds to divert the flow of water. In the fertile fields patchworking the valley, farmers tend their corn and squash and beans, as farmers have been doing for more than a thousand years.

When the French explorer Jacques Cartier led an expedition up the St. Lawrence River in 1535, there were already thriving villages there, including, most notably, the Iroquois settlement of Hochelaga. In his report to Francis I, Cartier recalled being met along the banks of the river by a crowd of hundreds. Men, women, and children formed three successive rings, singing and dancing to the beating of drums, welcoming their visitors. It was "as good a welcome as ever a father gave to his son," wrote Cartier.

When the Frenchmen went ashore in Hochelaga, they were led into a circular village enclosed by tiers of a wooden palisade. There was only one gate, and within the high walls were galleries stocked with stones of various sizes, presumably for the inhabitants to defend themselves against attack. The log structures were large, their chambers carpeted with bear hides, the walls lined with sheets of bark. Interior corridors connected the separate dwellings to a central longhouse, where the inhabitants would gather for meals. Pottery was decorated in rich, varied dyes, and both the men and women wore elaborate beaded necklaces. Inside a limestone smokehouse hung strips of venison and elk. Cultivated fields expanded outward from the palisades.

Cartier found the inhabitants to be a trusting people, as generous as they were prosperous. When the French expedition prepared to leave, the women lowered baskets of fish and threw loaves of corn bread into their longboats. Cartier would later remember the bread falling around them like heavy rain from the clear blue sky.

Three-quarters of a century later, the explorer Samuel de Champlain would find no trace of Hochelaga. To this day, no one is sure what happened to the original Iroquois of the St. Lawrence River Valley. Some scholars argue that they returned to their nomadic lives or that they were wiped out by diseases passed to them by the French; others believe that they were conquered by a neighboring tribe, most likely the Mohawks, who came to dominate the region and by the nineteenth century were known and feared for their strength. About the

Mohawks, the anthropologist Henry Schoolcraft would proclaim that their name "was a synonyme for cruelty and dread. No tribe, perhaps, on the continent, produced better warriors, or have ever more fully realized, as a nation, the highest measure of heroism and military glory to which hunter nations can reach."

UNTIL THEN

"Everyone, please, if you will, quiet down, friends. Order in the house, please. Mr. Unsworth has come all this way to talk to us."

"We want him to listen to us!"

"We know what's going on!"

"We don't need experts to tell us what is happening to our cattle."

"To our fish!"

"To our people!"

"Mr. Unsworth, as an Elder, I remember when our farms were large and grew plenty of food. Fish stocks were abundant, and medicines could be gathered in wetlands. We sold baskets made from black ash and sweet grass. We could always rely on the river to support our families. It was our insurance policy. And then the power authority changed its flow, and the factories moved up and poisoned the water."

"They took the river from us!"

"Where is the prosperity they promised?"

"Mr. Unsworth is on our side, we need to hear what he has to say. The more information we have, friends, the stronger our claim. Mr. Unsworth, thank you for being with us today. My people, please give Mr. Unsworth a hearty Akwesasne welcome."

"Thank you, ladies and gentlemen. I am on your side, believe me. I know the frustration when the government refuses to recognize the harmful effects of industrial pollution."

"If we complain to the state government about the dredge spoils along our shoreline, we are told to talk to the Seaway Board. The Seaway Board tells us to talk to Canada. Canada tells us to talk to the U.S.!"

"I'm here to help you build a case and gather evidence."

"You want evidence, here's some. Ma, stand up, let him see your goiter."

"Come to our farms if you want evidence."

"Friends, let Mr. Unsworth continue."

"I will certainly come to your farms. You will get tired of seeing me, I expect. I will take water and soil samples. The key is to trace wastes to their discharge points. I will be looking at the Grasse River, and of course the St. Lawrence, and Turtle and Robinson Creeks, and the Massena Power Canal."

"It comes through the air, with the wind. What is the white dust that coats our pastures and kills our cattle?"

"I will be tracking atmospheric transport and deposition. In addition, I will be looking for disposal areas on and around industrial properties."

"The discharge flows right from the plant down a natural ravine and into the bay."

"It is yellow liquid, hot, hot...hot enough to burn. What is the liquid coming out of the plant?"

"I need to do tests to identify the contaminants."

"How long is this going to take?"

"I will be working assiduously on your behalf, I promise."

"How long do we have to wait until they stop poisoning our land and our rivers?"

"I need to gather samples over time, since I don't have previous samples to compare. I ask for your patience. I must be thorough with the research and produce indisputable evidence."

"Mr. Unsworth, how long until we can expect reparation?"

"I believe we'll have conclusive results within ten years—sooner, if I get help gathering samples."

"How long did he say?"

"Ten years!"

"And until then?"

"I say we blow up Alumacore with dynamite!"

"Until then, friends, we will protect our territory as best we can. Mr. Unsworth, we thank you for your help. We thank you for your candor, for taking the time to visit us today, for your work on our behalf. Let us give Mr. Unsworth a hearty thank you."

Virginia Slims

God, it was cold in Visby. Who decided residents should stay put during winter? *The birds got it right; they knew when to ditch the place,* Robbie Whittaker said to himself as he jerked the car into park outside the 7-Eleven.

He was sixteen, and driving was a novelty to him. He hardly ever had a chance to drive. He wasn't allowed to keep a car at school, which was a total drag, in his hardened teenage opinion. At home, he found any excuse to take the car out, though it was always the old Ford station wagon, not the Cadillac; his dumb-ass parents wouldn't let him drive the Cadillac.

The snow swirled in gusts in front of the store window. Robbie pulled his ski cap down tighter and went out into the cold with such momentum that his sneakers slipped on the ice right beside the door. He went flying backward, knocked against the car, and landed hard on his rump.

He was thankful that no one had witnessed his humiliation. He picked himself up, brushed off the snow, and headed into the store.

He was on an errand for his mother, buying her cigarettes. He hated that she smoked, but it gave him a reason to drive. And since his mother believed that the only way Robbie would learn to drive in the snow was by getting firsthand experience, she let him go. She was really craving her Virginia Slims.

As for his father . . . Robbie hardly interacted with him. Fuck, he wasn't even his real father. And he had all these conservative beliefs, like if you're queer you're less than a man. He'd once asked Robbie if he was a fag, and Robbie said yes just to goad him. Ha-ha, Dad, April fool's. When Robbie was home on holidays, he looked for every opportunity to pick a fight. They'd had a good argument about abortion the previous night. Robbie knew just what to say to get Bob Whittaker going, and Robbie would get going back. Slamming doors would clang through their stupid aluminum house. He hated that house and resented his adoptive dad for making him grow up in Nowheresville. His mom he could put up with, though not with her smoking, except when she gave him the car keys and sent him to the 7-Eleven to buy her cigarettes.

This was back when cigarettes hadn't been moved to the shelves behind the counter. They were right up front, in a colorful arrangement next to the candy.

Robbie Whittaker reached for the Virginia Slims.

Beside him, Brigid Finney reached for the red Twizzlers.

Their hands outstretched, they looked at each other in surprise.

"Brigid?"

"Robbie?"

They hadn't seen each other in, like, three years, maybe more. They openly assessed their new selves, peering, clearly judging as their gazes raked up and down and back up again.

"You look great," Robbie said, and immediately thought, *Oh my God, did I really say that?* What an idiot he was. With her blond ponytail, her furry black earmuffs, her cheeks glowing from the cold, her pillowy ski jacket, her slender legs in bell bottoms frayed at the cuffs, Brigid Finney did look great, but you weren't supposed to come right out and say that to a girl. Talk about awkward.

She ignored him. She was absorbed with the effort of ripping open the bag of Twizzlers. "Want one?" she offered, thrusting the bag in front of him.

"You gotta pay for those first," said the cashier.

Brigid rolled the top of the bag to close it. "So, um, what are you up to these days?" she asked, moving ahead of Robbie to examine the items on display. He followed her.

"Um, not much. School and stuff."

"Yeah. You go to school in Massachusetts, right?"

"Connecticut."

"Oh."

"And how's life at Visby High?"

She turned down the aisle. Blocked from the cashier's hawk-ish eyes by the stack of magazines, she surreptitiously removed two Twizzlers and gave one to Robbie.

"You know, it's the usual."

"Yeah."

"Yeah, well..."

They wandered down an aisle, chewing on the licorice. Brigid stopped to examine the cereal boxes.

"What kind of cereal do you like?" she asked abruptly.

"Uh, I guess, well." He hesitated, worried he would sound foolish. "Froot Loops, I'd have to say."

"Me too! Wow!"

When she giggled, her cheeks ballooned like a squirrel's. She struck Robbie as irresistibly cute and poised at the same time. He wanted to stay in her company for as long as possible. He followed her up the next aisle and stood beside her when she lifted out a gallon of milk. He followed her to the counter and waited while she paid. He meant to keep following her, but the cashier stopped him, calling, "You can't just walk out with those cigarettes!"

Brigid and Robbie halted just inside the door. She gave him another long, appraising look. He was embarrassed about everything, but mostly because he was carrying a pack of Virginia Slims. "They're for my mother," he said mournfully.

"Oh." She lifted the bag in her hand, accepting her turn to explain the contents. "Dad isn't feeling great, so Mom is home taking care of him. We needed milk."

"Yeah. I hope your father feels better soon. I'll be seeing you around."

"Actually not, since you go to school in Connecticut."

"I guess." Was there anyone stupider than Robbie Whittaker? Other boys his age would have been suavely condescending in the company of a fourteen-year-old girl. Robbie was as clumsy as a kindergartner. Then he suddenly had a brilliant idea. "Do you need a ride?" he asked.

She thought for a moment, glancing through the glass door at the snow. "Sure," she said.

SOUND WAVES

With three large manufacturing plants in the area, Visby had enough wealth to support a small country club. The golf course, in fact, was famous for its long, sweeping hills and views of the islands and the huge locks in the distance. Unfortunately for developers, much of the best acreage in the area had been sold by the lumber company to the state and was protected under the St. Lawrence Power Project's land-management plan. For those who wanted to make their homes to the northwest of the industrial plants, upriver and in the opposite direction of the prevailing winds, the land adjacent to the golf course was prime, and in the 1950s and 1960s it was quickly snapped up by wealthy residents. The Whittakers were lucky to have a piece of it.

The Whittakers enjoyed their aluminum home for just short of twenty years. The aluminum counters in the kitchen were easy to clean. The aluminum sills reflected the sunlight and brightened the rooms. Aluminum trim throughout the house gave it a stylish contemporary look that never seemed to get old. The aluminum siding withstood the blizzards and hailstorms that damaged wooden structures. In the enclosed courtyard, white moths that had mysteriously infiltrated the space fluttered like scraps of paper blown about by a fan.

Those in the upper crust of Visby thought Mrs. Whittaker was rather "tightly wound," as the women at the country club would say among themselves. Similarly, Bob Whittaker's bluster, along with the cowboy hat he'd taken to wearing, drew muttered insults from his golfing buddies. But overall, the Whittakers were thought to be typical of their narrow segment of the social strata in Visby. They enjoyed the usual luxuries: a Hatteras yacht to motor out to the islands on weekends, boarding school for their child, and of course a fine home—one of the finest in the county, as even the most jealous neighbors had to agree after *Town and Country* featured it in an article about exceptional properties along the St. Lawrence.

Kay was a proud homeowner and kept her dissatisfactions, primarily the fact that aluminum intensified the littlest noises, to herself. She could hear her husband belch in the den when she was on the other side of the house. From behind the closed door of her bedroom, Kay could hear when the maid, Maria, dropped a penny on the kitchen floor. Unexpected sounds had always made her jump. That she spent almost two decades in a house where sound waves reverberated off every surface, electrifying her ears' sensitive cochleae, had an inevitable effect on her nerves. She couldn't help it if she was more delicate than other women. As the years went on, she grew ever prouder of her aluminum home and ever more appalled by its amplifications.

During her lowest points, she relied on those vodka tonics to help quiet the sounds. And her kindly GP offered help when she confided to him that she thought she would go crazy living in that aluminum box. Valium and vodka plus Virginia Slims together took the edge off all kinds of noise. There was a period back in the late 1960s when she was often so far gone that she would not even hear the garage door open or the doorbell ring. Sometimes she was already in her nightgown, tucked between crisp white sheets redolent of the lilac-scented detergent Maria used for the laundry, when her husband came home at the end of the day.

The Channel to Chinnampo

Can you blame Bob Whittaker for feeling lonely in those days? In 1969 he was thirty-eight, strong and healthy, already with a fortune that surpassed his wildest dreams. Yet after all he'd done to escape the pigsty of his youth, look what he came home to: Hamburger Helper congealing in a pan, and a wife who couldn't be roused.

Other men in his situation might have looked at some pretty young secretary licking the flap of an envelope and seen in her a potential relief from loneliness. But Bob Whittaker had already sown his wild oats when he was a young accountant back at the headquarters in Albany. He wasn't about to get his hands dirty all over again.

That Pauline. She was a fun girl, a real mustang. He still thought of her after all these years. He often wondered about the child that was half his own. He liked to think the child was a girl, to differentiate her from the adopted son who shared his name. Never having met her or even seen a photograph, he had nothing to imagine, so he was left picturing a daughter like Tom Finney's eldest girl, the one to whom Robbie had taken a fancy. A strawberry-blond sweetheart who would never know that Bob Whittaker was her father.

Had Pauline Moreau married someone else? Probably, and Bob's bastard child was growing up thinking her stepdaddy was her real daddy. Sometimes Bob would drive himself into a silent fury imagining her deprivation. A little girl as pretty as Brigid Finney. Bob's little girl, a child who called someone else Daddy and who wasn't there to greet him after a hard day of work when he stepped into the aluminum box that was his home.

Bob didn't think about Pauline and her daughter often, though. As he ate dinner alone at the kitchen table, the metallic quiet of the house would remind him of his navy days, of the tense, lonely silence that gripped a crew of hundreds as they swept the channel to Chinnampo for contact mines, listening for any scrape or bump that might precede a catastrophic explosion.

The darkness at sea had its own unique effect on a man's imagination. The crew had glided along, watching, waiting, silently praying that they would live to see the morning. Their radar was outdated; they trusted their eyes more than the sensors. No one ever spoke above a whisper.

Living in an aluminum house in Visby was not unlike serving on a minesweeper in the Korean War, Bob mused, then he wondered how he'd gotten to a point in life where that equation was possible. He had sacrificed everything to move up in the business world, and this was the result: a house that echoed like a minesweeper. No wonder Kay was jumpy. He couldn't blame her for seeking relief. He didn't blame Kay for any of it, not even for failing to produce a child from their marriage. She shared Robbie with him. That was enough. She had been a loyal wife, always supportive. She didn't care that he came from nothing, as long as he made good. And he had made good. He had an aluminum house to prove it. A house like a ship, the USS *Whittaker,* gliding soundlessly in the deadly sea.

He put his trust in God. God got him out of the trouble with Pauline. God kept the feds from finding out about that price-fixing scheme. God helped him double the profits of the plant in Visby. And on he sailed, praying for safe passage through the channel to Chinnampo, feeling as divided from his fellows as if he were a planet stuck in its orbit in the night sky, the darkness as silent as deep space—except for the tired chirp of one lonely cricket.

It was a hot, humid night in Upstate New York. Down in

the city, the elevator operators at the World Trade Center construction site were on strike, and earlier that day a construction
worker known as Chickenbone had ridden a floor plate to the
top of the North Tower.

They would need plenty of aluminum for the World Trade
Center. They would need aluminum for pipes and door handles. They would need aluminum for fixtures. The design called
for sheathing the two towers from top to bottom in aluminum
alloy.

Alumacore was the supplier for the Port Authority, a contract
that would keep the potline running up in Visby. But Bob Whittaker wasn't thinking about what was going on in New York. He
was thinking about sweeping clear the channel to Chinnampo.
He was thinking about their sister ship that hadn't made it,
and the flesh and bone and metal that had been blown into a
million pieces. He was thinking about the men on that ship,
wondering what it must have felt like in that final flash, when
you know you are going to die.

God had spared him. God had a plan for him. He was put
on this good earth to make a profit for Alumacore. Thank you,
God, for blessing Bob Whittaker with the savvy and guts to
make the Visby plant a reality. He had so much to be thankful
for, yet he couldn't deny his misery, despite his good fortune.
How alone he was in the world. His wife was asleep when he
came home after a busy day. He hardly knew his son, who went
to boarding school and then summer camp and for the few
days when he was in Visby preferred to read a book rather than
throw a ball with his dad. What boy likes to read? Wearing
those wire-rim spectacles, he resembled his real father, who in
old photos looked like a faggot, in Bob's opinion.

Please, God, don't let Robbie be a faggot.

On he sailed, a burly man on a metal ship, dedicated to his

dangerous mission yet hating every minute of it, death bobbing just beneath the surface. The stars burned dimly behind the veil of fluoride gas. The solitary cricket chirped feverishly outside the screen of the kitchen door.

Bob swallowed a spoonful of Hamburger Helper. Another spoonful.

Bob Whittaker had been home for nearly an hour. He'd worked later than usual to finish up an inventory report in the office, and his wife had given up waiting for him. Now she was sound asleep. She who jumped at the slightest noise. Nothing could wake her, not even the doorbell.

Someone was ringing the fucking doorbell. What time was it? After nine. Who could be calling at the Whittakers' aluminum house in Visby on an August night after nine o'clock?

A vague premonition made him hesitate to open it. He who by nature would have been a boisterous free spirit if everything had gone his way was, by middle age, a willfully cautious man. He had learned from his mistakes. God had forgiven him his sins and offered him redemption in Visby.

Visby, New York.

An aluminum house overlooking the golf course.

The loneliest place in all the world.

No one had ever come to visit the Whittakers at night unannounced. Why now? Maybe Bob didn't want to know. An unexpected visitor brings only bad news.

The doorbell rang again, insistently. In her bedroom, Kay Whittaker stirred and went back to sleep. In the kitchen, Bob weighed his options. He had to be honest with himself and recognize that he had only one option: to see who had come to bother him.

Passing through the dining room, Bob glanced out the window and saw only the family station wagon in the driveway. He had put the Cadillac in the garage. Whoever was at the door must have walked there.

The ship kept slipping stealthily along the channel, its internal lights sweeping side to side to illuminate the infinite darkness of the depths.

Every night Bob Whittaker said a silent prayer of thanks. And then he'd join his wife in bed, and after a period of uncomfortable wakefulness, during which he suffered from the existential terror that was used to explain everything in those days, he would finally fall asleep. In the morning he would get up and do it all again.

Every night was the same until the night in August 1969 when Bob Whittaker opened the door and saw Pauline Moreau standing there.

KAY WHITTAKER DREAMING

Meanwhile, Kay Whittaker dreamed. She dreamed of catching snowflakes on her mitten. She dreamed of waltzing with a boy named Phil at the high-school prom. She dreamed of feeling Robbie kick excitedly inside her to the music of the Albany Symphony Orchestra when she was eight months pregnant. She dreamed of nursing Robbie in early morning, when the bedroom was just beginning to brighten with dawn. She dreamed of Bob in his navy uniform, all crisp white. She dreamed of the sweet music of a train whistle in the distance. She dreamed of seeing her name on the cover of a book. She dreamed of making love. She dreamed of Vivien Leigh and Clark Gable. She dreamed of her mother rolling out a pie crust. She dreamed faintly of her father holding the back of her bike, trying to teach her to ride a two-wheeler.

Joanna Scott

She heard a distant ding and took it to be a single note on the piano. She sank deeper into her pillow and went on dreaming. She dreamed of the voices of young children playing in the yard. She dreamed of the previous day, when she'd watched a fly dipping its proboscis into ketchup on a plate she'd left behind on the patio table. She dreamed of the current of the St. Lawrence rippling backward in a lock. She dreamed of a meadow full of goldenrod at sunset. She dreamed of a winter so cold that words froze in the air. She dreamed of a river of liquid aluminum flowing into the sea.

XI

A PIECE OF PAPER

Mr. Raymond Quipley, it should be noted, had an aversion to paper lying around. He was generally a tidy man and liked to keep his office immaculate. As soon as he had glanced at a document, he insisted it be filed or discarded. Everything for Mr. Quipley had to be in its proper place. We were still at our Eighth Avenue location when he announced that, in preparation for the move downtown, he wanted everything in our department cleaned up, reorganized, and streamlined.

I'd perceived from the moment he took over as director that Mr. Quipley had it in for Pauline. Perhaps he resented her for the favoritism shown to her by Mrs. J. At any rate, he frequently gave Pauline menial, mind-numbing tasks. He moved her from reception back to filing. He chose her more often than anyone else to fetch his dry cleaning and empty his ashtrays. I remember one conversation that went something like this:

"Pauline, get in here!"

"Yes, Mr. Quipley?"

"Did you tell Tozzoli I was out when he called yesterday?"

"When did he call, Mr. Quipley?"

"For Christ's sake, how should I know? Don't you keep a log?"

"No, Mr. Quipley."

"You're telling me you don't keep a log of phone calls?"

"Yes, Mr. Quipley."

"Yes, you do keep a log?"

"No."

"You do not keep a log?"

"Oh, now I remember! Mr. T called when you were out at lunch yesterday."

"I didn't go out. I ate lunch in my office."

"You were in the restroom when he called. But I didn't think you'd want me to tell him that, so I told him you were at lunch."

"And you didn't tell him I'd call him back?"

"Yes, I did."

"How could I call him back if I didn't know he had called in the first place? Miss Moreau, I'm asking you—"

"I heard you."

"There are a lot of girls out there who'd like to work at the P.A. You're easily replaceable, Miss Moreau. I could replace the whole lot of you in a heartbeat! I don't know how Lee Jaffe got anything done around here. From now on, things are going to be different. I'm in charge. You better do what I tell you. And when the director asks to speak with me, I'm going to speak with him."

"What should I say if you're out when he calls?"

"I told you, I was in my office!"

"But what if, the next time—"

"That's enough. I don't want to hear another word. I swear, cross me again and you're done for. Now get out of my sight!"

"Yes, Mr. Quipley. Oh, by the way—"

"What is it?"

"Oh, it's not important."

"Then why'd you bring it up at all? You better screw your head on tighter, Miss Moreau."

"Whatever you say, Mr. Quipley."

By then most of us were used to Mr. Quipley, the same way one gets used to a neighbor's vicious dog snarling on the other side of a chain-link fence. Pauline, however, liked to irritate him, even as she was always looking for incentives to quit. I did everything I could to convince her to stay, and for a good four years following Mrs. J's retirement, Pauline did stay, enduring Mr. Quipley's insults. She needed a steady salary for Sonia's sake. Sonia's medications were expensive, plus she had started going to an after-school dance program that she loved. Who would pay for Sonia's dance classes if Pauline quit the P.A.?

Pauline stuck with the job, satisfying herself by thumbing her nose at Mr. Quipley behind his back, causing the rest of us to burst into laughter that we quickly suppressed when Mr. Quipley whipped his head around in search of his ridiculer. Beneath furry brows, his eyes would scan the room and alight on Pauline, who by then would be sorting through a file drawer, her back to him.

Many of the girls who had worked for Mrs. J left during Mr. Quipley's tenure. Some got married; others found better jobs or transferred to different departments in the P.A. Among those of us still there at this point, most were excited about moving to one of the glorious new towers rising into the air, hopeful that the headquarters would be up on one of the high floors with great views. Pauline, though, seemed to have grown more settled in her ways by then. She thought our location on Eighth Avenue was just fine and said so repeatedly to anyone who would listen, as if her insistence would make a difference. She complained that the move was an unnecessary inconvenience; I suspect she just didn't want to return to the downtown neighborhood where Mrs. J had first found her.

The strain of weathering the tyranny of our director made the staff in our department more reticent than before, and more resentful. I'm sure we got less work done than we had under Mrs. J. We worked as inefficiently as we could without drawing attention to ourselves. Mr. Quipley liked to call himself a detail man, so we lingered over details. We typed slowly. We took our time with the most trivial tasks. We would pretend to study documents that held no interest for us, just for the sake of annoying our boss.

That's what Pauline was doing—pulling out papers from the folders, leisurely reading letters and memos Mr. Quipley had ordered her to sort. I remember that our fans were whirring, but still I heard the shouting from an antiwar protest passing on the street below. I remember smiling to myself as I watched Pauline deliberately wasting time. I remember I asked Pauline if she wanted to join me for lunch and believed her when she said she wanted to leave early that day and so wouldn't take a lunch break, which meant I was out of the office when Pauline slipped a folded piece of paper she'd found in one of the files into her purse.

AND THEY'RE OFF!

Not long after Pauline swiped that piece of paper from a P.A. file, she developed a passion for horse racing. She wasn't interested in Belmont or Aqueduct; she preferred the holiday atmosphere of Saratoga Springs in August. Before she left for the track, she would rub Sonia's head for good luck, kiss her good-bye, and thank me for taking care of the girl.

I remember listening to a radio broadcast of a race I assumed Pauline was watching in person. I pictured her standing high up in the bleachers, a lone woman fingering her ticket when the horses thundered out of the gate, keeping her mouth shut as the crowd cheered the odds-on favorite, Linda's Chief. It was Linda's Chief who led the pack with bullish strength for half a mile while the rest of the horses struggled to keep up; Linda's Chief was still the front-runner as the horses reached the final stretch, at which point Secretariat, the two-year-old everyone was talking about, came out of nowhere, drove between Trevose and Northstar Dancer, sailed past Linda's Chief, and crossed the finish line two lengths ahead.

I pictured Pauline tucking her lucky ticket safely inside her pocketbook, lighting a cigarette, and studying the glowing end just like Mrs. J used to do. Then, in my imagined scene, Pauline stretched her arms and said to anyone who was listening, "I think I'm done for the day," before going to collect her earnings.

But what do I know about horse racing? I've never even been to a track.

An Anonymous Beauty

It had been ten years since Bob Whittaker had seen her. Her hair was bobbed, and her face had a more chiseled, mature look. The circles under her eyes had darkened a shade. He almost didn't trust the instantaneous blast of recognition. But with recognition came a rush of fear so strong that he couldn't take the time for second-guessing. Pauline Moreau had tracked him down in Visby. Now he had to hide her before anyone found out.

"What...what are you doing here?" he demanded in a hoarse voice, at the same time ducking outside and hastily closing the door behind him.

"I was in the neighborhood," Pauline said. "I thought I'd stop by and say hello."

He stupidly took her seriously for a moment. "At this time of night?"

He was slowly making sense of his predicament, gauging her intentions through an intense effort of interpretation. Her expression was nonchalant, even amused. But she hadn't sought him out to be amused.

"You can't be seen here," he hissed. He took her arm and pulled her out of the pool of light shining from the security fixture above the door. He felt her stagger a step, one foot turning on its impractical high heel. He held her upright.

"Ouch," she said, though without much conviction.

"Did you hurt yourself?" Bob's emotions were combining in a turbulent concoction. Mostly, he feared for his own reputation, yet he also felt a strong current of compassion mixing with the fear, and even some pleasure that he'd been found. With Pauline there, he wasn't alone anymore.

He couldn't hear that cricket from the front of the house. Overhead, a waxing moon lit up the edges of a cloud. It was unusually hot and humid—that must explain why there was sweat clinging to the black hairs on Bob's arms, like dew on grass.

"A sprained ankle would be the least of it," she murmured. Bob heard a bitterness in Pauline's voice that hadn't been there ten years earlier.

"We have to talk," she said.

"We can't talk here."

"Then where?"

"You didn't walk here, did you? You couldn't have walked. Where's your car?"

"I took a cab."

"Oh, for Christ's sake, you told a Visby cabdriver to bring you here?" His thoughts were churning, moving through speculation, memory, anticipation of the scandal that would erupt when the cabdriver mentioned at the diner that he'd driven an out-of-towner to the Whittakers', a nice-looking girl, and no, she hadn't said her name. The village chin-wags would be buzzing by morning. Kay would get wind of the gossip...

"Let me get a car key. Wait here, don't move," Bob whispered, his voice a hiss of panting sounds that he worried weren't intelligible, so he repeated, "Wait here," and added, "I'll be right back."

He didn't want to open the garage door and risk waking his wife, so he went looking for the key to the station wagon. He found it hanging in its proper place on a hook in the kitchen. In the minute or so it took him to return to Pauline, his panic veered in a new direction, making him fear that he would lose her all over again.

He threw open the door. He didn't see her and with a delirium that cast itself as common sense, he thought that he'd imagined the whole thing, that the doorbell hadn't rung, Pauline Moreau hadn't come to his home that night. But he looked again and there she was, in the shadows by the house, right where he'd left her. And she willingly went with him, leaning a little on his arm as he helped her across the yard. He felt her stagger as her heels sank into the soft ground.

He drove east toward the Alumacore plant, thinking he might find privacy there before remembering the obvious fact that the night crew would be on duty. Miles from the plant, he pulled into a dirt lot behind an abandoned warehouse.

Pauline, who hadn't spoken for the whole drive, said, "I don't like it here."

Bob obediently drove aimlessly on after deciding that inside a car was the safest place for them to be right then. He had to shake his head a little to keep steady. The dots of the divider had a dizzying effect as they unfurled ahead of the car. Luminescent moths zigzagged through the beams of the headlights. On either side, a wall of trees gave the asphalt the look of a tunnel.

He didn't glance at Pauline when he finally said, "What do you want?"

She had come for money, of course. That was all. Just money to help her and Sonia get by.

Sonia. Sonia was the name of their child. Bob had been right to imagine a daughter. A daughter named Sonia.

"How much do you need?"

Bobo was ready to give Pauline whatever she asked for. He hadn't forgotten her promise that she wouldn't ever bother him again; he just didn't care. He was relieved that money would keep her quiet. He had plenty of money. Giving money to support his daughter would assuage his lingering guilt.

She said he owed her one hundred and fifty dollars. He kept himself from laughing aloud. One hundred and fifty measly dollars. Dear girl, Bobo would give you that, and more! He was happy to share his income with Pauline, as long as she kept quiet about it. She would keep quiet, wouldn't she? Good, then they understood each other. He'd have to figure out a way to get the money to her. He obviously couldn't write a check with her name on it. He was ready to give her all the cash in his wallet, but that wasn't much, forty dollars and change.

After an hour of driving around, he finally dropped her off at a motel in Massena, as she'd requested. He promised her that within a week, a considerable sum would be on its way to the PO box she'd written down for him. He didn't specify exactly how much, only that it would keep her and Sonia comfortable for a good long while.

About Sonia—

As Pauline opened the passenger door of the Ford, Bobo asked her ever so gently if she happened to have a picture of Sonia.

Remember those nice pictures that Pauline had pocketed when she couldn't figure out something to write on the labels at Photomat? Well, there was one of a cute little girl, a dark-haired anonymous beauty with perfect teeth, that Pauline kept in her purse.

She had brought the picture with her for this precise purpose, to show Bobo if he asked, though not because she was ashamed of Sonia. The stock photo was a strategic ploy on Pauline's part to fool Bob Whittaker. Pauline wanted to make sure that if he ever came looking for his daughter, he wouldn't recognize her.

PAULINE QUITS THE P.A.

"Pauline, get in here."

"Yes, Mr. Quipley?"

"I can't find the Jackson report. It was here somewhere." He cast his hand over his desk, neatly arranged, with sticky frames affixed to the surface to keep the blotter in its proper place. "Someone must have thrown it out," he said. "Go look for it."

He nodded toward the blue plastic receptacle against the

wall of his office. This was 1969—no one made the effort to recycle, and the garbage bin didn't contain just paper; it also served as the dumping place for the contents of ashtrays, the wrappings around deli sandwiches, tissues, bent pushpins and paperclips. Mr. Quipley even tossed the remnants of his coffee into that bin.

It would be dirty, smelly work, going through that trash. But you already know that Mr. Quipley wasn't the only person who associated Pauline with trash.

"Well, don't just stand there. The report is probably in the garbage. Go find it."

"Yes, Mr. Quipley."

His phone rang. Soon he was absorbed in a conversation, and he didn't look up to watch Pauline go through the garbage bin in search of the Jackson report. He didn't notice when she picked up the whole container, which was about half her size and bulky, so it was hard to carry, but she did carry it, all the way across the room to Mr. Quipley's desk. She lifted it high above her head.

I don't know who first had an inkling of what was going on in Mr. Quipley's office, but a ripple of astonishment passed among the staff, and we all hurried to the glass partition separating the office from the rest of our department. We were there in time to watch as Pauline shook the contents of the garbage bin onto Mr. Quipley's desk. Out spilled reams of paper muddied from coffee, along with the pins and clips and sandwich wrappings, all of it falling amid a puff of powdery gray cigarette ash that expanded in a gritty bubble in front of Mr. Quipley's astonished face.

Whether he ever did find the Jackson report, I don't recall.

A Fairy Tale

Pauline Moreau, who had been living on the edge of poverty, was suddenly rich—so she said—after coming into an inheritance from a distant relative she hadn't even known existed. She bought herself a nice new wardrobe. She transferred Sonia to a private school where she'd get better services. She took us all out to dinner at her favorite clam bar on Mulberry Street, where Tammis asked her outright if she had ties to the Mob.

"Long as you don't mess with me, you're safe," Pauline squeaked, failing in her attempt to mimic a mobster's growling voice, causing us all, even Sonia, to erupt in such hilarity that other diners cast us annoyed glances.

It seemed a fairy tale, the way Pauline's life was magically transformed. This went on for five years, and somehow I kept convincing myself that I believed her when she said she was just lucky.

Mrs. J in Her Retirement

Several weeks after Pauline disappeared in 1974, I went out myself to see Mrs. J. Because of the circumstances, I forgot to be curious about the Jaffes' wealth. I couldn't have cared less about the furnishings and did not bother to notice the tile work or wallpaper or chandeliers as the maid led me down the hall and out the rear door.

I found Mrs. J lounging poolside, a lemonade in her hand, Giuseppe on her lap, his round brown eyes rimmed with red, weepy from age. On the far side of the yard, a gardener trimmed a hedge, flattening the top. A broadcaster on a radio playing in the house could be heard through an open door, announcing a ball game.

"Maggie, dear." She sat up and turned her deck chair to face away from the sun so she could remove her glasses. She was not the kind of woman who liked to hide behind dark glasses. She took the hand I offered and pulled me toward her, bestowing on me the first kisses I ever received from her, one on each cheek, in the European fashion.

I'd written to her asking if I could visit, and she had replied quickly, inviting me to Great Neck. She must have known I had come to discuss some sort of trouble, but first she wanted to make sure I was comfortably settled and my thirst had been quenched with fresh-squeezed lemonade the maid brought out for me.

Across the yard, the gardener put down his trimmer and mopped his head. Mrs. J waved at him. When he waved back, I recognized Isidore, Mrs. J's husband.

"He just can't get enough of yard work," she said. "Now, tell me, how are things in the department. Is Quipley liked?"

"Not really." I didn't know how far I could go regarding Mr. Quipley, but Mrs. J was already ahead of me.

"He's horrible," she said. "He does only one thing well: he can talk to the press. Not many people are able to do that. But how are my twins?"

Her twins were the World Trade Towers. "I like our offices. The view is spectacular," I said, forcing enthusiasm into my voice.

"I miss all you girls, though I don't miss having to explain the bills we racked up at the Golden Door. Having to justify expenses got tiresome. Do you ever think of moving to a new department there? I could help you get placed somewhere else, if you're interested."

"Thank you, Mrs. J, but I'm all right for the time being. Well . . . I'm not exactly all right. Something has happened, you see . . ."

She waited for me to get through my hesitancy. She didn't try to interrogate. She just sat there patiently, partially reclining in the chair, kneading the silky fur on Giuseppe's neck. If I had been in the right mood, I would have been amused to see that blue ribbon tied in a bow around the ponytail of the dog's forelock.

I wanted to say, *You put me in charge of Pauline and I failed you.* I wanted to confess the shame I felt when I was with Pauline in public. I wanted desperately to apologize.

"Pauline Moreau has disappeared." There—that was the most important thing to say, and I'd said it. Mrs. J stared off into the distance, taking in the news. I couldn't determine what she was feeling. My gaze went to her fingers, and I saw that they lay motionless, the tips buried in Giuseppe's fur.

"Pauline?"

"You know that she quit the P.A. back in 1969."

"Yes, I'd heard."

"After that, she didn't keep a job, but she had money. She had a relative who'd died and remembered her in his will, apparently. And sometimes she'd get lucky at the track. She went up to Saratoga every August."

"To gamble?"

"It's strange, I know."

"Are you sure her benefactor was a relative?"

I registered the implication in her voice. "She never went back to the clubs. At least, she assured me she was done with that. It's just . . ."

"You didn't entirely believe her." This was an observation, not a question.

"About going up to Saratoga Springs. I know she was lying."

"How do you know?"

"Because when she didn't come home, I checked with all the hotels there. She had not stayed at any of them."

"Could she have used a different name?"

"I don't think so. I think she went someplace else. Mrs. J, I think she came to some kind of harm. I . . . I'm sure of it. Something terrible has happened to her." I had to shut my eyes to calm myself.

"You've called the police, of course." It was Mr. J who said this. I hadn't noticed that he had joined us by the pool.

"Yes, I called them, but they're no help at all. The police believe Pauline wanted to abandon Sonia and went into hiding. That is ridiculous!" I so swelled with fury that I half rose to my feet.

"Pauline would never leave Sonia," Mrs. J agreed, her anger more muted and because of that more powerful than mine. "What has happened to Sonia?"

"I'm taking care of her."

"You can do that?"

"Absolutely, I will assume full responsibility for her. If Pauline doesn't come back, I will raise Sonia myself."

Mrs. J's face looked more drawn than before, even grayish, as if cast in shadow. Mr. J remained silent, watchful. I had no request to make of them, nothing I could ask them for. I was sorry to convey such terrible information, but I knew Mrs. J needed to hear it.

"Maybe we should get Probst on this," Mr. J said quietly to his wife.

"Yes, Probst. He's the best there is. . . . You're right, something must have happened to her. I am so sorry." I heard a gulping sound from deep within her throat. Her husband rested his hand on her shoulder.

"A woman can't just disappear into thin air," I said in desperation.

"We'll talk to a detective we know and get him on it right away. He'll have questions for you, I imagine. If we could just find out where she actually went when she said she was going to Saratoga Springs..."

Mrs. J cheered herself by trusting that a full investigation would bring results, and right then, I was hopeful too. I'll tell you outright, though, that nothing came of Detective Probst's investigation. He could not find out any more than I had. Pauline left no trail—easier to do back in 1974 than now. There was no security-camera footage to go through, no receipts or phone calls to trace, and by then I was already sure that she had been murdered. Only that would explain why she hadn't come back for Sonia.

At the end of our conversation, Mr. J offered to drive me to the station. After I said good-bye to Mrs. J, she reset her dark glasses over her eyes and turned her face to the sun. I followed her husband through the French doors, across the dining room, and into the expansive marble hall. On one of the walls hung the painting of Pretty Boy and Giuseppe. I hadn't seen evidence of the bird and was just about to ask Mr. J about him when I heard a loud wolf whistle from an adjacent room.

Mrs. J had worked all sorts of magic in her life. She had given each member of her staff an unimpeachable sense of worth. She had jump-started the P.A. on its most ambitious building project ever. She had provided everyone who knew her with a model of confidence and grace. She turned potential into actuality and persuaded us that exceptional achievement was within our reach. Mrs. J could make wishes come true, but even she couldn't bring back Pauline. Nothing was accomplished by my visit to her at her home on Long Island. Yet... come to think of it, I'm wrong about that, there was one change: When I went into the office on Monday, I discovered that Mr. Quipley had been transferred to another department.

THE HUNT

By 1977, those two Mohawk boys who used to spend their free time hunting for legless mudpuppies had outgrown their childish habits. The one named Max was working at the family gas station. Jimmy was parking cars at a hotel in Potsdam while he finished his degree at the local community college.

Though the legend about the horned monster that lived in the river continued to be passed on from generation to generation and there were more diseased mudpuppies than ever in the creeks and canals, the younger children had been cautioned against trying to catch them. They weren't supposed to play in the water at all. The water, they'd been told, had been poisoned by the factories. The children, however, had their own explanation for the prohibition: they believed that the great horned monster was back in the river, lurking just below the surface.

Being children, they still wanted to hunt for something even if they couldn't hunt for mudpuppies, so the scientist in charge of the pollution study gave them the important task of joining him in the hunt for soil samples. The children were told that their work would help clean up the land and the waterways. As long as they were dutiful and followed protocol, they would get results. One day, they would once again be able to eat all the fish they could catch.

The children took the challenge to heart. As soon as they were released from school, they would spread out into the meadows and woods, as if on an Easter egg hunt.

Let's follow two boys in particular, Mike and Rory, as they set out one fine spring day on their bikes, pedaling along just like Max and Jimmy had done a decade earlier. Let's try to keep up with them as they, like Max and Jimmy, race each other down what is left of the old lumber road, bumping over potholes and pebbly ridges before throwing their bikes aside at the trailhead.

The whole week had been unseasonably warm, and only pockets of snow remained in shady corners of the forest. The meadows were already deepening into a rich green. The creeks were swollen from the melt-off, and the redbuds were blooming three weeks earlier than normal.

That day, Mike and Rory chose to comb through the wooded area near Raquette Point. They wore the special gloves the scientist had given them, and they came armed with augers and spades and plastic bags. They really thought of themselves as hunters. They were hunting for evidence to use against Aluma-core, and they preferred to hunt together, for they were better than other children at paying attention to details and making sure the soil samples met the scientist's requirements.

The boys had been bagging plugs of soil for some time and were near enough to be within hearing range of each other when Mike found what he thought at first was some kind of treasure—a dimpled, round form that turned out to be white when he brushed it off. It was only a golf ball. He threw it away in disappointment and looked for another patch of earth to attack. The black flies had hatched too early in the season, and he pulled the rim of his cap lower to shield his face. He heard the crackling as Rory moved through the underbrush nearby.

"How many bags you got?" he called just to make some noise of his own.

"Six. You?"

"Five."

They couldn't feel the breeze down at the forest floor, but the top branches were rustling. There were no birds to be heard.

"Old Baldy gave Manny detention," Rory said idly in the distance.

"Yeah, why?"

"Manny set a desk on fire."

"Wow, really?"

"He filled the pencil groove with isopropyl during lab," Rory explained. "When Old Baldy wasn't looking, Manny went out of the room and got..."

Rory went on talking, but Mike stopped listening. He had spotted the surface of some kind of woven cloth, the fabric worn so thin that the meshwork was visible, like the intricate veins of a decayed leaf. He reached down to tug the cloth free, moving a stone that partially covered it.

"...but because it was burning inside his desk and not outside yet, Old Baldy didn't notice for a while, and everyone was like, uh, what are we gonna do..."

With the stone pushed aside and a layer of insulating moss tugged away, Mike saw more cloth, and then something that looked like a deflated balloon, a flattened leather balloon, and something that looked like bone, and teeth, and holes where the eyes should have been.

"And there's Old Baldy at the board..."

"Rory."

"And the fire's burning just inside the groove there because the whole thing is metal, so—"

"Rory, I think I found something."

"You did?"

"Come over here."

"Where are you?"

"Here."

There was the sound of twigs snapping, bushes being pushed aside, and Rory appeared, breathing heavily from the suspense, his features bright with expectation as he followed the direction of Mike's gaze and saw what Mike saw and kept staring for several more seconds before turning his head to the side and vomiting.

ON SUCH A NIGHT

Where were we, Mr. Whittaker? We were talking about money, as I recall, and that special quality it has for repairing every problem.

Remember that your problem with Pauline Moreau began at the end of the 1950s, when our society was using different criteria to measure morality. A man could be brought down by scandal more easily back then. Think of that story about the maneuverings preceding the hiring of Mrs. J at the P.A., when Frank Ferguson destroyed Edelstein by fabricating evidence of an illicit affair. Maybe you hadn't heard anything about Ferguson and Edelstein, but still, you understood the danger. A visiting preacher at your church had used the word that stuck with you: *perfidy*. What made *perfidy* even worse was that you'd gotten a leg up in the business world because of your wife's connections. If it came out that you'd betrayed your wife, you'd lose your wife's connections.

You weren't rich back then in 1959, but you managed to raise the cash for Pauline by legitimate means, scraping the money together from two different savings accounts. You'd promised Pauline one thousand dollars but had come up short. Still, in Pauline's assessment, eight hundred and fifty wasn't nothing. And really, paying off a girl you'd knocked up had its own kind of thrill. Made you feel powerful, in control of fate.

You dodged a scandal. The transfer to Visby was convenient. You got out in the nick of time, settled into life up north, enjoyed the trajectory that saw your income doubling yearly in tandem with the success you had in continually doubling the plant's output.

You made your money with aluminum—the useful, lightweight material that is everywhere. Today I put foil over an open aluminum can to protect the leftover refried beans. I turned the aluminum handle of the kitchen faucet. I stuck a card to the bulletin board with an aluminum pin. Even the pencil I am writing with right now is tipped with an aluminum ferrule. Who knows—maybe the aluminum on this pencil was produced in Visby.

The Visby plant became the most productive plant in Alumacore's history. Everybody kept asking you how you did it. You would respond with complicated answers about supplies and the energy assets of the region, but in fact it was really very simple: you increased the bauxite and just kept adding pots to the potline. The extra waste you threw into landfill and pumped into the creek.

Life went on without notable incident. You played golf because it was expected of you, but you didn't much enjoy it. You preferred to spend your weekends boating around the Thousand Islands, you and Kay together; Kay, in her cat's-eye sunglasses and that sweet striped dress tied with a red belt, stationed at the bow, her face turned to the wind. You had some good times with Kay. Yes, you did. And your namesake, Robert Whittaker III—he had a sharper mind than you and Kay together, you had to admit. If only he weren't so easily influenced by all those socialists who called themselves intellectuals.

You at the helm, in your topsiders and letterman jacket. Oddly, you felt safe and free out on the river. It was in your aluminum house where you needed to be on guard for dangers lurking just beneath the surface. Though you were so full of blinding bluster, you identified your place of weakness. You were right: It was in your home where you were most vulnerable. It was in your home where Pauline found you.

Consider that by then it was 1969, and people weren't so worried about perfidy anymore. Their attention was directed toward the war, race riots, rising poverty, famine in Biafra. Who would have really cared that you, Robert Whittaker Jr., was the father of a love child?

Yet you chose to fortify the secrecy enveloping your affair with Pauline, even welcomed the possibility of its renewal. That Pauline wouldn't let you touch her only made her return more thrilling. You saw yourself as the star of the movie about your own dramatic life. You were being blackmailed by a beautiful woman. In your imagination, she was cruel and glamorous. She appeared every twelve months or so, without warning, threatening to expose your dirty deed, and you adored her for it. You didn't feel so lonely now that you had Pauline at the center of your fantasies. She wasn't even out of her twenties. She was like a wild animal you were gently trying to domesticate. You gave her everything she asked for, plus some, in hopes that she would soften toward you. You didn't try to force yourself on her—she had grown too powerful for that. You worshipped her for her power, entreated her to forgive you for having abused her trust, prayed to your friendly God that He would open Pauline's heart as well as convince her to part her legs for you, and told yourself after Pauline's latest rejection that you just had to be patient. She would come around one day and welcome your aging yet eager body as well as your money. The long wait was in itself pleasurable, maybe even more rewarding for you than any real intimacy would have been.

Money was the problem, wasn't it? You had more than enough, yet you couldn't draw directly from savings to support Pauline, since the bank statements came to the house. Kay knew exactly how much spending money you had to throw around and would have noticed if five thousand dollars went missing.

Five thousand dollars? Wow, that was a lot of money in 1969. Five thousand dollars, times five, because Pauline kept showing up once a year. Twenty-five thousand dollars Pauline extorted from you.

Extortion, blackmail—these were your words, not Pauline's. Pauline called it child support.

If only she hadn't been so greedy, you'd say to yourself later. You did all you could to help her out, even going so far as to recall those little illegal maneuvers you'd learned in your accounting days at Alumacore's headquarters and applying them to the Visby accounts. In this case, you reentered numbers in order to inflate prices and skim some cream from smaller contracts.

You weren't a fool—you understood the danger—but what's a man at the mercy of a glamorous blackmailer to do?

Five times five. She wouldn't even let you kiss her, and she always brought the same photograph of your daughter, as though the girl named Sonia were forever fixed in time, always the same age, while you grew older, Kay grew older, even Pauline grew older, more poised, more regal, pretending that she had learned her manners from the queen herself. How long could this go on for? That way madness lay, and still Pauline kept coming round, 1970...1971—the year when Alumacore's profits plummeted and they sent out flunkies to demand explanations from their plant directors.

What could you say? It wasn't your fault that the Port Authority had finished paying its bills for all the aluminum you'd sent from Visby. Tell the executives in Albany to land another big client and send you the contract, you told them. That was their job. You made the aluminum—you didn't have to sell it too.

They wanted to take a look at your books. What books? Darn, you couldn't lay your hands on them. Seems they had been misplaced, alas. Sorry about that, boys. They'd turn up, you promised, your bruised heart pounding, your face purple.

You okay, Mr. Whittaker? Do you need to sit down?

And at the same time there were murmurings on the reservation. Babies were being born too early; the cattle's bones were rotting; a big die-off of muskies was attributed to some viral hemorrhagic disease. The Indians were blaming Alumacore for everything that was wrong in the valley.

Then stop cooking with those aluminum pans, goddamn it!

It's not like you were taking advantage of an addict's cravings. If people didn't like aluminum, then they didn't have to buy aluminum products.

1972 . . . 1973.

How long could this have gone on? Your enemies were closing in. You could hear them taunting you. You who had been born in a pigsty. They were going to pick you up and throw you back, headfirst.

1974. A summer's night, and the day's heat broke with a terrible storm. Crackling lightning lit up the Grasse River on the other side of the embankment. The torrents beat against the aluminum overhang of the motel outside of Massena. You gave Pauline her money; she shut the door on you.

Oh, on such a night! The rain dribbled over the rim of your cowboy hat. In the stormy darkness, your eyes blazed, but no one could see because no one was looking. You who gave all you had to give, who sought only forgiveness for your youthful errors, you who wanted comfort, company, a sympathetic soul to soothe your private turmoil; you, old man, so painfully alone—you said to yourself, *I will endure.*

On such a night, to shut you out.

How could she.

You were a big man; you could have rammed in the door. You would have done it, too, on that tumultuous night at the motel on Route 37—you would have folded your arms tight and leaned in with your bulky shoulder and taken a running start and crashed with all of your two hundred and thirty pounds against that wooden door so cheap it lacked a solid core, and with your great strength you would have battered it down and entered Pauline's motel room by force that fatal night if you hadn't first tried the knob and discovered that she had forgotten to lock the door behind her.

XII

A Condolence Ceremony

The chanting could be heard across the valley, doleful yet comforting, like the sound of a village bell. Feathery clouds made prints that glided across the meadows. Puffs from milkweed blew about in the breeze. It was a day that would have registered as beautiful if its warmth hadn't seemed so out of sync for the season.

The Elders wore traditional beaded vestments and feather headdresses; the sachem wore a more elaborate headdress, with an array of eagle feathers fixed to antlers. Chants were sung first by the women, then by the men, then by the women again as the sachem led the procession through the gates and into the cemetery, where a coffin had already been laid in an open grave and a small campfire was burning.

Ordinarily the group would have been divided into two moieties representing the clear-eyed and the mourners. But because the deceased had no family, the two boys who had found the body were the designated mourners. Even though the identity of the deceased was unknown, the remains were treated with the highest regard.

The sachem began with the song of Welcome at the Wood's Edge, his strong voice jumping effortlessly from the monophonic tone up to a higher register for three strong syllables and back down again. Next, the clear-eyed recited verses of the Requickening Address. For each verse, a brightly colored wampum string—yellow, turquoise, red—was passed over the fire from the clear-eyed to the two young mourners.

Grief blinds—here is wampum to dry the eyes.
Death causes sickness—here is wampum to gather up remains
    for burial.
Death defiles—here is wampum to sweep clean the house.

The young mourners repeated each verse. They wiped their tears with the string and returned the wampum to the clear-eyed.

As eulogy, the sachem raised a wampum belt and recited the final plea of the Requickening, calling to an audience not present but whom the sachem charged with these faults: blocking flowing rivers with locks that violated treaties, poisoning the water and the land, filling the minds of children with lies about the past, and delighting in the dispossession of the First People. Finally, to he who had cast the body of the deceased into the forest to rot without the honor of a proper installation in the sacred earth, the sachem sang: "With this string of wampum we take away the fog that surrounds your eyes and obstructs your view, that you may see the truth."

The hole was filled with dirt by the two boys; the clear-eyed doused the campfire. Following the closing of the ceremony, the procession continued to the longhouse for a funeral feast in honor of the dead.

This could be the end of the story I have to tell...but there is more. I want to tell you how the truth, though lost, did not stay buried. The truth had been invoked, and so the sacred earth expelled it, spitting it out of the grave. Set adrift from what should have been its resting place, the truth lived on past Pauline's death. Like a ghost animated by no more than the desire to be seen, the truth rose into the air and wafted with the puffs of milkweed seeds far into the sky, where it would travel with the wind currents, circling the world for years to come.

THE WOMAN IN THE YELLOW WRAP DRESS, BY KAY WHITTAKER

Another way to think about the truth is to consider it through the eyes of Kay Whittaker, writer of fictions. Kay had always found her imagination deliciously satisfying. Her one published novel was a saucy production, full of panting and heaving, with an ending that shrugged off all the sadistic antics and sent the viscount and milkmaid cantering off into the sunset. Its sex scenes made even the editor at Harlequin uncomfortable. If the ladies of the Visby Country Club had known about it, they wouldn't have viewed Mrs. Whittaker as quite so tightly wound as they'd assumed.

In the long interim between finishing *Lavender Serenade* and beginning *Unplayable Lie,* Kay satisfied her love of fantasy by dreaming. Along with the vivid dreams she enjoyed when she was sleeping, she liked to indulge in the idleness of daydreaming. In contrast to her husband, she wasn't afraid that her nightmares would come true, nor did she want to run off and have an affair. The realms of imagination and reality became muddled for her only when some small disruption in her life provoked her to be suspicious and she was called upon to search experience for clues to understand it. Then she didn't just try to *read* reality for the truth; she tried to *write* it in order to give it a shape that made sense.

The first vivid story Kay imagined involving her husband and another woman took shape in August of 1974, the day after Bob Whittaker had gone uninvited into Pauline's motel room. Waking that morning, Kay discovered that her husband hadn't come to bed at all during the night and wasn't home yet. And so Kay's busy mind went to work; she began telling herself a story.

Given her affection for romance, Kay authored a somewhat predictable tale. In it, her husband had joined some friends for a drink in the bar of the Windsor, Visby's one upscale restaurant. This in itself wasn't unusual, so it struck Kay as a logical first step in her imagined narrative. All stories need logic, she believed. It followed logically, she told herself, that there was a woman among the group of businesspeople at the Windsor. The woman had a nice figure that she showed off with her stylish wrap dress. In Kay's mind, the dress was lemon-colored with a black sash. The woman laughed too loudly and ran her index finger with its perfectly manicured nail around the rim of her wineglass before inviting Bob Whittaker up to her room.

Was the woman someone from Visby or an out-of-towner? Kay would have had to do some investigating to figure out this part of the tale, unless, as was the case, she preferred to remain in the dark about certain details.

Kay suspected that her husband had been less than faithful to her in previous years, but he had never gone so far as to stay out all night without explanation, and so she had not yet had reason to make up a story to explain his behavior. While she waited for him to return that August day in 1974, she indulged her love of logical connections and traced the effect that was his current absence back to its presumed cause. Yet she preferred to keep the tumult from becoming too destructive, which meant she had a knack for telling herself the kind of stories that end happily.

When Bob finally came home that evening, Kay was waiting for him. She met him when he entered the kitchen and without any greeting coldly searched his face. In the manner typical of her creative intelligence, she invented for him a demeanor of exhausted remorse. Yes, he had cheated on her. Yes, he had spent the night with a high-end whore. He shouldn't have had that third drink. But really, she herself wasn't always as abstemious as she might have wanted to be. She was ready to admit her own unfortunate tendency to seek out aids to help her sleep. Who was perfect in this world?

Look at him: He obviously felt overwhelmed with guilt. He had a wretched appearance, with dark swollen half-moons under his bloodshot eyes. His lips were so parched that Kay could see dried blood at their cracked corners. And how did he get that scratch on his forehead?

As Bob sank exhausted into a chair, Kay's saucy imagination flew off in the direction of whips and voluntary bondage. *Snap. Grunt. I know what you long for, darling.*

"Where have you been?" she asked, only because that's what a wife was supposed to ask.

"It's not what you think," Bob replied. He should have known such a statement was futile. Kay was always one giant step ahead of him. Obviously it *was* what she thought, for she had taken charge of the story.

"Who is she?" What a question—straight out of a million

books, Kay thought with a touch of mortification. But her husband's response was not what she expected, not the flinching, craven blink of a remorseful man eager to put his debauchery in the past. There was something wild and unfathomable in his red eyes; she was reminded of the eyes of a timber wolf she'd once seen in a zoo. He looked so strange and terrible to Kay, so different from the character she had been prepared to imagine, that she had to turn away.

He said something about perfidy. He said something about his regret for having caused such terrible suffering.

"Never mind," she said. She didn't like this story, not at all, and with the most illogical maneuver chose to bring it to an abrupt close.

With her back to him, she said, "I swear, if you let it happen again..." She didn't know how to finish the threat and so just let it hang in the air. The inarticulation was mutual—neither of them could add another word.

It didn't seem to matter then, back in 1974, that the reason for the guilt that Bob felt did not match the reason for the guilt Kay imagined for him. With the marriage broken, Kay saw no other recourse but to try and repair it. Her husband responded with love she didn't know he could feel. She made it evident that she was ready to forgive him. He wanted only to win her back. He was the one who suggested that they go away on a vacation, a second honeymoon, and forget all their troubles. The distractions of travel would be healing, he assured her. She wasn't so sure that *escape* was the answer, but she couldn't come up with a better suggestion, thus setting the stage for their troubles to return.

THE BOY WHO CRIED WOLF

Until now, the wolf has known only captivity. You might think freedom is preferable, but set him loose from his cage, and he runs crazily, lost in Daedalus's labyrinth, up a stony *calle* that ends at the murky expanse of a canal, back in the opposite direction, his paws sliced and bleeding from broken glass unseen in a dark passageway, his tongue hanging out of his parched mouth after lapping at the salty canal water, his yellow fangs pocked from age, his red eyes glowing. In this dark maze of water and stone he has lost his bearings. He can only run. He will run for the rest of his life in an effort to flee from the nature of his soul, murder an irresistible instinct. A wolf is a wolf. He can't help who he is and hates himself for that, runs in a desperate effort to escape from the impulse that drove him to kill. He runs late into the night, across bridges, past shuttered stores, down dank alleys, like a man trying to escape a horde of angry bees.

He is not a man, and there are no bees. He is a wolf with red eyes that glow in the dim light of the streetlamp, momentarily entrancing a young boy, who stands frozen at the entrance to the campo.

Red eyes bobbing like twin planets in the night sky. Red eyes like party lights strung above a trattoria. Red eyes of a ravenous wolf.

Wolf!

The boy is stirred to action. He flees across the campo and around a corner, propelled more by the self-importance of a messenger than fear.

Wolf! Wolf! the boy cries. Of course no one believes him.

One Gallant

Danny Sullivan, the doctor I once fancied I would marry, called me a few days after Pauline went missing in 1974 to ask me to come join him in New Jersey for the weekend. I told him I was busy with extra duties at work. I blamed the despot in charge of our department at the P.A. for making my life so difficult. How about the next weekend, then? Danny asked. My parents are coming into town, I lied.

What else could I say? I had kept Pauline a secret from him. How could I explain that now I was in charge of her daughter?

I tried to reassure him even as I fumbled from one poor excuse to another. He asked me outright if my feelings about him had changed. I didn't want to lose him. I told him I would see him soon, once my parents had gone back to Cleveland. When were they leaving? he asked. I told him I didn't know. They would stay a couple of weeks, maybe more.

After two weeks had passed, Danny called again. Was I alone yet? Could he come into the city and take me to dinner? How about that clam bar on Mulberry Street I'd said I liked? I put him off again. I wasn't feeling well, I said—a poor choice of words. Never lie to a doctor and tell him you're not feeling well. I had to struggle to invent an array of symptoms that would seem consistent—a headache, a sore throat, a fever…just a low-grade fever, nothing serious, and yes, maybe some aches and pains. Over the phone he diagnosed influenza, though he said I should be checked for tonsillitis. I thanked him for his concern and promised to talk with him in a few days.

I stopped answering the phone. I had so much to think about as I tried to keep from losing my job and at the same time to fill the vacancy left by Pauline in Sonia's life. I didn't know how to explain to Danny why I had never told him about Pauline, much less how to reveal that I was in charge of a young girl whose limitations were such that she would never be able to live independently.

I was still longing for someone to tell me I had been wrong to stop waiting for Pauline to return. The detective in charge of her case was no more accepting of the facts. He had made up his own excuse to justify his inaction, telling me with the condescension that comes from years of experience that Pauline wasn't the first mother who had run away from a child with special needs. He didn't say *special needs*. He used the common word of that time, *retarded,* to describe Sonia, who in his assessment of the case was the clear reason why Pauline would never come home.

You can see how I was floundering, unable to convince the authorities to launch a concerted search for Pauline, convinced by a dream that Pauline was gone forever, yet still wanting to believe that the buzzer to my apartment would ring and through the intercom would come Pauline's apologetic voice—

"Maggie, it's Danny. Can I come up?"

It was a gray November afternoon. I'd set up Sonia with a tape recorder after discovering that she loved to hear herself singing. She was singing into the microphone, making up words to the tune of a popular song, "Time in a Bottle." In Sonia's version, I remember, she sang, "If I didn't have any homework...then I could just sing all the time..." She added a lot of *la-la-la*s to finish the song, then played it back.

I remember laughing with her as we listened to her song. We were laughing almost as hard as we used to laugh together when we'd played Twister. It was the first day since Pauline disappeared that a future with Sonia was beginning to look conceivable. And then Danny arrived to find out why I wasn't answering my phone.

I buzzed him in, and in the short interval it took him to climb the stairs, I considered hiding places for Sonia—the closet, under the bed, the bathroom—before recognizing with a wave of remorse how stupid and selfish the impulse was. Sonia wasn't dirty laundry; she was the child Pauline had left me to raise.

When Danny knocked at the door, Sonia was certain that the visitor had to be her mother. She rushed to the door and struggled to open it. I approached, meaning to help, but she pulled it open on her own, welcoming Danny with a smile that could only ever be genuine.

"Well, hello there, miss," he said, unflustered by the drool on her chin, his manner so gentlemanly and calm that in an instant my belief that I needed to keep Sonia a secret transformed into relief that my secret had been revealed.

"Danny, this is Sonia."

"Pleased to meet you. And where is your home, Miss Sonia?"

"Here?" The rise in the voice that turned the word into a question led Danny to think she was just confused.

"You like it here?" he asked, looking ever so gallant with his mop of curly brown hair and the thick sideburns that reached almost to his chin. "Yes?" he offered in encouragement. Sonia hadn't been asked that question before, it occurred to me. Did she like it here in my apartment on Jane Street? She wasn't sure of the right word to say and so just gave a nod.

"That's good." There was a touch more impatience in his expression as he looked to me for an explanation.

"Want to hear me sing?" asked Sonia, who trusted every stranger she met enough to take his hand. She led Danny to the table where she'd left the tape recorder and took a minute to fumble with the buttons before she found Play, then discovered from the sound of static that she'd already listened to the recorded part of the tape. I helped her rewind it, and we all listened to her voice singing "If I didn't have any homework..."

I could tell Danny thought Sonia passably amusing. But he hadn't come to talk to Sonia, and when I offered to make him coffee and went to the kitchen to prepare it, he followed me.

I stood facing the counter in the narrow galley kitchen as I filled the coffee filter. Danny slid his arms around me from behind. "Is the girl out there why you haven't answered my calls?"

I bristled, finding fault in his generic phrase *the girl out there.*

"Who does she belong to?" he persisted.

"I don't know."

"What do you mean? She's not a stray you picked up off the street, is she? She's not an alley cat you made the mistake of feeding." He laughed feebly at his bad joke.

I winced. "She's mine!"

He released me from his embrace. "You have a child?"

"I do now."

"I don't understand."

"I'm raising her."

"You adopted her?"

"I'm going to."

"I don't understand," he repeated.

To be fair, how could he understand? He knew me as the friend of his friend's wife, a secretary who worked at the Port Authority; he had hinted that he was ready to get married. He was confident that I would make a good wife for a doctor—yet I was adopting the poor damaged child in the living room?

In the kitchen, I explained the history as best I could, describing Pauline as a "friend from work" who had gone missing while on a vacation upstate. As Danny listened, he kept fiddling nervously with a bowl of oranges on the opposite counter, making a move to pick one up and then deciding against it and just rolling the orange around on top of the others. I filled two mugs with coffee and held mine to warm my hands without sipping it while I continued to describe Pauline's life, omitting the portion about how she had once worked the streets but including the detail about Mrs. J asking me to be her friend.

"I wasn't always a good friend to her," I said limply, without disclosing the extent of my failure.

I'm not sure if Danny surmised much beyond my narrative, if he guessed why I had never mentioned Pauline to him, but as I kept talking, I began to sense, or imagine, a chilliness in his gentlemanly comportment. Was I right to perceive him withdrawing from me with the most infinitesimal movements, leaning slightly away in the narrow galley? Maybe he was trying to observe me from a better distance, to bring me into sharper focus. Maybe he felt a repulsion so slight that he might not even have been conscious of it. Maybe I invested in him the emotions I expected him to feel, and he was mirroring my own effort at detachment.

Later, I would wonder if my affection for Danny had been motivated more by the convenience he presented. He was "a good catch," as my mother had said when I'd told her about him, and he'd come into my life at the right time. But maybe we weren't as compatible as I had hoped, and Sonia, by her mere presence in the apartment, saved me from a marriage that would have been difficult, or worse. It seemed that's what Danny thought, for though he stayed for dinner and continued treating Sonia with his effortless chivalry, he declined to spend the night. He stopped calling after that. I never saw him again.

YOUNG LOVE

Robbie Whittaker had spent every summer for the past ten years at sleepaway camp. In 1975, he finally tried to put his foot down and insist on spending the summer in Visby. Tough luck; his parents made him sign away his life and agree to be a counselor. Eight weeks he'd lose teaching little boys how to tie clove hitches and bowlines. And then he'd be shipped off to dreaded college. By the time he graduated, one Brigid Finney of Visby, New York, would surely have forgotten him. Robbie who?

He called her and asked if she wanted to hang out for the day. He didn't have a plan in mind; he just wanted to see her. She was reluctant to leave her father, who was awfully sick, but her mother said it would do her good to get out of the house.

Robbie picked her up at noon. She was already heading out the door when he arrived, but then she seemed to forget something and went back inside. With his window down, he draped his arm over the frame and tapped the wooden side panel of the Ford while he waited. A minute later, she reappeared, holding a brown paper lunch bag.

"You brought your lunch?" he asked as she slipped into the passenger seat.

"I have something for you, stupid. A going-away present."

Robbie smiled to himself, thinking about the present he had in his pocket for Brigid.

"How's your dad?" he asked as he drove.

"Not so good."

"I'm sorry."

"It just sucks."

"Aw, Brig." He reached his right hand toward her shoulder to caress her.

"Let's not talk about it, okay?"

They drove on in silence. It was the end of June, a typical summer's day in the St. Lawrence River Valley, scattered clouds overhead, the flags at the car dealership they passed snapping in the strong breeze.

"You hungry?" he asked.

"Kind of."

They stopped at Dutchess's. They both ordered cheeseburgers and shakes—strawberry for Brigid, chocolate for Robbie. She picked the sweet pickles off her cheeseburger one by one and gave them to Robbie. They traded tastes of their shakes. They talked about a rerun of M*A*S*H they had both happened to watch the previous night and compared their expectations for the coming season. They talked about the summer. Brigid was fifteen by then and already had her lifeguarding certification. She'd be working at the Y in Massena. Robbie would be tying lots of knots.

After lunch they drove to the high school to look at the new tennis courts. There were a few people playing, and Robbie and Brigid sat quietly for a few minutes, listening to the sounds of the balls and the players calling out scores.

They drove on, unsure where to go next. They decided to go to the swimming hole at Turtle Creek, though swimming had been prohibited for years because of the pollution. The water burbling down the narrow falls looked crystal clear, but a pink foam lapped against the rocks. There was no one else around. Robbie and Brigid sat together a few feet back from the creek, where the pines had dropped their needles to make a soft carpet. The sounds of the water and wind were so pleasant, Robbie didn't feel the need to speak. He put his arm around Brigid and drew her close.

"Here," she said, handing him the bag. He opened the bag

and removed the present. The wrapping paper was blue, decorated with pictures of baby shoes. "Sorry!" She gave a giggle. "That was the only paper I could find."

He could tell the gift was a book even before he opened it. He was surprised to see that it was a used book, and he puzzled over the title, thinking it was in a foreign language, before realizing it was an American Indian word. The rest of the book was in English. He paged through it, feeling increasingly pleased and proud that Brigid understood him so well that she would give him a history book. He loved history and accepted this gift as her recognition that he had the potential to do important work in the subject.

"'It was their boast,'" he read aloud from a random page, "'that they occupied the highest part of the continent. Situated upon the head-waters of the Hudson, the Delaware, the Susquehanna, the Ohio, and the St. Lawrence flowing in every direction to the sea, they held within their jurisdiction as it were, the gates of the country, and could, through them, descend at will upon any point.'

"Thanks," he said. He felt strengthened by his certainty that he and Brigid would be together for the rest of their lives once they'd gotten past the temporary obstacles of camp and college.

"Here, this is for you." He took the velvet box from his pocket. He hadn't thought to wrap it, but she didn't seem to mind. Nor did she seem displeased that he was giving her a necklace instead of a book. He would give her a book next time, one he'd choose as carefully as she'd chosen the book for him. He watched her face, hoping she liked the necklace. He thought she looked happy as he closed the clasp behind her neck for her. There were three strands of green and blue crystal beads mixed with blue and gold glass beads divided by delicate brass separators.

"It's beautiful," she said, fingering the beads, rolling them against her skin.

He rested his hand against the side of her cheek, traced the strong line curving toward her perfect cheek. She folded her hand over his and closed her eyes. Their lips met in a kiss.

Robbie would never forget that kiss on the bank of Turtle Creek in June of 1975. He would often remember it in the years to come, conjuring the memory for comfort, for pleasure, and with the nostalgic amusement of hindsight when he was old and remembered kissing Brigid Finney for the first time, their soft lips pressed together, breathing in each other's breath, sharing tastes, warmth, the conviction that they were born for this, to love each other, to defend each other against the world's venom, never to feel alone again because even when they were apart, both would know that they were the subject of the other's thoughts, their young bodies not even full-grown and yet their whole future confirmed in an instant as they thought separately, in unison...

So this is what everybody is always talking about. This is why people sing. This is why poems are written. This is why our hearts pound and there's a hunger deep inside. We get it now. This is why the stars look brighter, why attention sharpens, why colors look more vivid than before. This is the source, like the pure water in an underground spring before it reaches the surface. This is the reason little kids tease us and friends talk behind our backs. Go ahead and talk. We don't care. This is the point in the story that is as slushy as a milk shake, as syrupy as the puddle on pancakes. We know, it's just a kiss, and kissing is only a prelude to the point, but we're not at that point yet, we're just starting out, so go ahead and skip over this page if you prefer, it's none of your business anyway, this kiss in the shady woods above Turtle Creek, this kiss that binds the two of us with joy, through memory, this kiss that neither of us will ever forget.

TRAITOR

He was remembering that kiss years later as he watched Brigid approaching across the yard of her family's house in Visby. He was praying that when she saw him waiting on the porch for her, she, too, would remember that kiss.

She had the water samples in her wooden basket. There was a focused fury in her eyes and an emboldening energy that made her seem taller, stronger than she should have been with her small frame, even scary to Robbie, leaving him nearly speechless when she asked in the commanding voice of some-one pointing a gun at a trespasser, "What are you doing here?"

"Um..."

"What do you want?"

"I have to talk to you, Brigid. Please."

She brushed past him and threw open the screen door with a bang, then pushed the interior door and marched inside. The small living room was dark; she brightened it by pulling up the shade. She stomped into the kitchen, deposited the basket with the test tubes on the counter, opened cupboard doors for rea-sons Robbie couldn't fathom, muttering to herself, and finally asked him, "Want some coffee?"

"Sure."

He watched her pour the morning's cold coffee into a mug; she impatiently stuck the mug in the microwave to heat it up. The handle was almost too warm when he took it from her, but he didn't want to complain.

"The purpose of science is to clean up the mess science leaves behind," she announced, out of the blue.

She was consumed by her purpose. Her father had been poisoned by the toxic fumes at the aluminum plant; he had suf-fered a terrible, drawn-out death because of Alumacore. The man who could have stopped it before Tom Finney was sickened, the one who should have known of the dangers, who was responsible for the poison that had caused tumors and premature births and destroyed the livelihoods of dozens of farmers on the reservation, was Robbie's dad. In her eyes, Robbie belonged to that world from which she'd withdrawn in order to launch an attack. She would sacrifice him as collateral damage.

"I'm sorry, Brigid."

He had been the one to spell out the truth for her in the first place. Long before the Restoration and Compensation Determination Plan had been submitted to the Department of Environmental Conservation, Robbie Whittaker had assembled all the available data and understood the extent of the charges that eventually would be directed at Alumacore.

Who didn't know that the manufacturing plants in the St. Lawrence River Valley were a source of pollution? All you had to do was stand next to one and smell the air. There had been an advisory against eating the local fish for years. The real issue was that the Visby plant in particular had neglected to install proper emissions filters and had been dumping waste illegally. It would take decades, even centuries, for the harm to be repaired. And there were some things that couldn't be fixed. You can't fix a dead man and bring him back to life.

In her blind rage, Brigid confused Robbie with the enemy. He selfishly wished he had never told her about Alumacore's wrongdoings. Didn't vengeful goddesses always blame the messengers? Though she had long dreamed of living in Paris and had been concentrating her academic studies on the language and history of France, she had suddenly developed a fascination with chemistry. Now she was filling the kitchen of this dingy little house in Visby with test tubes and jars and soggy pH sticks in an effort to identify poisons.

She was busy. *Go away, Robbie,* her brusque manner conveyed, along with the unspoken accusation *you traitor.*

He was on her side! How could he convince her? He'd give up everything for her. *Brigid, please, don't you remember that kiss?*

She would remember, and she'd say so eventually, but Robbie had to be patient. They would revive their love and kiss again. First, though, Brigid Finney needed to admit to herself that she had not descended from Olympus to exact revenge, and that some crimes will go unpunished.

LIARS!

It took time, but, in the end, fluoride, cyanide, and PCBs, along with alumina, would be identified as poisonous by-products of Alumacore's production system. The company would admit that waste from the plant was pumped into Turtle Creek and released in unfiltered emissions. Eventually, Alumacore would agree to clean up the contaminants within a thirty-mile radius and compensate residents for the losses in agriculture and tourism. They would not, however, take responsibility for adverse health effects in the local population, since attribution of industrial toxicity could not be verified.

"You're kidding me!" Brigid would whisper upon hearing the details of a report. She and Robbie were at a public meeting late in 1987, five months before the fire at the Visby plant. "Seriously? They're saying they put chemicals in the soil and water, but no one got sick because of them?"

"I think that's what they said."

"Liars!" she cried out, jumping up and pointing to the lawyers who were onstage representing Alumacore in place of Alumacore executives like Robert Whittaker Jr.

"Brigid—" Robbie was ready to stand by her, but he didn't think the best strategy was to scream out at a public meeting on the reservation.

"Liars!"

The audience murmured. People swiveled in their chairs to stare at her.

"You know who killed my father!" she shouted at the two lawyers, who in their embarrassment responded by twitching their lips into ridiculous smiles.

"Alumacore has been cleared by the EPA—" began one of the lawyers.

"Liars!"

"Brigid..."

"Liars!" shouted a Mohawk woman from the row behind, rising to her feet.

"Liars!" called a man in the front.

"Liars! Liars! Liars!" the audience chanted, stamping and clapping.

Nothing was accomplished by the rebellion. The state had already signed off on the reparation deal, and the Elders did not want to put the agreement at risk. But what a lot of noise the people made. Even with the windows of the longhouse closed against the cold, their voices could be heard a mile away.

THANK YOU, MR. WHITTAKER

Imagine Robbie having to go back home after that meeting. What could he possibly have to say to the man who wasn't even his real father? Bob Whittaker had led an assault on the environment. He had ravaged the land and water for the sake of profit. His defense was that the world needed aluminum, and when the world stopped buying it, he would stop selling it. The plant's failure to dispose of waste responsibly Bob blamed on the Alumacore executives in Albany. They wouldn't give him the money for the scrubbing equipment. Not that Bob Whittaker ever flat-out asked them.

Robbie still felt a strong loyalty to his mother, and so he suffered the presence of Bob Whittaker and tried to stifle his repugnance when he was visiting. He would go so far as to make a mental list of his thanks to his adoptive father, for his mother's sake:

Thank you for paying my tuition.

Thank you for paying my rent.

Thank you for taking care of my mother.

Such gratitude was a torturous effort and in some fundamental way felt wrong to him, unearned even if warranted, yet he tried to make it feel right. He was all grown up now. He had to be civil.

He braced himself as he entered the house. They wouldn't want to hear about the meeting on the reservation. What, then, would they talk about?

Luckily, Mr. and Mrs. Whittaker were already in bed by the time Robbie returned, and the house was silent.

A house made of aluminum. He ran his hand along the banister on his way upstairs. It struck him as impossible that he had ever felt at home here. Surely he wasn't the same boy who used to imagine that Visby was paradise and who spent his school vacations happily scouring the woods for Indian treasures. But of course, there had been only one Whittaker son, and he was a man now, a stranger in his parents' house, at home only with Brigid.

A PRAYER

A few minutes later, he was idly scanning the shelf above his bed, surveying his collection of broken pottery and carvings and arrowheads, when the phone on the nightstand rang. He grabbed it before the end of the first ring, hoping his parents hadn't been woken.

"Robbie?"

"Brigid, hi."

She wanted reassurance that she hadn't embarrassed him at the meeting. He said he thought she had been wonderful. They talked about the results of her work and agreed that something had come of it—there would be a substantial penalty for the company to pay, and improvements would be made on emissions and waste disposal at the plant.

"I just had to have the last word, I guess," Brigid said softly.

"You got everyone up on their feet!"

"I've had experience. I was a cheerleader once."

"You were a cheerleader? How could I not know that?"

"First year of junior high. Go red, go blue, and so on. Hey...I miss you." She was staying at the Finneys' house, which stood empty except when Brigid came to Visby. She and Robbie would be driving back to New York together in the morning. In January, Brigid would leave to study in Paris for the semester. Having by then joined Robbie in graduate school after returning to her original academic focus of French history, she'd been awarded a fellowship to study at the Sorbonne.

"I miss you too. I'm going to really miss you when you go to France."

"You'll come visit!"

"Of course I will."

"Bye, Robbie."

"Bye, Brigid. See you tomorrow."

He hung up the phone and lay back on his bed. Restless, he again focused his attention on the Indian relics on his shelf. His favorite object was the soapstone carving of a woman, and he picked it up to examine more closely. Puffed cheeks and hollow eyes gave the woman a masklike face. She was smiling and holding her plump belly, seeming to be in the midst of shaking with laughter. He didn't know if she was supposed to represent a spirit of the forest or if the figure had been modeled on an actual person. He had often wondered whether the carving was thought by its original owners to have magical powers...not that he believed in magic, *pshaw*. It was true that as a boy, he had once cupped the figure in his hands and secretly asked the stone woman to convince Brigid Finney to fall in love with him. And it had worked, Brigid had fallen in love with him! He laughed out loud at the idea. The stone woman laughed with him. And then, in a furtive whisper, he asked the stone woman to convince Brigid Finney to say yes when Robbie asked her to marry him.

OLD PETE

On the porch of the veterans' home on Main Street in Visby, a man known as Old Pete creaked in his rocker and watched the world go by. He called, "Hey there, chickies!" to the children on their way home from school. They used to run from him, but over time they had gotten used to the strange old man with the foot-long white beard, and now they just waved. He tipped his cap to every truck driver who passed by, and some of them tooted back a hello. He sat there even in winter, cocooned in a ratty parka, carrying on a conversation about baseball with the boy who came to shovel snow and accepting the home's bundle of mail from the postman. He chugged whiskey from a water bottle, and none of the attendants tried to stop him. Sometimes he sang drinking songs. When the president of the Visby bank drove by, Old Pete called out, "Steal from the rich and give to the poor!" When the mayor drove by, Old Pete stood up and saluted. When the managing director of the Alumacore plant drove by in his Cadillac, Old Pete would say, for reasons no one ever understood, "There goes a man who can't tell where he's going."

ZIGZAG

How do we sense when we are secretly being followed? Is it that our deepest instincts give us a special ability to spot a predator? Do we have some delicate sensory ability that allows us to perceive what we can't see? Could the reflective aspect of a solid body cause light to bounce off the surface of our follower, aiming in our direction? Are we good enough at noticing things around us that a difference in the routine catches our attention? To what extent is our imagination creating the scenario that then turns out to be real? Does a threat convey itself as some kind of palpable energy? Is it just that we've seen too many movies with those clever shots cutting back and forth between the hunter and the hunted while the sinister music on the sound track builds toward a climax? Do our dreams magically alert us to the danger so that, though we might not remember them upon waking, we spend the day on guard, more watchful, better prepared? Do we just see what is obvious and then recast it as stealth?

In the fall after her mother disappeared, Sonia went back

to school. Every day after I picked her up, I had the feeling that we were being followed. As I walked with Sonia down Broadway toward the Seventy-Second Street subway station, I would keep stealing glances behind me. Too often, I saw a man in a cream-colored letterman jacket and cowboy hat walking about thirty yards back. He wouldn't be watching us. He would just walk along, minding his own business—or pretending to. Sometimes we would stop at the grocer's to pick up fruit or we'd go into the pharmacy, and when we came out he would have disappeared, but after we walked a block or so, there he would be, paying for a magazine at a newsstand. Of course, he wouldn't look directly at us, but I thought I could see his eyes sliding to the side, and then, without him moving, his gaze would quickly slide to the other side to catch sight of us after we'd passed behind him, even as he accepted his change from the vendor and craftily pretended to ignore us.

I'd hold Sonia's hand as we made the descent into the station. We would plant ourselves among people waiting on the platform and push our way onto an overcrowded car. More than once I looked back through the set of windows into the car behind us and saw the cowboy gripping a pole and staring in our direction. When that happened, I would get off with Sonia a stop early and zigzag through side streets back to my apartment in the most haphazard way, dragging the poor girl with me. I never saw the cowboy after we left the subway and was comforted by the belief that he didn't know where we lived. But then a few days later, the chase would begin all over again when I picked up Sonia from school.

Have you ever thought you were being followed, only to discover that you were wrong?

Joanna Scott

The Appointment with the Podiatrist

He had found the name of the school in a letter in Pauline's purse. He waited until the following year, until he could not stand waiting any longer. Then he announced that he had a meeting in New York and would be staying there for a few nights. The lie was risky, he knew, for Kay was extra-sensitive, constantly looking for evidence that her husband had returned to his cheating ways. But even more dangerous than lying to Kay was putting himself within arm's length of Pauline's daughter just so he could see her. That was almost like the criminal returning to the scene of the crime.

Consider, though, that the real crime had occurred far from New York City and had gone unsolved. There was no reason anyone who had known Pauline Moreau would recognize him. He was as anonymous as any stranger in the city. He just needed to see his daughter. Not even to talk to her. She was his only blood-child. He had done a terrible thing to her, depriving her of her mother. He needed to know that someone would take care of her.

Such a little beauty. The photograph Pauline had carried with her was somewhat tattered by the fall of 1975. By then his girl would almost be a young woman. A beautiful young woman. Someone had better be taking good care of her. Risky as it was, Bob had to assure himself of this. He who knew himself to be vile and pathetic and destined for hell just wanted confirmation that his beautiful daughter was doing all right. And so he told the lie to Kay as plainly as he could, giving a few details about the objective of the meeting but not too many, to avoid contradicting himself.

In October he drove himself to the city, tuning in whatever news station was in range as he covered those four hundred miles, letting the newscasters' voices fill his consciousness to block out thoughts he didn't want to think. He heard about the traffic, the weather, the president's intended veto of the Privacy Act, a veto that Bob Whittaker agreed was a blatant infringement of civil rights. A man's private business was a man's private business. The longer he listened to the report, the more indignant he became. It was a good, healthy, distracting feeling and kept him going for miles, sustaining him like fuel, then burning itself out so that by the time he arrived at the hotel on Fifty-Sixth Street and gave his key to the valet, he was worn out, empty, sick of himself, on the point of a disorienting collapse, sure that the only thing that could bring comfort to him was to see his beautiful daughter. Just to see her. Not even to talk to her.

And so the next afternoon he was waiting across the street when the door opened and the children were released. He tried to be inconspicuous and avoided lingering in one place. He'd walk one direction for a few strides, then back, then study the name of a podiatrist on a brass plate affixed to the building behind him. If anyone asked, he would say he had an appointment with the podiatrist and was waiting outside to enjoy the lovely afternoon.

It was a small school and in Bob's eyes the students seemed normal enough. They came out shouting, laughing, greeting their parents or babysitters. Few were left to go home on their own; even the teenagers were met by adults. That seemed logical to Bob, given the dangers of a city like New York. As he watched the children from across the street, he would convince himself that a particular one was Sonia and then decide against it after comparing the girl to the one in his photograph. Always, the girl in the photograph was more beautiful. He would wait long after the last student had come out of the school in hopes that the door would open one more time and his beautiful daughter would appear.

He didn't see Sonia that day, or the next. Three days he returned to his post across the street and waited for his daughter to emerge. On the third day he saw two adults in the doorway, teachers, presumably, and one was pointing in his direction. He left abruptly.

He gave up trying to see Sonia without ever learning that the photo he'd taken from Pauline was of a different girl entirely. Sonia and I must have walked right past Robert Whittaker for three days straight. He saw only what he took to be a sadly deformed girl being led by the hand by a woman who, in her wool suit and practical shoes, had the look, he might have thought, of a librarian. It never occurred to him to follow us.

XIII

IN THE EVENT OF A HURRICANE

I was slow in emptying Pauline's apartment. After the initial visit, when I'd cleaned out the refrigerator and grabbed what I could carry of Sonia's belongings, it took me several weeks before I returned with Tammis and her husband, Jerry, to remove everything else. I paid a month's rent and the landlord gave me an extra month's grace period because of the circumstances, so it wasn't until the end of October that we gathered at Pauline's place and loaded up a van.

Tammis declined to take any of the furniture, though she did ask for one memento of Pauline's—a pair of woven, beaded, high-heeled shoes, cream-colored, with sets of jingle bells on the toes. Tammis couldn't fit into the shoes, but she liked the memories they evoked of Pauline at her most jubilant.

I didn't have room in my apartment for much. We packed Sonia's bed in the van, along with the desk Pauline had painted pink with black polka dots, and we gave the remaining furniture to Goodwill. I took some of the kitchenware and the *World Book Encyclopedia* set for Sonia. I collected the stock photos that Pauline had framed and hung them around the rooms of my own apartment. I still have them. There is one of horses grazing, the grassland rising in the distance behind them to meet the sky. Another shows a juggler entertaining a crowd. Something about the lighting in this one gives the faces of all the people a plastic sheen, except for the juggler, who, though he is wearing a red clown's nose, has a more honest, realistic face. A third picture that used to hang above Pauline's bed is of a woman and child sitting side by side on a pier overlooking a lake, dangling their legs as they watch the sun set. Though this picture is black-and-white, you can see the evidence of varied colors in the fine gradations of gray.

I'd made sure to gather odds and ends, like the scrapbook Pauline had made to document Sonia's early years, and a silver-handled mirror that Sonia was very glad to have. I hastily grabbed any papers and statements and bills lying around. These I went through carefully back in my apartment. I paid outstanding bills and worked with the bank to transfer Pauline's money into a small trust for Sonia. Over the next weeks I read and reread all the documents, searching for a clue that might help me understand what had happened to Pauline. Mostly, they were papers regarding Sonia's education and health care. There was a copy of Pauline's lease, and a document certifying that she had been tested and found negative for tuberculosis.

Resolved as I was to hide my grief from Sonia, I tried to do the things Pauline would have done for her daughter, who was now mine. On an unseasonably warm winter's day, I took Sonia to collect shells along the beach at Coney Island. We went to the circus. We rode in a carriage through Central Park. A little more than a year after Pauline disappeared, I arranged, with

Tammis's help, to celebrate Sonia's sixteenth birthday with a party at Windows on the World.

By then, Tammis was a hostess in the restaurant at the top of the World Trade Center. That's right: Tammis, who swore she'd never set foot on an elevator, was working at Windows on the World on the 107th floor of the North Tower. When I had learned through a P.A. notice that the restaurant management was advertising for a hostess, I'd told Tammis about it. Tammis was bored at home with her husband working long hours and her son at school, so she had started looking for a part-time job. She applied reluctantly for the hostess position and vowed she wouldn't accept it if they offered it to her. The salary made her forget her resolve.

The first time she rode in the express elevator, to get to her interview, she fainted. Going down, she held on to a stranger's arm and remained on her feet. For her next ascent, she brought a stopwatch and occupied herself watching the second hand tick. It took fifty-eight seconds to get to the top—and fifty-eight seconds to come down. By the third day she was used to the elevator. She brought the stopwatch for every subsequent ride and was comforted by the sameness—fifty-eight seconds up, fifty-eight seconds down. Over the years, she almost came to enjoy the elevator. She especially liked accompanying first-time visitors and witnessing their awkward attempts to mask their fear with enthusiastic jabbering as they were whooshed into the sky.

On the day of Sonia's party, Tammis had set a big table for us overlooking the harbor. Along with Tammis and Tammis's son, Sam, our small group included Brenda Dowdle and Eugenia Gilmore—two of the secretaries I'd worked with under Mrs. J, who were now in other departments at the P.A. We ate tea sandwiches and drank root-beer floats. For her gifts,

Sonia received a charm bracelet, a book about tigers, striped kneesocks, a transistor radio, and, from me, a stuffed elephant. It was midafternoon, between meals, so the restaurant wasn't full, but there were enough patrons to join us in a loud round of "Happy Birthday" when Tammis brought out a cake.

I held Sonia's hand and we made the first slice together, sinking the knife through the thick ridges of white frosting. She scooped a dollop of frosting into her mouth with her finger before she attacked the cake with her fork.

"Do you feel the tower sway?" Tammis asked us all as we were eating the cake. The rest of us laughed, but Sonia grabbed the edge of the table in a feeble attempt to keep us all upright. Tammis didn't mind scaring Sonia, or anyone else for that matter. She liked to tease diners at Windows on the World who were scared of heights. Did they feel the tower sway? If her customers were drunk she would assure them that their imbalance was due to the movement of the floor. The stronger the lateral force of the wind, she explained, the more the towers swayed, meaning that there was no reason not to go ahead and order another scotch. And for those nervous customers who asked what might happen in a hurricane, Tammis told them what she told us that day:

"These buildings are as strong and elastic as palm trees," she said. Nothing, she assured us, flashing a comforting smile at Sonia, would ever bring down the towers.

A ROSE FOR SONIA

I watched Sonia's face furtively, trying to see beyond her joyful surface as she opened her gifts. In my estimation, she'd grown more subdued since Pauline had disappeared. Even if she didn't fully register the finality of her mother's absence, she seemed to experience periods of quiet grief. I could never tell if I was projecting upon her the pain I expected her to feel, but I worried that she didn't have the ability to recognize unhappiness for what it was and so might let it grow out of control. There were times when she would start shaking her head all of a sudden, and I'd imagine she had turned her gaze inward and was trying to ward away demons.

She was late to develop, but by sixteen she had a young woman's body. Her left leg was shorter, with a knee that didn't function probably, so she walked with a lurch. But she had acquired more strength than the doctors had predicted for her when she was little. Her fingers gripped strongly, and in dance class she had learned a signature move that combined hops and skips in a spiral, resulting in a series of twirls.

After her party at Windows on the World, she twirled her way between the tables and back to the elevator. All my secret probing of her expression had turned up nothing. She seemed only happy and hadn't asked about her mother. I carried the bag of presents and held her hand as we stepped out of the elevator. I led her across the lobby and out the door. I meant to hail a taxi and in my hurry didn't notice the woman approaching us from across the plaza, not until she said, "Spare some change?"

She was draped in a ragged blanket and wore oversize loafers that looked like clown shoes. She was about thirty, maybe Haitian or Dominican, with hair that had been chopped irregularly, as if with a knife. She carried a single pink rose that someone must have given her in lieu of coins. Sonia stared openmouthed at her. She stared back at Sonia, then handed Sonia the rose. While I was scrambling to find my wallet in my cluttered purse so I could give her some money, the woman turned and ambled away. Sonia lifted the rose to her nose, closed her eyes, and inhaled deeply. Moisture seeped between the corners of her lids. It was the only time I ever saw her cry.

A Is For—

It took me fourteen years after Pauline Moreau disappeared to figure out what had happened to her. By then, 1988, Sonia was happily employed as a sweeper at her favorite bakery in Morningside Heights and sufficiently independent to ride the subway uptown as well as help with some of the cooking at home.

When I returned from work that day, Sonia was at the dining table with her reading glasses on. I'd started a stew in the Crock-Pot that morning, and the apartment smelled of curry. I came in from the cold rain and left my boots outside the door so I wouldn't track water across the floor.

"Hi, sweetie." I gave Sonia a kiss on the top of her head and glanced over her shoulder at the book she was reading. She had recently developed a fascination with the set of encyclopedias and was slowly making her way through the first volume, reading the articles one by one, skipping if she got bored, pausing to study the pictures.

Volume A. *A* for *Aachen,* manufacturing city in Cologne District, Germany. *A* for *aardvark*—Sonia would giggle when she said the word aloud. *A* for *Aborigines,* the indigenous inhabitants of Australia. *A* for *abstract art, Achilles, Adam and Eve, Afghanistan, Agra, Alps, aluminum.*

Al. Element 13. A silvery metal, the most abundant metal in the earth's crust.

"What's the paper there, Sonia? Is that yours?"

"It was in the book."

She had set the paper aside on the table. I picked it up and unfolded it.

"You found it in the book you're reading?"

She nodded and went on reading, excited by the prospect of learning everything there was to know about the world.

I glanced at the piece of paper and decided it didn't make much sense. But the age and quality of the paper drew me back to study it more carefully. From its waxy surface, I recognized a mimeograph. The type had bled slightly but was still legible. As far as I could tell, it was a page from a longer document, some sort of official agreement, it seemed, probably the final page, since there were two signatures of contractual parties. The realization that Pauline must have swiped it when she was working for the P.A. intensified my concentration. I turned the paper over, then turned it back. It included the last part of a restitution clause regarding refunds and then a final promise that "this contract shall be performed in the spirit of good faith and fair dealing," followed by the authorizing signatures of buyer and vendor.

Austin Tobin was the buyer. I probably would have recognized his signature even after all these years, but to help me out, his name was typed in neatly beneath the line, along with the address of the P.A. when it was still on Eighth Avenue. Both names had been typed. I didn't recognize the name of the vendor: Robert Whittaker Jr., signing on behalf of a company called Alumacore. He was identified in the lines below as the managing director for a manufacturing plant based, according to the address on the contract, in a town called Visby, New York.

WHITE SPACE

This mimeograph of a single contract page might have been inexplicable to others. Not to me; I understood the whole of Pauline's life and death in the time it took to swallow. I remembered that she had once worked at the Alumacore headquarters in Albany. My mind leaped over all the questions I should have had, and I recalled the past Pauline was fleeing when she ran into the arms of Mrs. J. I pictured her slipping the mimeograph into her purse while she was filing at the P.A. I saw beyond the lies she told about her distant relative to the real source of her money. I understood her refusal to admit that the funds came from her former Alumacore boss, whose predictable demand for secrecy would have made most women only more inclined to confide in their friends. But Pauline's friends could not forget that she had worked as a prostitute. She must have worried that we would have been disgusted to learn that she was seeking compensation for her own promiscuity. She was right to worry. If I had known that Pauline was extorting money, yes, I would have been disgusted. Just as there was lawful marriage, there were legal venues for a woman seeking support from the father of her child, I would have coolly reminded her. But Pauline must have expected that she would lose in court if she went up against a wealthy Alumacore executive. And so she did not tell us where she was really headed when she said she was going to the track in Saratoga. But now I knew. She had gone to a town called Visby. I had no doubt about this. She had sought out the director of the Visby plant. He was associated with a company where Pauline had once been employed, and so, putting the name together with my knowledge of Pauline's past, I saw that he was the father of Sonia. I guessed that he had been secretly giving her money ever since she quit the P.A.

I saw beyond his name, in the white space between the letters, that Pauline had gone up to receive her payment from him for the last time in 1974.

It might seem unlikely that I would decode so much from the name and address on the mimeograph. But at the time it was an easy equation: Alumacore + Robert Whittaker Jr. = the company executive who impregnated Pauline and then paid her to leave Albany. Years later, Pauline had recognized the name on the contract, and now it came with a new address in a town she'd never heard of: Visby. This, I thought, was the only way to explain why she had taken the page from the file.

The conclusion nestled snuggly in my mind, unshakeable. Whatever horror it should have stirred was supplanted by the hard rationality of my thinking. I should have known to be skeptical of certainty. When we forget to ask questions, we make mistakes.

SHEER COINCIDENCE

I saved all sorts of papers that are important to this story. I made sure to save the page from the contract that Pauline had tucked into the first volume of the encyclopedia. I saved the note Pauline had written when she went away for the last time, the one with the number of a hotel that didn't exist. I saved the unpaid bills she left behind. I saved Sonia's report cards and various medical instructions, along with the drawings she'd made over the years. I even saved the scraps of paper from the day Pauline had brought her little girl to the P.A., when I'd shown Sonia how to press the keys of the typewriter.

Look back at one of those scraps Sonia had typed on. Among the random letters are hidden words that must be there by sheer coincidence, since Sonia hadn't yet learned how to read. Starting with the *W* in the upper left corner, read down the diagonal line to the lower right-hand corner:

```
W R O # $ I G L J
P H F L E L B C N
J K O B N . W K J
P D K I M S K D L
M L # T S L S D K
R Y U N K P V B N
D M B N D X A L P
, C K D J $ I P F
Y T I ! ? 0 % Q A
```

A TEDDY BEAR

Though by 1988, our department at the P.A. was equipped with a single desktop computer, there was no Internet to search. One couldn't call up a newspaper article from 1974 just like that. I concede that it wouldn't have been all that difficult for police to search through old files and identify cases that remained unsolved and perhaps, through that, link Robert Whittaker to the murder of Pauline Moreau. But I couldn't trust the police after their conclusion that Pauline had disappeared intentionally. And when I called the private investigator named Probst with whom the Jaffes had put me in touch, I learned that he had long since retired. That left me untethered, alone with what I knew to be the truth. I couldn't even confide in Tammis, for I was sure she would have gone straight to the police on her own.

By then I was the executive secretary for Mr. Leone, our acting director. The new mood in our department at the P.A.

reflected the spaciousness and light of our offices. When we had staff meetings, Mr. L brought in doughnuts and cider. Things had run smoothly again since he had taken charge. We all liked coming to work.

The day after I found the mimeograph, however, I was easily distracted. I kept losing calls I'd put on hold. I deleted a letter on the computer and had to retype it.

I waited until everyone had gone to lunch before dialing the statewide telephone information service. I asked for the central number of the Alumacore plant. I called it and asked for Mr. Whittaker. The operator connected me to his secretary. The secretary asked for my name. I told her I was calling on behalf of the Port Authority of New York and New Jersey. She put me right through to Robert Whittaker. It was as easy as that.

"Hello?"

All those words I'd read into the blank spaces of the mimeograph—they all fled from my mind right then. I was stunned into silence by my own initiative. I couldn't believe I had him on the line.

"Hello? Hello . . ."

"Mr. Whittaker?"

"Yes, this is he. I'm sorry, I didn't get your name. You're with the Port Authority?"

"I am."

"And you are?"

"I am calling on behalf of Sonia Moreau."

Now it was his turn to be encased in a frozen silence.

"Sonia, the daughter of Pauline Moreau . . . Mr. Whittaker, don't hang up."

"Who did you say you were?" He must have been scrambling to protect himself by then, concocting a strategy of evasion, but

I jumped in before he could pretend that he didn't know any Pauline Moreau, had never heard of her ...

"Mr. Whittaker, I am calling about Sonia."

Again, silence, broken by the sound of his heavy breathing.

"I adopted her after Pauline ... " I was desperate to stay ahead of the man on the other end of the line; I couldn't let him know what I knew. "After Pauline ... "

"Pauline? Pauline who?" he asked.

"After Pauline left"—I heard, in the very blandness of my voice, a terrible euphemism—"I became Sonia's guardian."

I could guess what was going on inside that busy brain of his. He must have realized that continued evasion was in itself dangerous evidence of guilt, but he could not come right out and ask me what I knew about Pauline. He could only hope that he perceived a crucial ignorance in my request. Anyway, there was nothing to connect him to Pauline's disappearance in 1974. Fourteen years had passed. The caller would have gone to the police if there were any suspicion; instead, I had phoned him at work. There was only one thing I could have wanted— the same thing Pauline had wanted and that Robert Whittaker had plenty of, enough to spread around. If he was careful with the fragile threads of the conversation, he might at last be able to meet his daughter, who by then would be a grown-up Miss America.

"I'd like to come up to see you. To tell you about Sonia. In person, if you don't mind." My voice was producing speech without any contribution from thought. It was disorienting to be so out of control, the words tumbling without intention, soaring through the air in a free fall that could only be fatal. I felt physically dizzy. *Stop, Maggie. Hang up and call the police,* I told myself. But *myself* wouldn't listen.

"Sonia?"

The stranger on the other end wasn't quite ready to admit his paternity, so I spelled it out: "Your daughter," I told him. When he still said nothing, I spoke in his place, with a deliberateness that continued to shock me.

"I would like to talk to you about her."

"Does she need something?" Here was the first sign that he would relent, for the sake of seeing his daughter.

"You could put it that way. But I'd rather not explain over the phone." Why did I say that? To stifle the blatant accusation that would only have sent him running. I knew what he'd done, but to say it from four hundred miles away would only have scared him off, like a misfired shot. If he went into hiding, he might never be held accountable.

"I'll come there," he said hoarsely.

"No! I am heading to Montreal for the long weekend, I will be in your area Saturday," I heard myself say, inventing a plan out of the air.

"Here . . . you can't come here, not to my home, but . . . if you go to the Super Eight in Massena, I can meet you there. This Saturday? Does that work for . . . who am I speaking with again?"

"That works."

"Will you bring Sonia, please? I'd like to meet her."

What a teddy bear he seemed, acting like a gentle, wayward dad who wanted to make it up to the child he had neglected. Whoever had gotten through to his office by pretending to be calling from the Port Authority had voiced no suspicion. His reasoning, if I had successfully manipulated it, led him to believe that after tracking him down, I was using Sonia to get money from him. That was all right. As he liked to say, there was no problem that money couldn't solve.

XIV

AN OFFERING

Kay went out of her way to make a special dinner for her husband in the hours before the fire. She collected the necessary sundries at the supermarket in the afternoon, prepared the dough for an apple tart, and mixed up the marinade for the lamb. By the time Bob returned home that Saturday evening, the tart was cooling on the counter, the leg of lamb and the gratin were roasting in the oven, a plate had been filled with cucumber slices heaped with a crab compote, and the chilled champagne was ready to be uncorked.

Bob Whittaker wanted to know why Easter had come a day early this year. Kay assured him that the special meal had nothing to do with the holiday; rather, she knew that her husband had been under stress at work, and she had prepared this banquet to show him that she was supportive. These were trying times, what with the company threatening to shut down the plant in the wake of the reparation agreement. At best, it was a break-even prospect, with the profit from the plant just enough to pay the fines. Kay's heart ached for her husband, who was no villain, despite his flaws. Her goal tonight was to remind him that he was loved. She said she had been thinking about their lives together, their beautiful home, the land. They'd had good years in Visby. How about those summer days when the two of them went boating around the islands. Bob didn't have to be reminded. Those, he agreed, sipping his champagne, were some of his favorite memories. And don't forget how special autumn was in the St. Lawrence River Valley, with the mosaic from the forest canopy reflected in the numerous waterways. There would never be a lack of fresh water in the region, potable or not, depending...Winters were hard, yes, but there were days when the snow was fresh and the sun came out and the sky was a deep slate blue Kay was sure you couldn't see anywhere else.

Friends downstate didn't hide their pity for the Whittakers. From their safe distance, they confused Visby with a gulag. They didn't know any better. They hadn't bothered to come up and watch the sunset from the Whittakers' patio. Downstate, they suffered through their traffic jams and the high cost of living, they endured the muggings, the crowds, the stink of garbage that piled up when the sanitation workers went on their yearly strike. Upstate, life was easier. The Indians figured it out long ago. They made this fertile valley their own. They were the Keepers of the Eastern Gate and saw the valley as a garden that was their responsibility to tend. And then came the great dam harnessing the river's power. It was too bad, really, that so many industries chose to locate here. Not that Kay meant to suggest that Alumacore was at fault in any way. She wanted to assure Bob that she agreed the company was a force for good. It produced the things that society required, and at the same time, it employed workers who otherwise would have

had trouble finding jobs. Young people like Robbie blamed industry for all the world's ills, neglecting to recognize their own
complicity as happy members of a consumer culture. "But our
son will come around," Kay assured Bob. She emphasized *our*,
communicating without saying outright that she was grateful to
Bob for treating Robbie as his real son. It was too bad that Robbie had fallen under the influence of that Finney girl...though
Kay didn't mean to imply that she didn't like Brigid Finney. It
was just that Brigid...had strong opinions. That was one way
to put it. Still, she was a nice girl, she would calm down eventually. She would make Robbie a good wife.

Wife?

Well, yes. Robbie and Brigid Finney were engaged. But before you object, Bob, try to let your imagination take you
beyond the present, to, say, a decade hence, when Robbie and
Brigid have their own children, making it necessary for them
to forget their youthful resentments. It will take time, but think
about a future when there are grandchildren whose very presence will serve as glue to put their family back together. For
what was more important than family? Family, and at the center
of it marriage—that rare and delicate thing that Kay and Bob
had been in danger of neglecting of late, their most valuable
possession that could so easily be destroyed, knocked down
and shattered by something as small as a woman's fist swinging
wildly upon hearing that her husband was having another affair.

Oh, she hadn't meant to turn the conversation in such an
unpleasant direction. That wasn't her intention at all. It was the
eve of Easter, and she just wanted to make a nice dinner for her
husband. Before you begin protesting, Bob, listen to Kay.

She wasn't setting out to accuse you. She really meant it
when she said that she wanted to protect the fine thing the two

of you had worked so hard to create—your marriage, with all its ups and downs, like the decorations an expert potter paints on the vase, pigments swirling, flowers bursting open against a blue not unlike the winter sky in Visby after a snowstorm. Kay hadn't intended to mention her suspicion. But there, she couldn't help it, out it had burst. Just a moment while she wiped up the spill. She didn't want to talk about your most recent affair. Oops, she said it again, and now she would need another napkin. It was just...just...she really hadn't meant to bring it up, but you see, Bob, a postcard had arrived in the mail that day, without a signature. There were just four words on the postcard beside Bob's address. He could go find it for himself— the postcard was on the table in the hall. Someone had written four words with vast meaning that was easily interpreted.

I will be there.

It was amazing, really, how sometimes the simplest language can mean more than the rest of the dictionary put together! Oh, Kay hadn't sat you down just to accuse you. Yet out it came. Blame the champagne. All day long since the mail arrived she had been thinking about that postcard, and thinking about you, Bob, and the fine thing you and Kay had made together that was called marriage. The whole dinner, so thoughtfully prepared, was not meant as a trap to put you at ease so you would forget yourself and admit that you had been unfaithful yet again. That really wasn't her purpose. The dinner was an offering in honor of your marriage. The loving preparations were designed to show you how much she loved you, despite your habit of sneaking off to have an affair. Oops, she said it once more, and this time, feeling a little wobbly from all that good champagne, she bumped the pedestal when she bent over to wipe up the spill, so to speak, and down went that rare vase, crashing to the floor.

THE POSTCARD

I had found his home address as easily as I'd gotten his work number. You could do that back in those days. You could call Information and ask for anyone's address. I had bought one of the postcards and a stamp from a souvenir shop in the lobby and sat on a bench in the World Trade Center plaza. I'd used a black felt-tip marker and written the four words in careful cursive to make sure his wife could read it. I had wanted to taunt him, to coax him to fear me, and I meant to get at him through his wife. I had carried the postcard with me all day before mailing it. And then I'd finally done what I should have done earlier: I went home and called Mrs. J.

ACCORDING TO SCRIPTURE

Bob Whittaker contemplated his crime with a directness that exhausted him. Over and over, he remembered slapping his hand over Pauline's mouth, grabbing her around the neck in the crook of his arm, strangling her until she went limp, hauling her to his Cadillac and depositing her in the trunk, then driving to the end of the lumber road and, in the storm, carrying her into the woods and covering her with moss and sticks because he had no shovel. He punished himself by rewinding the memory and viewing it repeatedly. He despised himself for what he'd done and had spent that awful night in 1974 after the crime aimlessly driving hundreds of miles into the mountains and back out again, thinking about evil, thinking about guilt. His self-loathing left him drained, and he began to welcome the prospect of imprisonment. He was surprised that the police weren't waiting for him when he returned home late in the afternoon the next day. If he'd been arrested then, he would have come right out and confessed. But the police weren't there, and the worst sin his wife thought he was guilty of was adultery. He had to suppress his laughter. Adultery! He accepted the charge without even entering a plea. He let his wife tell the story she wanted to tell, and then they went abroad, travel an effort of purification. It worked for Kay and failed for Bob. No one guessed what he had done, yet there was no escaping memory.

A Christian man who believes he was forced to do evil by his own nature, who sees himself living out a destiny prophesized for him at birth, will, after committing that evil, inevitably compare himself to Judas. Bob imagined hanging himself from a tree, like Judas. With some exploration, though, he learned that, according to Acts, Judas did not hang himself. Rather, in that book of the Bible, Judas used his blood money to buy a field to cultivate but then tripped and fell and somehow managed to disembowel himself on the rocks.

The two fates struck Bob as not just different, but morally contradictory. Further research presented him with another possibility: according to Papias, an early Christian, Judas had been crushed by a chariot.

How did Judas die? The question became an obsession for Bob Whittaker. He gingerly asked his parish priest, who suggested, following Augustine, that the accounts of Judas's death offered different interpretations of the same event, to wit: Judas hanged himself, then the rope snapped, and he was disemboweled.

Bob wasn't satisfied. He wanted to know: Did Judas die by his own hand or by accident? He pondered the question for months, then years. He was still wondering about it when he heard that two Indian boys had found Pauline's remains in the woods, three years after Bob had dumped her there. He was secretly glad that she had been found. She deserved a proper burial. He would have given her one if he hadn't been controlled by the devil. He'd been born to belong to the devil, just like Pauline had been born to tempt him. They were both fulfilling their destinies in their different ways. Everyone is born to fulfill the promise contained within him, Bob had come to believe. And so he went on comparing himself with Judas, thinking he would follow in his footsteps. But had Judas committed suicide or had he just been reckless? Bob Whittaker was desperate to ascertain the truth, and so he cried out for it, wherever it was, begging the truth to return to him.

THE CONFESSION, PART I

Back at the Whittakers' aluminum house in the hours before the Visby fire, while the fine dinner of roast lamb and potato gratin that Kay had prepared grew cold, Bob blinked with startled eyes at his raging wife. He had never seen her so animated, so angry, so willing to give up on him. Weakened by years of the turmoil he'd kept private, he could no longer bear the isolation created by his wife's misunderstanding. She thought he was a wicked man because she believed he had cheated on her and had sex with another woman. She was shouting, threatening divorce because she assumed he had a mistress. She didn't know the half of it.

That half was too heavy for Bob to carry alone anymore. He had kept it inside himself for fourteen years—the weight of it had become intolerable. He couldn't stand hearing his wife rage at him for the wrong reason. She needed to know the right reason. He needed to make the confession he'd been longing to and finally either hang himself with his guilt or relieve himself of his guilt and let God decide what to do with him. And so as Kay roared at him from across the table, Bob Whittaker interrupted and said for the second time in his life, "It's not what you think."

THE CONFESSION, PART II

She listened, incredulous at first, then appalled. But as soon as she felt the surge of disgust, she suppressed it. She needed to hear all of what he had to say. He would stop talking if she revealed the effect his words were having on her. She had to hear every bloody detail.

He had retreated into a cave he made by curling his arms over his bowed head. His voice seemed to echo off shadowed walls. To keep him talking, she faced him with an expression of concern that almost had the flatness of placidity, just in case he looked up to see her response.

He never once looked up. He evidently didn't want to know what she was thinking; he just needed her to listen. And when he was done, he let her walk away without bothering to ask her what she thought. He had put himself in her hands. He left her to decide his fate unencumbered by any plea from him to be spared.

CARE OF THE PORT AUTHORITY

She shut herself in the bedroom. Bob didn't move from his chair. Hours passed, and the Whittaker house remained more silent than it had ever been. Even the second hand of the kitchen clock failed to make its usual ticks as it jerked relentlessly forward. It was the kind of silence one might experience in a courtroom when everyone is waiting for the jury to return.

Kay was writing out the verdict. She had always liked to write. She wrote with a Cross pen on a yellow pad. She found it freeing and absorbing. She especially loved writing stories, in which she could lay out the different parts one by one and take full charge of their outcome.

She had locked the bedroom door so she would have the privacy she needed to write a story in the form of a letter to a woman whose name Kay didn't know but who had promised to be waiting for Kay's husband in the Super 8 in Massena that night.

Here is Kay's letter:

Dear Ma'am,

My name is Mrs. Robert Whittaker Jr., and it is my duty to tell you the truth. I am sorry I do not have the courage to tell you in person. A stronger woman would not even have this letter to write because she would not have let any of this happen.

My husband, Robert Whittaker Jr., is employed with Alumacore, a company based in Albany. Mr. Whittaker worked at the company's Albany headquarters for four years, beginning in 1957. There, though Mr. Whittaker and I were only recently married, he met a young woman named Pauline and began an affair with her. She became pregnant. To protect his marriage and his job, he gave her what was then a sizable amount of money in an effort to convince her to go away.

The woman named Pauline left Albany. Where she went, I do not know. She gave birth to a daughter. She stayed away from my husband for ten years. In that time, Alumacore trans-

ferred Mr. Whittaker to Visby, where he was appointed director of operations for a factory that produces raw aluminum. In 1969, the woman named Pauline came to Visby to demand money from my husband. He agreed to take responsibility for supporting her and her child. This arrangement lasted for five years. In that time, my husband raised the money for Pauline through illegal means, by secretly inflating numbers reflecting the plant's expenses.

My husband believes Pauline was blackmailing him. She clearly believed he owed her child support. You will judge for yourself. As for me, I blame aluminum, and I will tell you why.

Toxic chemicals are inevitable by-products of aluminum production and are dangerous if not properly captured and disposed of. The aluminum factory in Visby has poisoned many people, including my husband. I believe the fumes destroyed his brain and petrified his heart. He is a damaged man. Nor have I remained unaffected. We live in an aluminum house. Aluminum blinded me to my husband's sickness. I could not see what he had done. The truth is, I saw something once in his eyes, for a moment, but then I was blind again. If I had not been blind, I would have seen that my husband went into a motel room one August night in 1974, in hopes of resuming the affair with Pauline. She was unwilling. In my husband's damaged state, he held her by the neck. He says he did not want to kill her, just to hurt her. The next thing he knew, she was dead. He hid her body in the woods near an old lumber road. The remains were found by two Indian boys three years later. She is buried in the Indian cemetery on Karahkwa Hill Road.

My husband lost his mind long ago. He doesn't fully understand the consequences of his actions, but he is ready to take responsibility. I believe he should be found not guilty by reason of insanity, but that is for a judge to decide. He has in-

dicated that he will be revising his will to include his natural daughter as a beneficiary of his estate. He wants to ensure that the girl named Sonia is provided for. You should know that he once tried to see the child, but he failed to find her among her schoolmates. He isn't so damaged that he does not worry about the well-being of his daughter.

It is my understanding that you are waiting for him at the Super 8. I am delivering this letter in his stead. Forgive me for not speaking to you in person. I have never had to tell such a terrible story as this.

Yours sincerely,
Mrs. Robert Whittaker Jr.

She sealed the letter and addressed it to the Port Authority of New York and New Jersey. It was close to midnight by the time she set off to deliver the letter to the motel. There was no one at the desk, so she left it on the check-in counter.

The letter was meant for me, but I did not receive it in Massena because, at Mrs. J's direction, I did not go to the Super 8 and wait for Robert Whittaker. Following Mrs. J's advice, I went to the police in New York instead, and by that weekend in April, the authorities in St. Lawrence County had only just begun to look into the matter.

LIQUID ALUMINUM

I picture Bob Whittaker at the table, as unmoving as a statue. But when he hears the car start in the driveway, he turns his head to gaze in the direction of the window. Kay prefers to drive the old station wagon rather than the Cadillac, convinced that it handles better in wet conditions, and so it is the station wagon that Bob sees backing down the driveway. His immediate impulse is to follow Kay, and he grabs the key to the Cadillac to do just that, though he isn't in a hurry because he already knows where she is going.

Given the complexity of the mission he believes she is on, Bob is surprised to see Kay already exiting the Super 8 when he pulls into the parking lot. He can't conceive of what she would have told the woman in such a short time. It doesn't occur to him that Kay had written down everything she wanted to say. He is puzzled by and fearful of the intensity of purpose expressed on his wife's face.

She plants herself back in the driver's seat of the Ford and starts up the engine. She doesn't look over at him or glance in her rearview mirror when he pulls behind her onto the road, but he assumes she is aware of his presence.

Where will she go next? Either to the police station to accuse her husband of murder, or back home. Those are the only possibilities Bob can fathom. He is surprised, then, when she continues on the road toward the center of Visby, past the police station, past the turnoff that would have led her home. She isn't going home. She is heading east, toward a destination that Bob, in his damaged state, doesn't guess, though it should have been obvious.

She enters the property of the Alumacore plant through the back gate. She parks in an unlit area far from the employee lot and lets herself into the building through a little-used rear door that has been left unlocked, as if for her convenience. Watching her from his black Cadillac, Bob wonders how his wife even knows there is a door there. And was that a bottle of water she was carrying? He is pondering these questions with such concentration that he wastes a precious minute loitering in the car when he should have been pursuing Kay into the foundry.

By the time he is inside the building, she is nowhere in sight. The production process is noisy, with metal banging against metal, gears grinding, iron wheels turning, chains clanking. He can't hear the voices of the night crew, but he knows they must be at their various posts throughout the building, so he is reluctant to call out for Kay. He skirts behind the potline, trying to keep hidden as he goes in search of her, his panic growing, for he is beginning to have a hunch about the quintain she is aiming at in her delirium. Rather than setting her sights on her husband, she means to attack the aluminum plant itself.

He must stop her before she causes harm far greater than that which a strong man can cause with his bare hands. Does his wife not understand aluminum? Did she never learn about the dangers of aluminum in its molten state?

Oh, but Kay Whittaker isn't stupid. She has read up on the element of which her own home is made. She understands aluminum just fine. She knows what she is doing when she climbs up to the mesh bridge clutching a plastic water bottle by the neck. Before Bob can reach her, she unscrews the cap from the bottle and reaches into the hellish fury beneath the safety hood, where the hot aluminum is cooking in its insulated pots. A moment later there is a loud popping sound, and Kay is suddenly in Bob's arms, transported as if by magic rather than by the force of the combustion she caused when she splashed the molten aluminum with water.

At the same time, droplets of aluminum have burst from a newly formed hole in the hood, spraying a nearby wall that happens to be coated with a cheap paste Bob had ordered for refractory coating to save money when the plant was being constructed. That paste proves its liability by bursting into flames.

Never having taken the time to consider the consequences of cutting corners, Bob is astonished to see how easily the building is ignited.

With his arms around his wife, Bob watches, mesmerized, as the flames spread. They watch together as the fire pours across the wall like brightly colored paint over a white canvas. They see the smoke thickening. A moment later, the horn of the alarm starts blaring. The Whittakers hear voices shouting in the distance. They both say a silent prayer that innocent people will not perish. And then Kay tries to wrench free from her husband's grip, stumbles, and they both fall backward.

EMERGENCY ACTION PLAN

In the years since Joe, supervisor of the night crew, started working at the Alumacore plant in Visby, the alarm had gone off seven times. In each instance, he followed the emergency action plan step by step, only to discover that the alarm had malfunctioned. Did the previous false alarms, then, make him negligent when the alarm horn began sounding for the eighth time? Emphatically no! In his testimony following the fire at the plant, he would maintain that he had stuck to protocol.

Step 1: Evacuate all employees.

"Holiday time, boys!"

"Aw, I was just about to take a nap."

"Up and out, all of you.

"Billy. Douglas. P.J. Carlos. Tony." He checked off the names, one by one, as the men exited the building, and then he counted the list. There was one missing. "Where's Walt? Hey, guys, anyone seen Walt?"

"He went to take a piss."

"Fuck's sake, doesn't he hear the alarm? Walt? Billy, could you go in and—oh, forget it, I'll do it. You boys wait here. I'm going back in."

"Hey, fellas, is that smoke?"

"Where?"

"By the roof. Yep, I think it's smoke."

"We gotta tell Joe! Where's Joe?"

"He went to get Walt."

"Someone needs to tell Joe this is for real!"

"Joe!"

"Walt!"

"I'll go."

"We'll all go. Let's stick together."

"Joe, Walt, where are you?"

"Whoa . . ."

"What? I can't hear you."

"Oh, Mama . . ."

"Walt, there you are! Where's Joe?"

"Why the fuck should I know?"

"We better get out of here!"

"Where's Joe?"

"Walt!"

"Joe!"

"Where were you, Walt, you shit? I been looking all over."

"What the hell . . ."

"Where's Billy?"

"What?"

"Billy, I said! Where's Billy?"

"He went looking for you."

"I told everyone to wait outside."

"The top of the line is burning. The whole thing's gonna blow."

"Oh, sweet Mama, where is Billy? Billy!"

"Billy, where are you?"

"Billy, there you are, you little prick. Get out of here. All of you, get out of here. Let's go!"

Step 2: Call 911.

"This is the supervisor over at Alumacore, we got a situation here, there's been some kind of accident, and it looks like it might be, um, significant. We have a fire in the foundry. A major fire. It appears to have ignited the potline. The pots...there is a danger of combustion...we have a dangerous situation here, ma'am. Please send help as soon as possible. Thank you."

Step 3: Disconnect the power circuit.

"I have to turn the power off."

"Joe, you can't go back in there."

"But I have to turn the power off."

"I'll get the hose."

"Oh, Billy, you sweetheart...you know that hot aluminum loves water."

"You can't go back in there, Joe."

"I left the line running."

"Whoa, man, look at that!"

"Move back, everyone."

"Here you go, Joe."

"Joe, you can't go back in there."

"Stay put, the trucks will be here any minute. I mean it, don't follow me in. Do as I say! I just gotta...there is the circuit switch...supposed to be...emergency operating...along this wall, umph, Mama, get me out alive...to disconnect... what...which way...umph...oh, sweet Mama, I promise I'll be good...off, right? Off...okay, I always wanted to go scuba diving, if I get out of here I'm gonna do it, do you hear, Mama, I'm gonna go scuba diving and swim with the sharks, sharks are fine, I like sharks, just get me out of here...I swear I'm gonna quit and go to Florida..."

"Joe!"

"Someone help me with him!"

"Joe, you okay?"

"Joe, your life is more important than fucking aluminum."

"Shut up, Walt."

"You okay, Joe?"

"I'm fine."

"Watch out!"

"She's blowing!"

"Fucking aluminum."

HAMMER AND FEATHER

In 1971, while standing on the moon, the astronaut David Scott opened his gloved hands and released a rock hammer from one and a falcon feather from the other. In the absence of air resistance, the hammer and feather accelerated equally, landing on the moon's surface at virtually the same instant, proving that Galileo had been correct about gravity. Similarly, Kay and Bob Whittaker fell at an equal rate, the difference between their weights insignificant. Let's imagine them, then, during this fatal synchronized plunge, when the force of gravity had a warping effect, seemingly expanding the distance between the mesh bridge and the floor and giving them time, in their final moments, to reflect.

Here's Bob, thinking back on all his misjudgments and indulgences, wishing that he had made other choices and faced a different destiny than the imminent one, wondering once more about Judas, wondering if the reality of hell resembled any human conception of it, experiencing his ignorance of the afterworld as a physical discomfort that caused him actually to wince in midair, the way the thought of the previous night's faux pas might make a person wince in the shower the next morning; the very act of wincing functioned like a floodgate, opening to let out a surging feeling of regret that soon filled Bob's entire being, saturating him, drowning him. It was regret that made him gasp and cough, regret that colored the sharp clarity of his thoughts, regret that reminded him in the last second of his life of something he had forgotten to mention to his wife: When she answered the phone earlier in the day and was greeted by silence, he had been the one calling, from a phone booth on Main Street, having made up his mind over the course of the morning to give up everything and make a run for it. Instead of meeting the woman who had contacted him under the guise of working for the Port Authority of New York and New Jersey, instead of giving her the money she had come to demand from him on his daughter's behalf, he was going to take the cash he had withdrawn from the bank and leave Visby, leave Alumacore, leave his family, and never look back. He had called Kay to say good-bye but, as he would have put it, *chickened out* when he heard the familiar voice on the phone. He could not bring himself to tell her good-bye. He could not bring himself to speak at all, not to the woman he thought was waiting for him at the Super 8 nor to his wife, and so he had just hung on the line, wearing the invisible cloak of a coward's silence while Kay said, "Hello? Hello, who's there?," his whole being transformed into a consuming blankness, the same blankness he relived as he fell and that engulfed him as a river does a man who has jumped off a bridge.

Meanwhile, Kay, falling beside Bob, was a woman who, by her own assessment, had offered herself for sacrifice in order to save the world. No way would she beat herself up for failing to see into the future. She had done the best she could, taking care of her family, accepting the transfer to Visby, and turning the dullness of inertia into a creative energy that found its expression in her aluminum house. Unlike her husband, she had no regrets. Just the opposite. As she fell, she was pumped with pride, savoring the knowledge that she had lived a righteous life and triumphed over a corruption that would have defiled the earth if she had let it spread. She understood her whole existence with the kind of insight that can come only in retrospect, when all she had were memories compressed by the speed of her descent into the crystalline satisfaction of having known love. She had loved Bob in spite of his faults. She had loved their time together. She had loved being alive every day. She had loved waking early on a spring morning to the *cheerio*ing of the robins. She had loved being a child. She had loved holding a snowball between her mittened hands. She had loved soaking in bath bubbles, walking in bare feet on a croquet turf, shopping for clothes on the Ville-Marie in Montreal, writing with a pen, raising her beautiful son. She had loved being a mother. She had loved making love and making life out of love. She had been treated to a perfect lover in the form of her first husband, hardly more than a boy himself when they had married, and she a grown-up girl confidently taking him into her arms and dissolving into a feeling that really deserves a better word to do it justice, a rapturous, multisyllabic neologism to capture the engulfing fullness that Kay experienced once more, in contrast to her husband's blankness, at the end.

THE GREAT HORNED BEAST RETURNS

For months afterward, the scientist took soil samples and tested the water to see if the noxious fumes from the Alumacore fire had saturated the environment with poisons. To his surprise, evidence of chemicals had diminished. The scientist hypothesized that the lack of wind that night conveniently allowed the fumes to drift north and rise high enough to disperse harmlessly above the seaway. The children, however, had a better explanation.

On the night of the fire, the children were woken from their dreams by the sound of roaring. They clutched their blankets, terrified, for they knew what the sound meant. The great horned beast had risen once more out of the river! They heard sirens in the distance and thought that their parents were trying to fight the beast, surely to no avail, for if the adults had listened to the stories, they would have realized the beast was unstoppable. There was no defense against the monster's wrath. The children could only wait for their parents to grab them and try to run. They lay awake for hours, already zipped in their parkas, ready to flee at a moment's notice. But no one came for them. Night turned to morning. When they heard their parents downstairs preparing breakfast, they knew that the earth had not been consumed by poisonous smoke.

Instead of emerging from the river for the purpose of destruction, the beast had come to save the earth, or so the children told themselves. They believed that the beast, whose heart clearly had been softened over the years by the children's attempt to care for the mudpuppies, was summoned by the sound of sirens. Seeing the fire at the plant, the beast took a deep breath, sucking in all the smoke that could have corrupted the earth for years to come, and then, with a great snort, blew the smoke into the deep space of the universe.

The children can't remember which one of them first told this story, but they kept telling it over and over until it fixed in their imaginations as fact.

FROM: <CUSTOMER SERVICE>, CUSTOMER.SERVICE@PANYNJ.GOV

The letter from Mrs. Robert Whittaker Jr. would sit unopened for months at the Super 8 in Massena. Management didn't know what to do with it. As far as their records showed, no one from the Port Authority of New York and New Jersey had ever stayed there, certainly not recently, and the sender had not included a name or a return address.

Finally the manager looked up the street address for the Port Authority and wrote it on the envelope himself. He added a stamp and put the letter in the mail. That was that. He didn't have to think about it again.

Any letter addressed to the Port Authority was forwarded by Customer Service to a specific department—usually Airports, Bridges and Tunnels, or Terminals—or to the Office of the Inspector General. A letter that had no specific recipient and without a return address was regarded with a combination of suspicion and indifference. Sometimes a secretary would go ahead and open it; other times she would put it aside.

Kay's letter was one of the letters that went unread. Weeks went by, then months, then years. It disappeared under a pile of mail. Finally, in 1992, I received one of the many e-mails that came daily, courtesy of the organization's new electronic-communication system, to everyone at the P.A. Usually the e-mails were general updates. This e-mail, however, was a request for anyone who recognized the sender's name, Mrs. Robert Whittaker Jr., to please contact Customer Service.

THE TRUTH MAKERS

"You mean my mother's letter sat unread for four years, yet no one bothered to throw it out?"

"That's right."

"But by the time you received the letter, you already knew that Pauline Moreau had been murdered?"

"Yes."

"You might know, then, that the man, the murderer, was not my actual father. My father died when I was an infant, and my mother remarried."

"I gleaned as much from the testimony at the inquest."

"I was not called to testify at the inquest and did not attend."

"I know. But I was there."

"Did it trouble you that the man who murdered your friend was dead and could not be held accountable?"

"You could say that he suffered a harsh justice."

It was the spring of 2000. After deciding to put this story in writing, and after writing as much as I could based on the available information, I had summoned the nerve to contact Robert Whittaker III, hoping that he might be able to answer some of my many questions about his parents and their lives in Visby.

We had arranged to meet in a café on Amsterdam Avenue a block south of the Cathedral of St. John the Divine. Rob

Whittaker was tall, with black wavy hair already streaked with silver, and brown eyes brightened with specks that reminded me of gold leaf. He had the demeanor of the professor he was and had come to our meeting wearing a denim jacket and black jeans. He struck me as a man who had taken a long time to grow up and still thought of himself as awkward even though he appeared to move through the world with an easy elegance.

He reverted back to his youthful awkwardness once we got to talking, and after dropping a sugar cube into his coffee, he began stirring it and didn't stop. At intervals, he would scoop up a spoonful of coffee, bring it to his mouth, then start stirring again. I did not blame him for his discomfort now that he was in my presence, but I was wrong to fear that he would resent my effort to dig into his family's past. He was a historian, after all, and the past was his business.

"Harsh justice, indeed!" His spoon rattled against the side of the cup. "In your letter to me, you described the fire as 'a desperate act born of a heroic impulse'...this strikes me as accurate in theory. But is it the truth?"

"Yes, I believe so."

"Some say truth cannot exist without truth makers. You are a truth maker—but does that make your hypothesis about the fire true? There is really no way to verify certain specific details regarding the chain of events."

"I understand your doubts. It must be very painful—"

"I think my mother would have liked your version," he interrupted. "She liked tales of heroism. She was a big reader—and writer. Most passionate readers become writers in one way or another. Did you know that my mother was the author of a romance novel? No? Given all that you do know about her, I'm surprised you missed this. You can find her first book if you look for it, *Lavender Serenade*. Oh, it's a racy Cinderella story. She was writing a new novel at the time of her death. She gave it the working title *Unplayable Lie*—when you read it, you'll understand. There's a strange, slanted resemblance to real events in the last pages she wrote—I mean, it doesn't match what actually happened, but I wonder if she felt the weight of her husband's guilt, even without knowing what he'd done. I thought you might be interested in reading the portion of the manuscript that she left behind, so I brought a copy along for you." He motioned to his messenger bag, pausing before pulling out the folder. "There are other things I could tell you that might be of interest," he offered.

"I am eager to hear anything you have to add."

I slowly came to understand that he shared my motivation and wanted to help me cover the whole canvas. He went on talking, sipping his coffee in spoonfuls as he told me about his mother and her first marriage, his boyhood adventures, his love for Brigid Finney, her father's death from brain cancer, her courage in standing up to Alumacore. He showed me photographs of Brigid and of his parents and the exterior of the Whittakers' house in Visby. He told me about the settlement between Alumacore and the Mohawks, and he handed over his mother's manuscript. "It's not fair," he said helplessly, "that she never got to finish it."

In the end, he gave me leave to use everything he had shared with me as I saw fit. And as we prepared to say good-bye outside the café, he offered one key piece of advice, almost as an afterthought. He said that if he were the one aiming to find meaning in the confusing morass of life, he just might consider arranging the pieces in accordance with the force of association rather than in obedience to the order of time.

Joanna Scott

Off the boulevard Saint-Michel in Paris, on a little side street called rue Pierre-Sarrazin, not far from the Luxembourg Gardens, where Brigid Finney and Robbie Whittaker agreed in the spring of 1988 that it would be a wonderful thing to celebrate their love with a modest wedding in New Jersey later in the year, there is a small museum. To enter the museum, you pass through gates and cross a stone courtyard. The Gothic building is remarkable in itself, built over Roman baths in the fourteenth century to house the abbots of Cluny. Astronomers used to gaze at the heavens from its towers. The roof is embellished with gargoyles and elaborately carved friezes. But the most valuable treasure is to be found inside. Covering the walls of a gallery are six huge tapestries woven in wool and silk.

The tapestries depict an unidentified lady amid a colorful menagerie. A unicorn with a sharp horn as long as its white body is stationed to her left, and a lion stands guard to her right. Each of the tapestries is different, with immense variations of color and intricately woven designs. The first five tapestries are commonly interpreted as allegorical illustrations of the five senses. In the sixth tapestry, which is wider than the others, the lady is holding a necklace, either depositing it into or lifting it from a chest. On the top of the canopy above her are the words *À mon seul désir*—to my only desire.

Brigid and Robbie spent a long time admiring the tapestries on that early spring day in Paris in 1988, one week before the Visby fire claimed the lives of Bob and Kay Whittaker. They walked hand in hand, slowly moving in front of the sequence and then returning to the beginning and studying the six tapestries all over again. They talked about the designs and noted where gold threads were woven in to give the impression of

light shining from above. They wondered about the relationship between the artists who had drawn the cartoons on paper
and the weavers in Flanders who had produced the tapestries.
They tried to identify all the animals and imagined what the
lady might say to them. They speculated about the meaning of
the allegories. They happily spent the better part of the morning in the gallery. Brigid compared the experience to rereading
the kind of book in which the end invites you to go back to the
beginning and read again, with new attention.

All the while, infusing their appreciation for the beautiful
tapestries was the knowledge that they were going to spend
their lives together. From time to time one of them would
squeeze the other's hand in a reminder of their love, and the
other would squeeze back.

SWEEPING

First, prepare the space by moving the unoccupied chairs and
tables to one side. When you are cleaning in the kitchen, be
sure to include the narrow areas between the ovens and the
cabinets. When you are cleaning in front of the counter, avoid
disturbing any customers and certainly don't ask them to move.
Open a window if it isn't too cold out, and tie back the cur-
tains. Check to confirm that the broom head does not shake in
the handle, and if it does, screw it in until it's tight. Don't rely
on the broom to support you as you sweep, otherwise the bristles will be permanently bent. Your goal is to collect the dirt in
piles, not to spread it from the floor to the chairs. Lean the handle forward and sweep with a brisk, confident sliding motion,
maintaining the tilt of the handle. Sweep horizontally in front
of you without sweeping over your shoes. Avoid jerking the

brush and stirring up dust. Be particular about corners. Sweep on alternate sides of the broom head to keep the bristles even. The broom will last longer if you sweep in a rational way, and the floor will get cleaner. Use a whisk brush to sweep the pile into the pan, and deposit the contents of the pan in the bin in storage rather than in the public wastebasket at the front of the bakery. After half the room is swept, move the furniture and sweep the other half.

This is what Sonia does day after day. She enjoys the work. She takes pride in the visible evidence of meticulous cleaning and is considered by her employers to be an expert sweeper. Her thoughts are occupied with the satisfying knowledge that she is doing something that needs to be done. Taking the train uptown to work, spending the day sweeping, and taking the train back home creates a pleasant rhythm for her waking hours.

Long ago, she processed the confirmation of her mother's death with a firm silence, as if the fact alone, impossible as it would have been for her to comprehend the cause, was enough to fill the vacuum created by her mother's absence. Now she does not dwell on the past or probe for answers to questions it doesn't occur to her to ask. She is good at what she does, and that is enough. *Swish* goes the broom, and a clean, gleaming band appears where there had been a film of dust. The results of her efforts are quickly apparent. There can be nothing pathetic or demeaning about work that produces such a strong feeling of purpose. She enjoys the conviction that her wage is commensurate and that everyone, from the owners to the bakers to the clerks to the customers, is appreciative.

If you ever have an interest in learning the correct way to sweep, you can find her at the bakery most every day, Monday through Friday. She will be happy to teach you what she knows.

Careers for Women

Let's not forget about my good friend Tammis, who retired from her job at Windows on the World in 1993. She hadn't been planning to go as soon as that, but she changed her mind all of a sudden, and here's why:

On the morning of February 26, 1993, Tammis attended a Food Service meeting in the cafeteria on the ninety-sixth floor of the South Tower. She was heading down in the elevator with five other passengers, all men, when a Ford van loaded with dynamite exploded in the basement parking garage of the World Trade Center. A thunderclap resounded through the buildings. Power in both towers went out, and the elevators came to a standstill.

Remember Tammis's fear of elevators? Well, you would think that she would have panicked when she found herself stuck in a black box halfway down the elevator shaft of the South Tower. The air in the dark elevator was filled with soot that was blowing throughout the building. When one of the other passengers pressed the emergency button, a recorded message came on: "Message has been heard; we will be responding." But no rescuers arrived. The passengers waited half an hour, their only illumination a single penlight. They tried to cheer one another up with bad jokes that got lewder as the time passed. Finally, two of the men wrenched apart the interior doors of the elevator to see if by chance they were at a floor level. They found themselves facing the back of the plasterboard of an interior wall.

The penlight went out. The passengers kept waiting for another ten minutes or so. Knowing Tammis as I do, I would have expected her to collapse in a faint. On the contrary, she did not come close to fainting. She waited and considered her predicament, and as her eyes became accustomed to the dark, she had an idea. She took out her nail file and thrust it at the plasterboard. The men joined her, using money clips and car keys. With the air so thick from rising dust, breathing was difficult. Some of the men would later testify that they didn't think they would make it out alive. Tammis, though, wasn't thinking about what might happen. She was concentrating on sawing and pounding with her nail file, and when the crumbled wall was thin enough, she stuck the file into the hole, twisted it, and felt the space on the other side.

She moved away when the men started kicking at the plasterboard and the tiles behind it. With the hole widened, Tammis, who at one hundred and fifty pounds was not a small woman, offered to climb through first. The men lifted her up; they pushed and she pulled, and she found herself sliding out over the plastic cover of a toilet seat in the women's bathroom. She stood up, tugged her skirt down over the run in her pantyhose, and dusted herself off. While she waited for the other passengers to follow, she swore, once more, never to ride in an elevator again. This time she kept her promise.

She gave notice that day and never went back to work. When I saw the fun she was having in her free time, I decided that I wanted to have fun too, and so in 1995, I finally retired from the P.A. Thanks to Tammis, I was not inside the World Trade Center on September 11, 2001.

SKYLINE

Sitting in her wheelchair on her balcony overlooking the deserted tables of a beachside tiki bar, on the eighth floor of Ocean Manor, clothed in a hand-painted kimono robe, Mrs. J threw her copy of the newspaper to the floor. She closed her aching eyes to ease the strain; a minute later she blinked with a start, as if jolted awake by an alarm. She composed herself and out of habit glanced at her wrist, though she was not wearing a watch. She clasped her hands and rested her chin on her intertwined fingers, directing her gaze between the trunks of two Barbados palms standing sentry behind the building. The breeze brushed her face with a feathery softness. The autumn sun, low in the sky, gave the shallow water near the shore a sepia tint, creating the illusion of an inviting split-toned warmth.

She was reminded of the luxurious buoyancy of floating in her pool in Great Neck during one of those rare intervals when she wasn't being called upon to make a quick decision about a minor crisis. It had been a good feeling, drifting through a summer afternoon on that padded lounge-chair sling while Izzy pruned roses nearby. She liked being lazy once in a while, though only briefly. All in all, she would rather be busy. Even at her age, she missed the thrill of giving orders, of being in charge and presiding over her court with her silver hammer and anvil. Time was, she put on a winning show; everybody thought so. She who was known for her finesse, her natural flair for diplomacy, her knack for purchasing fine clothes at discount prices, and her mind, described by reporters as a *steel trap*—she, a mere woman, had been the voice of the P.A. "I suppose I might be forgiven for imagining that the director of Public Relations of the Port of New York Authority, the largest port in the world, would be a big important-looking man," wrote one reporter in a profile. "Yet, when you come to think a bit more deeply, why should not the office be held by a slim, tactful woman?" Indeed, she proved that she had what it took. She knew how to make a case for almost anything, beginning with that water-front project in Brooklyn that cost eighty-one million dollars back in 1951. How do you convince the public to give up hard-earned tax money for the construction of nondescript warehouses and piers? By calling the marine development program *the greatest of its kind ever undertaken*. The skeptics were silenced; the public couldn't resist the pitch. And so she learned from her own success and was ready with advice when, ten years later, Austin Tobin came looking for direction.

Her career, as she assessed it in her mind, involved telling people what they hadn't yet realized they wanted to hear. *One thing is certain. You can't have good public relations unless you are giving a good performance.* An optimist by nature, she trained herself to fight against the kind of logic that offered despair as the pathetic answer to all questions. She spent her time at the P.A. casting news in glowing terms, with irresistible gusto. In every press release that came out of her department, there was always at least one exclamation point!

Yet the years had taken their toll. She had buried her beloved Izzy, her eyesight was fading, and she was deaf in one ear. By the world's measure, she had outlived her usefulness. She had lived so long that she had watched her well-meant machinations end in the cruelest outcome possible: the murder of poor Pauline. She'd lost the girl she'd tried to save. There had been nothing worse, no failed project that haunted her more, and still she was able to incorporate the memory of Pauline into hopefulness that remained vital at its core and, by her own example, to keep everyone who knew her invested in living, defiant, determined, until now...

...Now that her twins had been excised from the skyline in the front-page photo of the newspaper at her feet, what was left but grief? The worst that could happen had come to pass; this was the worst, and she, the forgotten author of the most famous memo in the history of the Port Authority, was nothing but an ancient dame with sour breath. How tempting it was to accept defeat. She could close her eyes and never open them again, relieving herself of the burden of memory, dissolving loss into oblivion.

This is how I pictured Mrs. J in the weeks after the attack: a grieving old woman alone on her balcony. Honestly, I didn't even know if she was still alive. I sent a brief condolence to an old address I had for her and was not surprised when I received no reply. The enemy was strong. The more I thought about her, however, the more convinced I became that Mrs. J was stronger.

THE DEADLINE GIRL

You can tell from the furrowed wrinkles of her forehead that she is plotting something. She scans the horizon for a minute before cinching the belt of her kimono tighter and lacing her slippers. She pushes herself out of her wheelchair and marches with all the strength of her conviction across the apartment and out to the elevator. On the ground floor, she exits the building and sets out across the beach. After testing the water with the toe of her slipper, she walks straight through the surf, climbing with each step until she is walking on top of the dimpled surface of the deeper water. With the shoreline in sight, she walks perpendicular to the waves, gently bobbing with each swell, her slippers gliding as if over ice. She walks through dusk and into the night, following the path of a moonbeam. She keeps walking north across the sea, tireless, unstoppable, determined to look upon the destruction with her own eyes. Nothing is going to get in her way. She is the Deadline Girl, after all, and has never left a job unfinished.

Morning finds her climbing over the embankment onto the island of Manhattan. Crossing Battery Park, she hears the bells of nearby Trinity Church ringing. Along State Street, a powdery gray ash coats the pavement, and the hollow windows of buildings that haven't yet been demolished seem to be emitting shadows, as if smoke were still pouring out. She stops to read a note written in dust on a wall: *Dad, I came looking for you. Matt.* She sees the remnants of memorials: photographs, stumps of burned-out candles, vases full of wilted flowers.

She merges onto Broadway and finds herself amid a crowd of people, all of them heading uptown. Some have a cloudy translucence, their clothes sticking to them like decals on frosted glass; others are solid flesh and bone coated top to bottom with ash. Two dusty women walk hand in hand, barefoot, each clutching a pair of stiletto pumps with her free hand. A fireman burdened with gear tries to wipe his sweating face, but the rag he is holding passes right through him, as if through a holograph. At the corner of Fulton, Neil Levin, the young director of the Port Authority, suddenly appears in front of her. According to a newspaper report from earlier in the week, he had not been heard from since he left his office to go to a breakfast meeting at Windows on the World on September 11. Mrs. J is saddened but not shocked to feel nothing there when she embraces him.

It's just fabulous! he says to her. I wake up each morning having no idea what challenges the day will bring. He salutes her and hurries on.

Others follow him, among them a hairstylist who owned a salon in the area for thirty years and used to cut Mrs. J's hair, and a man who ran a coffee cart in the lobby of the South

Tower. Here and there, ghosts in unsullied business suits march by. The mayor, accompanied by the governor and the president, leads a pack of policemen trailed by reporters and cameramen. Jerry Falwell strides rudely past, pushing the crowd out of his way. To all you pagans and abortionists, Jerry Falwell is shouting, you feminists and gays and lesbians and the American Civil Liberties Union: I point my finger in your face and say, You helped this happen.

Mrs. J scoops up a broken brick and throws it at Jerry Falwell but misses her target and ends up putting a hole in a window that is already broken. She walks on. Halfway down the block, she comes to the doorway of an abandoned building where a woman sits alone—the same woman who used to wander around the World Trade Center plaza begging for change. Of course she has grown older since Mrs. J last saw her, though it's hard to tell if her hair has turned gray from age or from the ashes covering her. She is dressed in an oversize trench coat and a pair of men's loafers. She is working purposefully on a torn piece of cloth, pulling threads loose from the frayed edge one by one. Mrs. J observes the royal burgundy color of the cloth through the woman's transparent fingers.

Mrs. J turns the corner onto Cortlandt and walks as far as she is allowed, until the street ends in a plywood fence hiding the site of the ruins. She peers between the hinges of a construction gate at the heap of crumpled debris topped by a steel trident, its edges jagged against the empty sky. She sees a fire engine, its rear end crushed, its ladder mangled. On top of the mountain of debris, she sees a single mud-splattered rubber boot. The reams of torn paper scattered about remind her of the bound reports she herself authored. She wrote five reports, each one a hundred pages or more, about Port Authority projects, the longest report being, understandably, about the Port Authority's tallest buildings, her beloved twins. She did not bother to save any copies for herself. She can only assume that all of her written work through the years has been destroyed.

The desolate scene is just as the newspapers have shown it in photographs, and for a minute she wonders why she came such a long way to see it for herself. But she finds her reason as soon as she blinks. Opening her eyes wide, she sees something unexpected: Orpheus sliding along the curved surface of a waterfall. Orpheus! She recognizes him from a painting she once saw at the National Gallery in Washington. She watches as the slim youth disappears over the spillway of a giant pit so deep that from the side it looks bottomless. She resists calling out to him.

Beside the first watery pit is a second deep pit with its own cascade. Mrs. J sees the tilted rim of the granite perimeters inscribed with names and, here and there, a fresh rose standing upright, its stem stuck in the lines of a letter. She sees two faint rainbows in the cooling mist blowing from the fountains, the water flowing into a system that returns it to the surface and propels it back over the wall again in an infinite cycle of renewal. She sees the warped reflection of the new tower undulating on the water's surface. She sees carefree children running in figure eights around the plaza, dogs pulling at their leashes, and, for an instant, Orpheus emerging from the Underworld for another ride down the cascade.

When she feels the presence of a man beside her, she steps back from the gate and faces him. He has the look of a prizefighter, with a thick neck and blunt nose dented on one side. She does not recognize him, but she can tell from the tools strapped to his belt that he is a plumber.

Did you help build these fountains? she asks him.

He nods, his lips slightly parting in a melancholy smile, his gaze turned inward.

They're beautiful, she says. You must be very proud, she adds, provoking the reply that will continue echoing in her mind on her long walk home over the sea:

I'll never build anything like this again in my life.

Acknowledgments

I wrote the first draft of this novel during a residency in Marfa, Texas. I thank the Lannan Foundation for giving me shelter, serenity, a big sky, and access to an invaluable library. I thank my editor, Reagan Arthur, for her keen navigation; Matt Carlini for his wise advice; Tracy Roe for her spirited comments and corrections; and Betsy Uhrig and the whole team at Little, Brown. I thank my agent, Geri Thoma, for decades of support; Robert and Peg Boyers and Michael Collier for their friendship and for building those sturdy platforms where writers can try out their words; all my colleagues at the University of Rochester, especially Stephen Schottenfeld, Jennifer Grotz, Kenneth Gross, and Russell Peck, for giving me so much to consider. To Alice, Kathryn, and Jim: thank you for everything.

About the Author

Joanna Scott is the author of eleven books, including *The Manikin*, which was a finalist for the Pulitzer Prize; *Various Antidotes* and *Arrogance*, which were both finalists for the PEN/Faulkner Award; and the critically acclaimed *Make Believe, Tourmaline, Liberation, Follow Me,* and *De Potter's Grand Tour.* She is a recipient of a MacArthur Fellowship, a Guggenheim Fellowship, and a Lannan Award.